# Praise for the novels of Sherryl Woods

"Woods' amazing grasp of human nature and the emotions that lie deep within us make this story universal."
—*RT Book Reviews* on *Driftwood Cottage*

"Woods' emotionally intense story of loss and love will appeal to a broad range of readers."
—*Booklist* on *Willow Brook Road*

"Once again, Woods proves her expertise in matters of the heart as she gives us characters that we genuinely relate to and care about. A truly delightful read!"
—*RT Book Reviews* on *Moonlight Cove*

"Woods employs her signature elements—the southern small-town atmosphere, the supportive network of friends and family, and the heartwarming romance—to great effect."
—*Booklist* on *A Slice of Heaven*

"Woods…is noted for appealing character-driven stories that are often infused with the flavor and fragrance of the South."
—*Library Journal*

"Woods delivers a charming novel…[a] unique blend of sparkling humor and family drama."
—*RT Book Reviews* on *Midnight Promises*

# SHERRYL WOODS

## *Priceless*

MIRA®

**MIRA**

ISBN-13: 978-0-7783-1876-7

Recycling programs
for this product may
not exist in your area.

Priceless

Copyright © 2004 by Sherryl Woods

For questions and comments about the quality of this book, please contact us at
CustomerService@Harlequin.com.

www.MIRABooks.com

**Printed in U.S.A.**

Dear Friends,

The Perfect Destinies series was originally issued as three Harlequin Special Edition books (Million-Dollar Destinies), with a longer follow-up book written for MIRA Books. I'm so pleased to have all of them available in these new editions from MIRA.

As many of you know, I've always loved writing about families. And in this case three sexy, very different brothers were raised by their madcap aunt Destiny after the tragic death of their parents. Think Auntie Mame, for those of you old enough to remember that wonderful movie. Or meddling Mick O'Brien, if you're a fan of my Chesapeake Shores series.

I hope you'll enjoy revisiting the Carltons if you've read these books before. And if you're new to the series, I hope you'll welcome the family into your heart as you have so many of my other families.

All best,

*Sherryl Woods*

## CAST OF CHARACTERS

*Mack Carlton*—He knows a lot of moves…on the football field and off. He took the game seriously until an injury forced him to the sidelines. Now he sits in the owner's box, usually with a gorgeous woman close by, and takes very little seriously. It's way past time for a reality check.

*Beth Browning*—As a pediatric oncologist, Beth confronts life-and-death struggles every day. She has no patience for frivolities such as football or the grown men who live for games. Beth is a more than even match for a man like Mack, but when it comes to fate, she's no match at all.

*Destiny Carlton*—Mack's aunt knows as well as anyone that life can take a tragic twist, so she's an ardent believer in living every moment to its fullest. It's Destiny's opinion that her beloved nephew Mack understands all about the rules of the game of football but nothing about the game of life. Until he loses his heart, she won't be satisfied that he's destined for victory.

**One fun-loving man, one woman who's suffered too much loss and Destiny's touch. Touchdown!**

# Priceless

# 1

Mack Carlton, who'd had more quick moves on a football field than any player in Washington, D.C., history, had been dodging his Aunt Destiny for the better part of a month. Unfortunately, Destiny was faster and sneakier than most of the defensive linemen he'd ever faced. She was also more highly motivated. It was a toss-up as to how long it would be before she caught up with him.

Ever since she'd succeeded in getting his older brother, Richard, married a few weeks back, Destiny had set her sights on Mack. She wasn't even subtle about it. A steady parade of women had been popping up all over the place. Not that that was an unusual occurrence in Mack's life—he did have a well-deserved reputation as a playboy, after all—but these women were not his type. They had "serious" and "happily ever after" written all over them. Mack didn't do serious. He didn't do permanent. Destiny, of all people, should know that.

Not that he had the same issues with love and loss that had kept his big brother off the emotional roller coaster. Mack preferred to think that his hang-ups had more to do with a desire to know lots and lots of women than any fear of eventual abandonment. Why limit himself to one particular dish when there was an entire buffet to be sampled? Sure, he'd been affected by the deaths of his parents in a small plane crash in the Blue Ridge Mountains when he was barely ten, but the trauma hadn't followed him into adulthood as it had Richard.

Not that Destiny or Richard believed that. Hell, even his younger brother, Ben, was convinced they were all emotionally messed up because of the crash, but Mack knew otherwise, at least in his own case. He just flat-out liked women. He appreciated their minds, their quick wits.

Okay, that was the politically correct thing to say, he conceded, even though there was nobody around who was privy to his private, all-too-male thoughts. Truthfully, what he really appreciated was the way they felt in his arms, their soft skin and passionate responses. While he enjoyed a lively conversation as much as the next man, he truly loved the intimacy of sex, however fleeting and illusional it might be.

Not that he was any kind of sex addict, but a little wholesome rustling of the sheets made a man feel alive. So maybe that was it, he thought with a sudden rush of insight. Maybe what he loved most about sex was that it made him feel alive after being reminded at a very young age that life was short and death was permanent. Maybe he had some emotional scars from that plane crash, after all.

He was still pondering the magnitude of that discovery when Destiny sashayed into his office at team headquarters, where he was now ensconced as part owner of the team for which he'd once played. He was so thoroughly startled by her unexpected appearance in this male bastion, he brought the legs of his chair crashing to the floor with such force it was a wonder the chair didn't shatter.

"You've been avoiding me," Destiny said pleasantly, sitting across from him in her pale-blue suit that mirrored the color of her eyes.

As always, Destiny looked as if she'd just walked out of a beauty salon, which was a far cry from some of the pictures around the house taken during her years as a painter in the south of France. In those she always appeared a bit rumpled and wildly exotic. Mack occasionally allowed himself to wonder if his aunt missed those days, if she missed the life she'd given up to come back to Virginia to care for him and his brothers after the plane crash.

As a child he'd never dared to ask because he'd feared that reminding Destiny of what she'd sacrificed might send her scurrying back to Europe to reclaim it. As he'd gotten older, he'd started taking her presence—and her contentment—for granted.

Now he gave his aunt a cool, unblinking look, determined not to let her see that her arrival had shaken him in any way. With Destiny it was best not to show any signs of weakness at all. "You're imagining things," he told her flatly.

Destiny chuckled. "I didn't imagine that it was your behind I saw scurrying out the back door at Richard and Melanie's the other night, did I? I saw that backside in too many football huddles to mistake it."

Damn. He thought he'd made a clean escape. Of course, it was possible that his brother had blabbed. Richard thought Mack had taken a little too much pleasure in Destiny's successful maneuvering of Richard straight into Melanie's arms. He was more than capable of going for a little payback to see that Mack met the same fate.

"Did you really spot me, or did Richard rat me out?" he asked suspiciously. "I know he wants me to fall into one of your snares the same way he did."

"Your brother is not a tattler," she assured him. "And my eyesight's twenty-twenty." She gave him a measuring look. "What are you scared of, Mack?"

"I think we both know the answer to that one. I also suspect it's the same thing that brought you to my office. What sort of devious scheme do you have up your sleeve, Destiny? And before you answer, let's get one thing straight, my social life is off-limits. I'm handling it very well on my own."

Destiny rolled her eyes. "Yes, I've seen how well you're handling it in every gossip column in town. It's unseemly, Mack. You may not be directly affiliated with Carlton Industries, but the family does have a certain social standing in the community. You need to be mindful of that, especially with Richard entering politics any day now."

The family respectability card was a familiar one. He was surprised she'd tried the tactic again, since it had failed abysmally in the past. "Most people are capable of separating me from my brother. Besides that, I'm an adult," he recited as he had so often in the past. "So are the women I date. No harm, no foul."

"And you're content with that?" Destiny asked, her skepticism plain.

"Absolutely," he insisted. "Couldn't be happier."

She nodded slowly. "Well, that's that then. Your happiness is all that's ever mattered to me, you know. Yours and your brothers'."

Mack studied her with a narrowed gaze. Surely she wasn't giving up that easily. Destiny was constitutionally incapable of surrendering before she'd even had a first skirmish. If she were so easily put off, Richard wouldn't be married right now. Mack needed to remember that.

"We appreciate that you love us," he said carefully. "And I'm glad you're willing to let me choose my own dates. It's a real relief, in fact."

She fought a smile. "Yes, I imagine it is, since the kind of woman *I* see you with is not the sort of mental and emotional lightweight you tend to choose."

He ignored the slap at his taste in women. He'd heard it before. "Anything else I can do for you while you're here?" he asked politely. "Do you need any team souvenirs for one of your charity auctions?"

"Not really. I just wanted to drop by and catch up," she claimed with a perfectly straight face. "Will you come to dinner soon?"

"Now that I know you've given up meddling in my social life, yes," he told her, deciding to give her the benefit of the doubt for the moment. "Is everyone coming for Sunday dinner?"

"Of course."

"Then I'll be there," he promised. At least there was some safety in numbers, in case Destiny had a change of heart between now and Sunday.

She stood up. "I'll be on my way, then."

Mack walked with her down the hall to the elevator, struck anew by how small she was. She barely reached his shoulder. She'd always seemed to be such a giant force to be reckoned with that it gave the illusion she was bigger. Then, again, he was six-two, so Destiny was probably a perfectly average-size woman. Add in her dynamic personality, and she had few equals of any size among Washington's most powerful women.

She was about to step into the elevator when she gave him her most winning smile, the one reserved for suckering big bucks from an unwitting corporate CEO. Seeing that smile immediately put Mack right back on guard.

"Oh, darling, I almost forgot," she claimed, reaching into her purse and pulling out a note written on a sheet of her pretty floral stationery. "Could you drop by the hospital this afternoon? A Dr. Browning spoke to me earlier and said one of the young patients in the oncology unit has a very poor outlook. The boy is a huge fan of yours, and the doctor feels certain that a visit from you might boost his morale."

Despite the clamor of alarm bells ringing in his head, Mack took the note. Whatever Destiny was really up to, it was not the kind of request he could ignore. She knew that, too. She'd instilled a strong sense of responsibility in all of her nephews. His football celebrity had made fulfilling requests of this type a commonplace part of his life.

He glanced at his watch. "I have a business meeting in a couple of hours, but I can swing by there on my way."

"Thank you, darling. I knew I could count on you. I told Dr. Browning you'd be by, that the other requests must have gotten lost."

Mack felt his stomach twist into a knot. "There were other requests?"

"Several of them, I believe. I was a last resort."

He nodded grimly, his initial suspicions about his aunt's scheming vanishing. "I'll look into that. The staff around here knows that I do this kind of visit whenever possible, especially if there's a kid involved."

"I'm sure it was just some sort of oversight or mix-up," Destiny said. "The important thing is that you're going now. I'll say a prayer for the young boy. You can tell me all about your visit on Sunday. Perhaps there's more we could be doing for him."

Mack leaned down and kissed her cheek. "You ought to be the one going over there. A dose of your good cheer could improve anyone's spirits."

She regarded him with a surprised sparkle in her eyes. "What a lovely thing to say, Mack. That must explain why you're such a hit with the ladies."

Mack could have told her it wasn't his sweet-talk that won the hearts of the women he dated, but there were some things a man simply didn't say to his aunt. If she wanted to believe he owed his social life to being a nice guy, he was more than willing to let her. It might keep a few tart-tongued lectures at bay.

"It's a game, for heaven's sake," pediatric oncologist Beth Browning declared, earning a thoroughly disgusted look from her male colleagues at Children's Cancer Hospital. "A game played by grown men, who ought to be using their brains instead of their brawn—assuming of course that their brains haven't been scrambled."

"We're talking about professional football," radiologist Jason Morgan protested, as if she'd uttered blasphemy. "It's about winning and losing. It's a metaphor for good triumphing over evil."

"I don't hear the surgeons saying that when they're patching up some kid's broken bones after a Saturday game," Beth said.

"Football injuries are a rite of passage," Hal Watkins, the orthopedic physician, insisted.

"And a boon to your practice," she noted.

"Hey," he protested. "That's not fair. Nobody wants to see a kid get hurt."

"Then keep 'em off the field," Beth suggested.

Jason looked shocked. "Then who'd grow up to play professional sports?"

"Oh, please, why does anyone have to do that?" Beth retorted, warming to the topic. She'd read about Mack Carlton and his rise from star quarterback to team owner. The man had a law degree, for goodness' sakes. What a waste! Not that she was a huge admirer of lawyers, given the way their greediness had led to hikes in malpractice insurance.

"Because it's football, for crying out loud," Hal replied, as if the game were as essential for survival as air.

"Come on, guys. It's a game. Nothing more, nothing less." She turned to appeal to Peyton Lang, the hematologist, who'd been silent until now. "What do you think?"

He held up his hands. "You're not drawing me into this one. I'm ambivalent. I don't care that much about football, but I don't have a problem if anyone else happens to find it entertaining."

"Don't you think it's absurd that so much time, money and energy is being wasted in pursuit of some stupid title?" Beth countered.

"The winner of the Super Bowl rules!" Jason insisted.

"Rules what?" Beth asked.

"The world."

"I wasn't aware they played football in most of the rest of the world. Let's face it, in this town it's about some rich guy who has enough money to buy the best players so he'll have something to get excited about on Sunday afternoons," she said scathingly. "If Mack Carlton had a life, if he had a family, if he had *anything* important to do, he wouldn't be wasting his money on a football team."

Rather than the indignant protests she'd expected, Beth was stunned when every man around her in the hospital cafeteria fell silent. Guilty looks were exchanged, the kind that said humiliation was just around the corner.

"You sure you don't want to reconsider that remark?" Jason asked, giving her an odd, almost pleading look.

"Why would I want to do that?"

"Because I'm pretty sure you mentioned when we started this discussion that you've been trying to get Mack Carlton in here to visit with Tony Vitale," Jason said. "The kid's crazy about him. You thought meeting Mack might lift his spirits, since the chemo hasn't been going that well."

Her gaze narrowed. "So? This community-minded paragon of football virtue hasn't bothered to respond to even one of my calls."

Jason cleared his throat and gestured behind her.

Oh, hell, she thought as she slowly turned and stared up at the tall, broad-shouldered man in the custom-tailored suit who was regarding her with a solemn, steady gaze. He had a faint scar under one eye, but that did nothing to mar his good looks. In fact, it merely added character to a perfectly sculpted face and drew attention to eyes so dark, so enigmatic, that she trembled under the impact. Everything about his appearance spoke of money, taste and arrogance, except maybe the hairstyle, which had a Harrison Ford kind of spikiness to it.

"Dr. Browning?" he inquired in an incredulous tone that suggested he'd been expecting someone older and definitely someone male.

Despite the unspoken but definitely implied insult, his quiet, smooth voice eased through Beth, then delivered a belated punch. She tried to gather her wits and to form the apology he deserved, but the words wouldn't come. She'd never have deliberately insulted him to his face, even if she did have an abundance of scorn for men who wasted money on athletic pursuits that could be better spent on saving mankind.

"She'll be with you as soon as she gets her foot out of her mouth," Jason said, breaking the tension.

Grateful to the radiologist for helping her out, she managed to stand and offer her hand. "Mr. Carlton, I wasn't expecting you."

"Obviously," he said, his lips curving into a slow smile. "My aunt said you'd had trouble contacting me. My staff shouldn't have put you off. I apologize for that."

Beth had read that he was a heartbreaker. Now she knew why. If his gaze could render her speechless, that smile could set her on fire. Add in the unexpected touch of humility and the sincerity of his apology, and her first impression was pretty much smashed to bits. She'd never experienced a reaction to any man quite like this. She wasn't sure she liked it.

"Would you...?" Exasperated by her inability to gather her thoughts, she swallowed hard, took a deep breath, then tried again. "Would you like a cup of coffee?"

"Actually I'm on a tight schedule. I found myself near here and wanted to let you know that I haven't been deliberately blowing off your calls. I thought I'd take a chance that now would be a good time to meet Tony."

"Of course," she said at once, knowing what such a visit would mean even if regular visiting hours were later in the day. This was one instance when she didn't mind breaking the rules. "I'll take you to his room. He'll be thrilled."

Jason cleared his throat. At his pointed look, Beth realized that her colleagues were hoping for an introduction to the local football legend. Amazed that grown men could be as enamored of Mack Carlton as her twelve-year-old patient was, she paused and made the introductions.

When it seemed that the doctors were about to go over every great play the man had ever made on the football field, she cut them off.

"As much as you guys would probably like to discuss football for the rest of the day, Mr. Carlton is here to see Tony," she reminded them a bit curtly.

Mack Carlton gave her another of those smiles that could melt the polar ice cap. "Besides," he said, "we're probably boring Dr. Browning to tears."

Now there was a loaded statement if ever she'd heard one. She didn't dare admit to being bored and risk insulting him more than she had when he'd first arrived and overheard her. Nor was she inclined to lie. Instead she forced a smile. "You did say you had a tight schedule."

His grin spread. "So I did. Lead the way, Doctor."

Relieved to have something concrete to do, she set off briskly through the corridors to the unit where twelve-year-old Tony had spent far too much of his young life.

"Tell me about Tony," Mack suggested as they walked.

"He's twelve and he has leukemia," Beth told him,

fighting to keep any trace of emotion from her voice. It was the kind of story she hated to tell, especially when the battle wasn't being won. "It's the third time it's come back. This time he's not responding so well to the chemotherapy. We'd hoped to get him ready for a bone marrow transplant, but we don't have the right donor marrow, and because of his difficulty with the chemo, I'm not so sure it would be feasible for him right now anyway."

Mack listened intently to everything she was saying. "His prognosis?"

"Not good," she said tersely.

"And you're taking it personally," he said quietly.

Beth promptly shook her head. "I know I can't win every battle," she said, as she had to the psychologist who'd expressed his concern about her state of mind earlier in the day. Few people knew just how personally she took a case like Tony's. She was surprised that Mack Carlton had guessed it so easily.

"But you hate losing," Mack said.

"When it's a matter of life and death, of course I do," she said fiercely. "I went into medicine to save lives."

"Why?" Before she could reply, he added, "I know it's a noble profession, but dealing with sick kids has to be an emotional killer. Why you? Why this field?"

She was surprised that he actually seemed interested in her response. "I was drawn to it early on," she said, aware that she was being evasive by suggesting that it hadn't been the motivating force in her entire life. With any luck, Mack wouldn't realize it.

"Because?" he prodded, not accepting the response at face value and proving once more that he was a more insightful man than she'd expected him to be.

"Why does it matter to you?" she asked, still dodging a direct answer to his question.

His eyes studied her intently. "Because it obviously matters to you."

Once again his insight caught her off guard. It was evident he wasn't going to let this go until he'd heard at least some version of the truth. "Okay, here it is in a nutshell. I had an older brother who died of leukemia when I was ten," she told him, revealing more than she had to anyone other than her family. They knew all too well what her motivation had been for choosing medicine, and they didn't entirely approve of her choice, fearing she was doomed to have repeated heartaches. "I vowed to save other kids like him."

Mack regarded her with what appeared to be real sympathy. "Like I said, you take it personally."

She sighed at the assessment. "Yes, I suppose I do."

"How long do you think you can keep it up, if you take every case to heart?"

"As long as I have to," she insisted tightly. "I only see a few patients. Most of my time is spent in research. Our treatments are getting better and better all the time." Sadly, Tony wasn't responding well to any of them, which was why she'd taken such an intense interest in his case.

"But not with Tony," Mack said.

Beth fought against the salty sting of unexpected tears. "Not with Tony, at least not yet," she admitted softly. Then she set her jaw and regarded Mack defiantly, blinking back those tell-tale tears. "But we're going to win this battle, too."

He gave her an admiring look. "Yes, I think you will," he said quietly. "Will my being here actually help Tony?"

"Hopefully it will improve his spirits," Beth assured him. "He's been a little down lately, and sometimes boosting a child's morale is the most important thing we can do. We need to keep him from giving up on himself or on us."

Mack nodded. "Okay, then. Let's go in there and talk football." He gave her an impudent grin. "I assume you won't be saying much."

Beth laughed despite herself, liking Mack far more than she'd ever expected to. She could forgive a lot in a person who had a sense of humor, whether about her foibles or his own. "Probably not."

His expression sobered. "Good. What I do for a living may not be medicine or rocket science, but I'd hate to have you dismiss it in front of a kid who thinks it matters."

Beth stared at him as his point struck home. Her opinion of football or of Mack Carlton didn't matter right now. "Touché, Mr. Carlton. I'll definitely refrain from comment. This is all about Tony."

He winked. "Call me Mack. My fans do."

"I'm not one of your fans."

"Stick around," he taunted lightly. "You might be, after this."

Beth bit back a sigh. Yes, she could be, she admitted to herself. Not that Mighty Mack Carlton needed another conquest in his life. The gossip columns were littered with the names of women who thought they had the inside track in his life. She'd noticed that few of them ever got a second mention. She wasn't the least bit inclined to test her luck in an already crowded field.

"Don't hold your breath, Mr. Carlton. Besides, the

only person whose adoration counts is Tony, and you've already got a lock on that."

"I wouldn't mind at least a hint of approval from you, too," he said, his gaze capturing hers and holding it.

Despite the obvious attempt to disconcert her, Beth felt herself falling under his spell. She found it irritating. "Why? Do you have to win over every woman you meet?"

He hesitated then, and an odd look that might have been confusion flickered in his eyes. "How well do you know my aunt?" he asked.

The out-of-the-blue question caught her off guard. "Your aunt?"

"Destiny Carlton, the woman you contacted who made sure I came over here today."

Beth shook her head. "I don't believe we've met," she said. "Though I recognize the name. I think she raises a lot of money for the hospital. I never spoke to her, though."

Mack seemed surprised. "You really don't know her?"

"No."

"And you didn't call her?"

"No. Why?"

He shook his head, obviously more puzzled than ever. "Doesn't matter."

Despite his denial, Beth got the distinct impression that it mattered a lot. She simply had no idea why.

# 2

Mack had been in his share of hospital rooms. He'd had enough football injuries to guarantee that—including one final blown-out knee that had ended his career on the field. Granted, his life had never been on the line, but even so, he hated the antiseptic smell, the too-perky nurses, the beeps and whirring of machines, the evasiveness of the doctors who never looked you in the eye when the news was bad. If he'd hated it, how much worse must it be for a kid, especially a kid who had to face the possibility that he might not come out alive?

During his football career, Mack had made it a habit to visit children in this hospital and others. The smiles on their faces, knowing that for a few minutes, at least, he'd taken them away from their problems, made his own discomfort seem like a small thing.

Now that his own playing days were over, he made fewer of these visits. Most kids wanted to meet the current players, and from his position in the team's front office, he made sure it happened, even if it made some of the biggest, brawniest players in the league cry afterward. Men who took a lot for granted suddenly started counting their blessings after a hospital visit to cheer kids facing the toughest fights of their lives. Nothing he'd ever encountered had given him a better perspective on what mattered in life.

Outside Tony Vitale's door, he braced himself for what he'd find inside—a pale kid, maybe bald, his eyes haunted. Mack had seen it too many times not to expect the worst. It never failed to make his chest tighten and his throat close up. Forcing himself not to react visibly had been one of the hardest lessons he'd ever had to learn.

"You okay?" Beth asked, regarding him worriedly. "You're not going to walk in there and pass out on me, are you?"

Mack gave her a disbelieving look. "Hardly."

"You wouldn't be the first man who couldn't take seeing a kid this sick," she said.

"I've been here before."

She gave him a look filled with understanding and commiseration. "It's always hardest the first time. After that, it gets easier."

"I doubt that," Mack said.

Her gaze stayed on his face. "You ready?" she asked finally, as if she'd seen some minute change in his demeanor that had satisfied her.

"Let's do it."

Beth pushed open the door, a seemingly genuine smile on her face. "Hey, Tony," she called out cheerfully. "Have I got a surprise for you!"

"Ice cream?" a weak voice called back hopefully.

"Better than that," she said, then stood aside to allow Mack to enter.

Admiring her performance and determined not to let

her or the boy down, Mack gave her a thumbs-up and strode into the room.

The boy lying amid a pile of pillows and stuffed animals was wearing a too-large football jersey with Mack's old number on it. He clutched a football against his scrawny chest. When he spotted Mack, he struggled to sit up, and for just an instant there was a glimmer of childish delight in his dull eyes before he fell back against the pillows, obviously too weak to sit upright.

"Mighty Mack!" he whispered incredulously, his gaze avidly following Mack's progress across the room. "You really came."

"Hey, when I get a call from a pretty doctor telling me that my biggest fan is in the hospital, I always show up," Mack said, swallowing the familiar tide of dismay that washed over him. The men who walked onto a football field every Sunday and allowed equally brawny men to tackle them and pound them into the dirt didn't know half as much about real bravery as this kid.

Tony nodded enthusiastically. "I'm your biggest fan, all right. I've got tapes of every game you ever played."

"That can't be that many. I had a short career."

"But you were awesome, the best ever."

Mack chuckled. "Better than Johnny Unitas in Baltimore? Better than Denver's John Elway? Better than Dan Marino in Miami?"

"Way better," Tony said loyally.

Mack turned to the lady doc. "The kid knows his sports legends."

She gave him a wry look. "Obviously, the two of you agree you're in a class by yourself."

"He is, Dr. Beth," Tony asserted. "Ask anyone."

"Why ask anyone else, when I can get it straight from

the horse's—" she deliberately hesitated, her gaze on Mack steady before she finally added "—mouth?"

Mack had the distinct impression she would have preferred to mention the opposite end of the horse. He had definitely not won her over. Not yet, anyway. That was a challenge for another time, though, one he was surprisingly eager to pursue. For now, his focus had to be on Tony.

"How about I sign your football for you?" he suggested to Tony.

The boy's eyes lit up. "That'd be great! Wait till my mom comes tonight. She'll be so excited. She's watched all those tapes with me a million times. I'll bet she's the only mom around who knows all your stats."

Mack read between the lines, but managed to keep his expression neutral at the hint that there was no father in this boy's life. He reached in his pocket and pulled out a valuable football card from his rookie year that he'd brought along. "Want me to sign this for your mom or for you?"

"Oh, wow! I saw that card on the Internet. It was selling for way more than I could pay," Tony said, obviously struggling to do the right thing. "Sign it for my mom, I guess. She can show it to all her friends at work. She'll probably want to put it in a frame on her desk."

Mack grinned at him. "Good choice. I'll bring you your own on my next visit. I think I can come up with one from my MVP year that's even more valuable, especially when it's signed."

"You'll come back?" Tony asked, his eyes wide with disbelief. "Really? And we can talk about all the guys you drafted for this season? We really need that defensive lineman you got."

"Tell me about it," Mack said.

"Has he signed yet?"

Mack grinned at his enthusiasm and his up-to-date knowledge. "Not yet. We're still bargaining."

"He'll sign," Tony said confidently. "Who wouldn't want to play for your team? What I don't get is why you didn't go after that punter at Ohio State."

Mack laughed. "Maybe I'll explain budgets and salary caps to you the next time I come."

"I can't believe you'll really come back," Tony said.

"I'll be back so often you'll get sick of me," Mack promised. "Nothing I like more than talking to someone who remembers all my great plays."

"And I do," Tony said. "Every one of them. That game against the Eagles, when you threw for a team record was the best ever, but I liked the way you scrambled for a winning touchdown against the Packers, when everybody said you ought to be off the field because of a shoulder injury."

Mack laughed. "That was a great one," he agreed. "I still get a twinge in that shoulder every time I think about it. I had to scramble, because I couldn't have thrown the ball if my life had depended on it."

"I knew it!" Tony said, obviously delighted to have his impression confirmed. "I told my mom before you ran that there was no way you were going to try a pass. How come the Packers' defense didn't get that?"

"Pure, dumb luck," Mack admitted. "And just so you know, I shouldn't have stayed on the field. I could have cost us the game."

"But you didn't. You won it," Tony said.

"That doesn't mean it was the smartest play. It means I was showing off."

"I don't care. It was a great play," Tony insisted.

Mack laughed at the kid's stubborn defense. "Too bad you weren't around to talk to the coach. He almost benched me for the next game because of that play."

Tony's eyes widened in disbelief. "Really? But that's so unfair."

Mack studied the boy's face and thought he looked even paler than he had when Mack had first arrived, despite his obvious excitement. Mack glanced at Beth and saw the lines of worry creasing her forehead. He was pretty good at reading cues and he definitely got this one. It was time to go.

"Listen, Tony, I've got to head to a meeting. You get some rest. Maybe next time we can go down to the cafeteria for some hot chocolate. I hear it's pretty decent."

"Really?" Tony asked, his voice fading as if he were falling asleep but struggling to fight it.

"If the doc okays it," Mack said, giving her a questioning look.

"No problem," Beth said, but she didn't seem too enthusiastic.

Mack took Tony's frail hand and gave it a squeeze. "Take good care of yourself, son."

By the time he released the boy's hand, Tony was already asleep.

A few seconds later Mack and Beth Browning were back in the hall. She scowled at him with fire in her eyes.

"Why did you do that?" she demanded.

"Do what?" Mack asked, confused by the sudden return of overt hostility. He'd felt good about the way things had gone during the visit. He was sure he'd lifted Tony's spirits and gotten his mind off of his illness for a few minutes at least. Wasn't that the point of his being here?

"Why did you say you'd be back?" she asked.

Mack was annoyed by the implication that he'd made a promise he had no intention of keeping. "Because if I was reading the signals correctly, that boy doesn't have a dad, and he needs someone around to support him," he retorted. "Do you have a problem with that?"

"Tony's not alone. You heard how he talks about his mom. She's great with him."

Mack regarded her with a steady look. "And I think that's fantastic, but now he has me, too."

Beth's expression faltered as the sincerity of his intentions finally sank in. "You actually mean that, don't you?"

"Yes."

"Why?"

"Because I know what it's like to grow up without a dad," Mack said honestly. "That was bad enough. To grow up sick and terrified without a dad must be a thousand times worse. If I can help by coming to visit, then that's what I intend to do. Any objections, Dr. Browning?"

She hesitated, her gaze locked with his, then finally she shook her head. "None, as long as you don't let him down."

"You concentrate on getting him well, Doc. I'll concentrate on giving him a few extra reasons to live."

That said, he turned and walked away, not sure whether he was more upset by Tony's situation or by the doctor who doubted his own good intentions.

Not until he was on his way to his business meeting did Mack allow himself to consider Beth's earlier claim that she had never spoken to Destiny. Was she telling him the truth? He couldn't imagine any reason she'd have to lie.

Destiny, to the contrary, might well be inclined to lie if this was another of her matchmaking plots as he'd initially suspected. The instant he'd met the doctor— pretty, brainy, serious—his suspicions had been aroused all over again. The fact that Destiny had never mentioned Dr. Browning being a woman raised all sorts of red flags, as well.

As he drove across town, he voice activated his cell phone and called Destiny.

"Darling, I didn't expect to hear from you again so soon," she said. "How did things go at the hospital? Were you able to meet Tony?"

"Yes. He's in rough shape."

"Then I'm sure your visit meant a lot. I'm so proud of you for taking the time to stop by."

"It's the least I can do." He hesitated, debating whether it was wise to ask his aunt any question at all about Beth Browning. She might make way too much of his curiosity. Still, he wanted to know what he was up against. Had she schemed to bring the two of them together? If so, she had to know that it was an unlikely match. The woman didn't even like football, much less understand it, and the game was an integral part of his life. And she seemed to have formed some very negative opinions about the kind of man he was.

"By the way, your Dr. Browning is not exactly a huge fan of the game," he said eventually.

"Really?" Destiny said.

He listened for a false note in her voice, but didn't detect one. "You didn't know?" he pressed.

"How would I know?"

"You did say you'd talked to her."

"Did I say that? Actually your secretary passed along all those messages."

Now she was getting her stories mixed up. Mack knew he was on to something. "Destiny, it's not like you to forget what tale you've told. What's the real scoop here?"

"I have no idea what you're talking about. I asked you to do a good deed. You did it. That's the end of it, isn't it?" Now she hesitated. "Or did you find Dr. Browning attractive?"

"In a quiet, no-frills sort of way," he said, considering that to be a bit generous. She had nice, warm eyes, pale blond hair in a chin-length style and lovely skin, but she didn't do much to accentuate her femininity, not like most of the women he knew. All of that made it much harder for him to understand the little frisson of attraction he'd felt toward her. Maybe it was nothing more than the obvious challenge she represented.

"Mack, didn't I teach you that the packaging is not what counts with a woman?" Destiny chided.

He laughed at that. "You tried."

"Perhaps you should reconsider the lesson. It was a good one."

"I'll keep that in mind."

"Well, if that's all, Mack, I've got to run. I have a million things to do before my dinner guest arrives."

"Anyone I know?" Maybe if his aunt had a social life of her own, she'd stop messing with his.

"No. This is just someone with whom I've recently become acquainted."

"A man?" he pressed.

"If you must know, no."

"Too bad. I could introduce you to some eligible bachelors anytime you say the word," he said, warming to the idea.

Destiny laughed. "Most of the men you know are half my age. As flattering as I might find that, I doubt it's very wise. There's nothing worse than a foolish old woman trying to be something she's not."

"I do know a lot of rich, powerful men who own their own companies," Mack retorted. "Though, frankly, I think a guy my age might find you more fascinating and challenging than some of the women they're currently dating."

"Ah, there's that silver tongue of yours again," she said, chuckling. "Thank you, darling. I must run, though."

Mack said goodbye, then went over the conversation a few more times in his head. Had Destiny actually admitted to knowing Beth or not? He had a hunch it was something he needed to know before he got sucked right smack into the middle of one of her schemes. Forewarned was forearmed with his aunt.

Beth studied the older woman seated across the elegant dinner table from her. So, this was Destiny Carlton.

Beth had been caught completely off guard when she'd returned to her office after Mack's visit to find a message from his aunt inviting her to dinner. Curiosity had compelled her to accept. Maybe tonight she'd learn why Mack had seemed so sure that Beth and his aunt were already acquainted.

So far, though, the evening had been filled with idle chitchat. Beth was growing increasingly impatient. She put down her fork and met Destiny's penetrating gaze.

"Pardon me for being direct, Ms. Carlton, but why am I here?"

Destiny's blue eyes sparkled with merriment. "I was wondering when you were going to ask that. I'd heard you were direct."

Beth wasn't sure what to make of that. Surely there hadn't been time for Mack to report back to his aunt. "Oh?"

"No need to look so worried," Destiny said. "As I'm sure you know, I do a lot of fund-raising for the hospital. I tend to hear about the rising stars on the medical and research staff. Your name has come up rather frequently in recent months. When I heard about your messages for my nephew, I decided it was time we met."

"I see." Beth was still a bit confused. "Are you interested in funding some of the research at the hospital?"

"Always, but my interest here has more to do with Mack. What did you think of him?"

"I'm not sure I understand what you're asking," Beth responded cautiously.

"Come, dear," Destiny said with a hint of amusement in her voice. "From all reports, you're an exceedingly brilliant doctor. Surely you have some idea of what I'm asking."

"Not really," Beth insisted, not sure she wanted to go down the path Destiny seemed determined to explore.

"Women have a tendency to fall all over themselves when they first meet Mack," Destiny said.

"I don't doubt that," Beth said, not that she intended to be one of them. She didn't have time for a man who took so little seriously. Even as that thought entered her head, she recalled just how seriously Mack had taken Tony's situation. Maybe he wasn't as much of a lightweight as she'd assumed, but that still didn't make him her type.

Not that she had a type, she amended. Not anymore. Not since she'd discovered that the kind of man she'd always been drawn to, men who loved medicine as much as she did, often had an ego that couldn't stand the competition from a woman in the same field.

That was how she'd lost her fiancé. Her team had inadvertently applied for the same research grant Thomas had applied for, and she'd won it. He had not taken the news well. Not only had she lost him, but a month later the grant had been withdrawn because of a vicious rumor he'd deliberately spun about her research methodology. Beth had been crushed by the betrayal, but she'd learned a valuable lesson about not mixing her professional and personal life.

"But you weren't impressed by Mack," Destiny guessed.

Now there was a minefield, Beth thought. Insulting him to his face was bad enough. Insulting him to his doting aunt, who raised millions for the hospital, was something else. Beth wasn't the most politically savvy creature on earth, but she knew better than to offend a major donor.

"Actually I didn't spend that much time with him," Beth said truthfully.

Destiny's lips twitched as if she were fighting a smile. "Very diplomatic. I like that."

"Are you trying to set me up with your nephew?" Beth asked bluntly.

Destiny's eyes widened in a totally phony display of innocence. "How could I do that? You and Mack have already met. Either something clicked or it didn't. I'm sure you know as much about chemistry as I do, perhaps more."

Beth chuckled. "Some forms of chemistry, yes. The male-female thing is definitely not my area of expertise."

"My nephew might make an excellent teacher," Destiny suggested slyly.

"I don't think so." Beth grinned at the determined woman. "Does Mack know you're sneaking around behind his back trying to fix him up?"

"As I said, how could I fix him up with you since you've met? You're two consenting adults capable of making your own decisions," Destiny said, as if the thought had never crossed her obviously devious mind.

"But a little nudge from you wouldn't be out of the question, would it?" Beth suddenly recalled Mack's earlier suspicion that she and his aunt knew each other. "He's on to you, isn't he? He thinks you deliberately got him over to the hospital today to meet me. Seeing Tony was simply a means to an end."

"You called his office," Destiny reminded her. "He came over there to meet Tony at your request."

Beth couldn't argue with that. "Would you have been as quick to intercede if the request had come from one of my male colleagues?"

"Of course," Destiny claimed. "We're talking about a sick child."

Beth wasn't entirely sure she believed her. Nor, she suspected, would Mack.

"Look, Ms. Carlton—"

"Please call me Destiny. I insist."

"I appreciate what you're trying to do, Destiny, or at least what I think you're trying to do, but it's a bad idea,"

Beth said emphatically. "I'm not interested. Mack's not interested. Let's just leave it at that."

Rather than the disappointment Beth had anticipated, Destiny's expression brightened.

"Perfect," Destiny said.

"I beg your pardon?"

"I said that was the perfect response. You're going to be a challenge," Destiny explained. "I love that. More important, it is exactly what my nephew needs in his life. Most women are all too eager to fall right into his bed."

"I don't have time to be the challenge your nephew needs," Beth said, beginning to feel a little frantic. She had a hunch that Destiny Carlton was a force to be reckoned with once her mind was set on something. Besides that, the whole image of falling into Mack's bed was a little too attractive. She needed to stay away from these two. They had money. They had power. And one of them at least had a plan for the rest of Beth's life, a plan she wasn't one bit happy about.

"Of course, you have the time," Destiny said blithely. "Everyone has time for love."

Love? *Love?* Sweet heaven, how had they gone from talking about the prospect of her even having a date with Mack to falling in love with him?

"Not me," Beth said fiercely. "I definitely do not have time for a relationship. Really, Destiny. I don't have a second to spare. My days are crammed. There are simply not enough hours for all the work I have to do."

"You made time to have dinner with me at the last minute," Destiny reminded her. "You could just as easily make time for Mack. Keep that in mind when he asks you out."

"He is not going to ask me out," Beth said confidently.

"And if he does, the answer will be no." A resounding no, she thought to herself. Bad enough to have to fight that little twinge of attraction she'd felt for him. She did not need to waste her time trying to fend off his aunt's machinations as well.

Destiny's smile spread.

"Stop that," Beth said. She could practically read the woman's mind. She was going back to that challenge thing again. "I am not saying no just to play hard to get. I am saying it because I am not interested. Period. That isn't going to change. I suspect your nephew has enough women saying yes that he won't waste too much time mourning my rejection, assuming he even asks me out in the first place. We didn't exactly get off on the best foot. I was being very insulting about him, and he happened to overhear me."

Destiny looked vaguely shocked by that. "You insulted him?"

"I never meant for him to hear me," Beth said in her own defense.

"But all the same," Destiny said. "He really is a fine man."

"I'm sure you believe that," Beth said, trying to extricate herself from the increasingly deep and murky waters of this conversation. "I only pointed out what he'd heard so you would understand why I don't think he's likely to ask me on a date."

"Oh, Mack has a thick enough hide. He has to, after being in the public eye for so long. He'll ask you out. He won't let a little unwitting insult stop him," Destiny said confidently. "All I ask is that you give the invitation some thought."

"Why me?" Beth asked, completely bemused that a

woman she'd barely even met seemed so certain Beth was right for her obviously beloved nephew.

"I think that will become clear in time," Destiny said enigmatically. "Just promise me you won't close any doors."

"I can't promise that," Beth said honestly. In fact, at the moment, with panic spreading through her, she was pretty sure that slamming the door on Mack Carlton and his meddling aunt, then bolting it tight, would be the smartest thing she could do.

Then again, she couldn't recall the last time she'd felt this little *zing* of anticipation humming through her veins. Sadly, it wasn't altogether unpleasant. Just dangerous.

# 3

Mack Carlton was as good as his word. It began to seem as if every time Beth went into Tony's room in late afternoon, Mack was there. It was evident he'd become a quiet, comforting, dependable presence in Tony's life, just as he'd promised he would. She began to feel the first faint hint of respect for him, despite her determination to keep her guard up.

Sometimes he sat quietly reading a book while the boy slept. Beth couldn't help noticing that Mack's taste ran to thrillers, rather than to the sports books she would have guessed. She even caught him totally absorbed by a recently released presidential biography. He rose another notch in her estimation that day. She tried to smother the reaction by reminding herself that she couldn't weaken, not with Destiny Carlton scheming in the wings.

Sometimes Beth arrived to find Tony in a spirited argument with Mack over the best football players ever. Mack listened intently to whatever case Tony made, and even when he disagreed, he did it in a respectful way that seemed to make Tony sit a little taller in bed, pride shining in his eyes at being taken so seriously by a man he idolized.

On more than one occasion, they played one of the electronic games that Mack provided. When they were caught up in the competition, they barely spared Beth a glance. That gave her a chance to observe the two of them a bit more closely. To her amusement, it was evident that Mack was having as much fun as Tony and was every bit as determined to win, not giving the boy an inch out of pity.

There was something a little too appealing about Mack with his hair mussed, his collar open, his expression totally focused as he concentrated on that little screen with such intensity.

To Beth's surprise Mack was also sensitive to Tony's level of exhaustion and his shifts in mood. Mack seemed to know just when to encourage a nap and just when to initiate some distracting activity. And he always left shortly after Tony's mother arrived, clearly attuned to Maria Vitale's need to spend time alone with her son.

The first time Beth saw Mack in the hallway outside Tony's room consoling an obviously shaken Maria, she caught herself looking for evidence of the kind of chemistry that Destiny Carlton had been talking about over dinner. If her reaction had involved anyone other than Mack, she might have labeled it a ridiculous twinge of jealousy, but with Mack that would be absurd. There was absolutely nothing between her and the ex-football star. Her interest was purely clinical, a chance to study how the male-female-chemistry thing worked.

After all, Mack was a virile man with a reputation for appreciating beautiful women. Maria was a gorgeous woman with a flawless olive complexion, a lush body and flowing waves of black hair. Only the exhaustion that was clearly visible in and around her eyes marred her beauty. For some men, Beth thought, that evidence of vulnerability would make her seem even more attractive. Beth couldn't help wondering if Mack was one of those men.

But despite her intense curiosity, Beth never saw the slightest sign that Mack was interested in the single mom. Even his attempts to comfort her were verbal, not physical. And rather than any hint of a growing closeness between the two, more often than not, he left mother and son together and sought Beth out when he left Tony's room.

In little more than a week, Beth had come to count on him dropping by far more than she should. While he'd shown no evidence of being attracted to her, he was giving her more attention than she'd expected from him.

Now, at the rap on her office door near the research lab, Beth glanced at the clock and saw that it was just past six. That was when Mack usually stopped in.

"Yes?" she said, fighting the little flash of heat that licked through her as she anticipated seeing him for a few minutes.

Her office door cracked open and, as expected, Mack peered around the edge. "Busy?"

Just this once she should tell him yes. That would be the smart thing to do. These brief little visits were beginning to feel too right, as if her day would be somehow incomplete without them.

"I have a few minutes," she said instead, telling herself that there was nothing wrong with indulging herself in the company of a sexy man in the privacy of her office. It didn't mean a thing. It just proved she was a woman, something she tended to forget when she was caught up in the whirlwind of her job.

"Long enough to go for coffee?" he asked, his expression hopeful. "I could really use a jolt of caffeine. It's been a long day, and I still have a dinner thing at eight."

This was something new. Beth wasn't sure what to make of the invitation. In her office, on her turf, she felt confident and in control of the situation. Even in a setting as thoroughly unromantic as the hospital cafeteria, with Mack buying her coffee she had a feeling that the balance of power between them would somehow shift.

Mack grinned at her hesitation. "I'm asking you to go for coffee, Doc. I swear I won't try to seduce you behind the vending machines."

"I was just thinking about everything I have to do before I can get out of here tonight," she fibbed.

Mack's grin spread. "If you're going to make a long night of it, then you need the coffee as much as I do."

"You're right," she said, telling herself that any other reply would make her seem churlish and ungrateful. After all, this man was coming here almost daily to bolster the spirits of one of her patients. The least she could do in return was share a cup of coffee with him. "I'll buy."

Her offer seemed to amuse him, but he stood aside as she brushed past him, then he closed her office door behind them.

As they walked through the hospital corridors, Beth noticed the stares of the nurses, which were accompanied by more than a few whispers. This, she realized, was what she'd feared about being seen with Mack. She needed to command respect among the staff, not be the subject of speculative gossip.

"Doesn't that sort of thing get old?" she asked as they passed another cluster of gaping females.

"What?" Mack asked blankly.

"The women staring at you, speculating about you, looking you over as if you were a piece of meat."

He shrugged. "I don't really notice it anymore."

Beth couldn't decide if that was ego talking or a weird kind of humility. In fact, she was beginning to think there were a lot of fascinating contradictions in Mack Carlton. Worse, she was beginning to want to unravel them.

He studied her with a penetrating look. "I'm sorry if it bothers you. It didn't occur to me that you being seen with me around here might stir up talk. Would you rather go somewhere else?"

She shook her head. "No, the cafeteria's fine. I don't have time for anything else."

As they approached the line, he regarded her with concern. "Have you eaten?"

"No, but I'll grab something later or take a sandwich back to my office."

He glanced at the board of specials. "Come on. They have meat loaf. How can you pass that up?"

Beth chuckled. "I've had it before. Trust me, it is not like anything you ever had at home."

"Ah, then no to the meat loaf." He glanced along the display of prepared foods. "The salads look fresh." Before she could decline, he reached for two and put them on a tray, then added two bowls of soup. "Crackers?"

Giving up the fight, Beth nodded. "Sure, but I thought you were going to dinner at eight."

"I am. Rubber chicken and a lot of schmoozing. I'll be lucky to get a couple of bites. Believe me, this is a

lot more appetizing, and the company is a thousand percent better."

Beth tried not to feel flattered by the compliment,
but it warmed her just the same. No wonder Mack had
women falling at his feet. His charm was instinctive
and natural, not the phony kind of lines she would have
expected him to utter. He was slipping right past her
natural wariness.

When he'd added apple pie and two cups of coffee
to the tray as well, he brushed off her offer to buy and
paid the cashier himself, then led the way to a table in
a far corner of the room where there were fewer people
around.

Once they were seated, Beth regarded him with curiosity. "Do you always get your own way?"

He seemed genuinely surprised by the question. "No,
why?"

"You just steamrolled right over me back there," she
said.

"I figured you were trying to be a lady."

She studied him with a narrowed gaze. "Meaning?"
she asked, expecting some totally chauvinistic remark
that would permit her to dislike him again.

"When it comes to food, my experience is that most
women would rather starve than admit to a man that
they're hungry. They seem to think we'll worry that
they're about to start putting on weight. Personally I
like a woman with a healthy appetite and a little meat
on her bones."

Beth bit back her impulse to point out that she had
neither. She should have known Mack wouldn't be so
reticent.

He gave her a thorough once-over, then added, "You

...d use a few more pounds, Doc. People might take you more seriously if you didn't look as if a strong wind could blow you away."

"The people who count seem to take me fairly seriously already," she said.

"But it's important to get lots of vitamins and minerals from food, right?" he said, placing her food in front of her. "Munching on a couple of vitamin caplets and drinking an energy shake does not constitute a healthy diet."

Beth almost choked on her first spoonful of soup. How the heck did he know what she usually ate? "What have you been doing? Lurking outside my office door at mealtime?"

"Nope. No need to. The industrial-size vitamin bottle's in plain view on your desk and the trash is littered with empty shake cans. If you ask me, that's a sure way to end up sick."

"What made you an expert on nutrition?" she asked irritably, because he was right and she didn't want to admit it.

"Destiny pretty much drilled the basics into us, but anything she missed, I got from the team doctors when I was playing football," he explained. "Food is fuel. Without the right fuel, the body isn't going to run properly, not for long, anyway."

She gave him a wry look. "I'll keep that in mind."

"You should," Mack said, his expression serious. "Tony and a lot of other kids are counting on you, Doc. You won't be able to help them if you get sick yourself."

"Point accepted," Beth said, deliberately taking a bite of salad to prove she'd gotten the message.

They ate in silence for several minutes, then Mack asked, "How's Tony doing? Any change?"

"You've probably seen for yourself that he's getting weaker every day. We're doing everything we can to build him back up so we can try another round of chemo, but nothing's working," she admitted, her frustration evident in her voice. "Maybe you could work some of your nutritional magic with him. He's not eating."

"I'm on it," he said at once. "Anything he can't have?"

"No."

"And I won't be breaking any rules by carting in takeout?"

"I'll save you from the food police around here, if you can just get him to eat," Beth promised.

"Consider it done. I think I have a pretty good idea what might tempt a twelve-year-old kid to eat. And I can always give him the same spiel I gave you about the body needing fuel."

"Thanks," Beth said sincerely. "These days he's much more likely to listen to you than me."

"It's a guy thing." Mack grinned. "Of course, I might have to insist that you stop by to split a pizza with us or maybe some tacos. Kids learn best by example."

Beth chuckled despite herself. "Still trying to fatten me up?"

"Just a little."

"It seems to me the women I usually see on your arm are all model thin."

Mack's expression darkened a bit. "Don't believe everything you see in the paper, Doc."

"Are you saying the pictures lie? How can that be?"

"Put an ambitious female and a sleazy photographer in the same room and all it takes is the click of a shutter to create a false impression," he said with an unmistakable touch of bitterness.

Before Beth could comment, he waved off the topic. "Let's not talk about that. Anything on the search for a bone marrow donor?"

Beth wasn't sure what to make of the quick change in subject, but she accepted that Mack didn't intend to say another word about the women in his life. Instead, she tried to answer his question about Tony honestly. "He's on the list, but we haven't been pushing because he's not a good candidate right now."

"Anything I can do?" Mack asked.

"Just keep coming to see him. It's the only time I ever hear him laugh," she said quietly.

Mack studied her intently. "What about you, Doc? How are you doing? This is getting to you, isn't it? I mean even more than it was before. You're scared, aren't you?"

Beth struggled with the emotions she tried to keep tamped down so they wouldn't overwhelm her. Mack had a way of bringing them right back to the surface, of forcing her to confront them.

"Terrified," she admitted finally.

Mack reached for her hand. "You know, even doctors are allowed to have feelings."

"No, we're not," she said, jerking her hand away from the comfort it would be far too easy to accept. "We have to stay focused and objective."

"Why?"

"It's the only way we can do our jobs."

"Without falling apart, you mean?"

She nodded, her throat tight. Now she was the one who was uncomfortable with the turn the conversation had taken. "Can we talk about something else, please? I can't do this, not tonight."

Mack sat back in his chair. "Sure. We can talk about whatever you like." He grinned. "Want to talk about football?"

She relaxed at the teasing note in his voice. "It would have to be a brief conversation, unless you intend to do all the talking."

"You know us jocks. We can go on and on about sports at the drop of a hat," he taunted. "But I'll spare you. How about politics? Any opinions?"

"I saw in the paper that your brother finally announced he's running for city council in Alexandria."

Mack's expression darkened a bit. "Yep, Richard's fulfilling the legacy our father left for him."

Beth heard the edgy note in his voice and studied him curiously. "You don't seem pleased by that."

"If it were what my brother really wanted, I'd be all for it, but the truth is Richard has spent his whole life living up to these expectations that were drilled into him when we were boys. Running Carlton Industries is one thing. That's the family legacy and he loves it. He was clearly destined for it. But politics? I'm not convinced it's what he wants. He'll do it, though, out of a sense of duty to a man who's been gone for more than twenty years, and he'll do it well."

"Have you told him how you feel?"

He gave her a rueful look. "Nah. You don't tell Richard anything. He's the one who tells the rest of us what to do."

"Do you resent that?"

"Good grief, no. If he hadn't taken the pressure off the rest of us years ago, I'd probably be behind some desk at Carlton Industries pushing a pencil. I'd not only be totally miserable, but I'd probably bring down the company."

"Singlehandedly?" Beth asked skeptically.

"No, I imagine Ben, our younger brother, would be even worse at it than me."

"I think I read somewhere that he's an artist. Is that right?"

Mack's eyes twinkled with knowing amusement. "Checking us out, Doc?"

"No, it's just hard to avoid the mention of the Carlton name in the local media. Even your reportedly reclusive younger brother's name pops up from time to time."

"If you say so."

"Why would I bother checking you out?" Beth inquired irritably.

"Some women think we're pretty fascinating men," Mack responded with a straight face.

"I'm not one of them."

"So you only tolerate me hanging around for Tony's sake?"

"Yes," she said.

His skeptical gaze caught hers and held until she flushed under the intensity. Only when he was apparently satisfied that he'd rattled her and proved his point did he finally glance away.

Relieved to be out from under that disconcerting gaze, Beth drew in a shaky breath. No man had ever unnerved her the way Mack Carlton did. For the life of her, she couldn't figure out why that was. Sure, he had the kind of body that would look great on a beefcake calendar. Sure, he even showed evidence of being kind and sensitive, two traits she admired in a man. He had a killer smile, an agile brain and a charming personality. With all of that added together, the question shouldn't have been why he unnerved her, but why she hadn't thrown herself straight into his arms.

That she could answer. Mack Carlton was a rich, ex-jock playboy, who didn't take anything seriously. His affairs were played out publicly, and she was a very private woman with a reputation to protect. So even if that glimmer of heat she thought she saw in his eyes from time to time was real, even if these brief hospital encounters implied a certain fascination on his part, she couldn't allow any of it to lead anywhere—assuming he even wanted to pursue it himself beyond the occasional cup of coffee or idle conversation at the end of the day.

Too bad, she thought, barely containing a sigh. Because something told her that Mack had the kind of moves that could make a woman not only forget every last bit of common sense she possessed, but could send her right up into flames.

A couple of days after his fascinating cafeteria dinner with Beth, Mack was sitting in the hospital waiting room while the doctors examined Tony when he looked up to see Richard striding toward him.

"What are you doing here?" he asked, standing to give his brother a hug. He glanced pointedly around the empty room. "No prospective voters in here to impress."

"Very funny. Actually I was in the neighborhood, and Destiny told me you might be here," Richard said. "What's going on? What are you doing hanging out in a hospital waiting room?"

Mack shrugged. "There's a sick kid I've been coming to see," he said as if it were no big deal.

Richard studied him intently. "You're here every day from what I hear. You getting too emotionally involved with this boy?"

"This isn't about me," Mack said defensively. "The boy doesn't have a dad to hang out with. He likes football. The least I can do is come by for an hour or so."

"I admire you for taking an interest, but is it really all about the kid?"

Mack stared at him, instantly suspicious. "What exactly did Destiny say to you?"

Richard's serious expression finally cracked. A grin spread across his face. "She mentioned that the boy's doctor is a very pretty woman with a brilliant scientific mind. Which hooked you, bro? Her body or her mind?"

"I am not hooked on anybody," Mack retorted defensively. "That's ridiculous. Next time you talk to her, tell Destiny to mind her own damn business."

"Ha," Richard said. "What are the odds of that ever happening?"

Mack scowled at his brother. "So the real reason you dropped by is to gloat. You think I'm about to get reeled smack into the middle of one of Destiny's schemes."

"That's what I'm thinking," Richard agreed unrepentantly. "If so, I want to be around to witness every second of your downfall."

"Destiny claims she doesn't even know Beth Browning," Mack said. "Beth said the same thing."

"Ever heard of the little white lie?" Richard asked. "What kind of manipulator would our aunt be if she didn't make liberal use of whatever tactic serves her purposes? She wasn't entirely honest with me or Melanie, either. She sucked us both right in and never suffered a moment's remorse because of it."

"Well, there's nothing like that going on here," Mack insisted. "I'm not the doc's type. She's not my type, either. If Destiny really is behind all of this, she got it wrong this time."

"We'll see," Richard said. "Any chance the doctor will be by anytime soon? I'd like to get a good look at her. Melanie will have questions."

"Too bad. I'm pretty sure Dr. Browning is at a medical conference on the other side of the universe today," Mack said just in time to see the very woman in question strolling their way. He sighed heavily. "On the other hand, she could be back."

Richard's eyes widened with appreciation and he let out a very soft whistle. "Not your type, huh? Maybe you should get your eyes checked."

Mack took another look at Beth and tried to see what his brother saw. She was pretty enough in a natural, wholesome way, but compared to the beauties he usually dated, she was fairly unimpressive. Her hair was straight and cut in a severe, simple style that clearly required little fuss. Her simple, tailored clothes did nothing to flatter a figure he'd already assessed as too thin. Her low-heeled shoes, a necessity for a woman on the run all day long, did nothing to enhance her legs. Mack was really, really partial to women in strappy spike heels that made their legs look endless. He simply didn't get whatever it was Richard obviously saw.

Eventually his gaze made its way to Beth's eyes, which were regarding him with a perplexed expression. He blinked and looked away guiltily.

"I thought you'd want to know that it's okay to go back in to see Tony now," she said.

"Thanks."

Richard looked from Beth to Mack and back again, then shrugged. "Dr. Browning, I'm Mack's brother Richard. He seems to have lost his tongue. It happens sometimes. I can understand it in your case. I imagine you render him speechless a lot."

Beth gave Richard a startled look and a blush tinted her cheeks. "Not that I've noticed."

Richard grinned at Mack. "Then it must be something I said."

Before Richard could explain that remark and further embarrass him, Mack clapped his brother on the back a little more forcefully than necessary. "Thanks for stopping by to pass on the message," he said. "I know how busy you are, though, so feel free to take off. Give Melanie a kiss for me. Go win over a few voters or raise a few million for your campaign. You're going to need it, since I intend to vote for whoever runs against you."

Richard barely managed to contain a laugh at the brush-off. "If it comes down to one vote costing me the election, I didn't deserve to win in the first place," his brother said, unperturbed. "And I'm in no hurry. I can hang here awhile."

"No you can't," Mack said, his voice a little tighter. "I'll walk you out."

He spun Richard around and aimed him toward the door. As they were leaving, he called back to Beth. "Let Tony know I'll be back in a minute."

"Sure," she said, staring after them with a puzzled expression.

Not until they were in the elevator did Mack face his brother, staring him down with a look meant to intimidate. "Don't get any ideas, big brother. None, you hear me?"

Richard returned his glare with a look of pure innocence. "I can't imagine what you're talking about. I just wanted to get to know your new friend."

"You say that as if you'd caught me on the playground with some girl in pigtails," Mack grumbled.

"Believe me, I am well aware that you're past being infatuated with a kid. Those are definitely grown-up sparks flying between you and the doc."

"You're crazy."

"I don't think so," Richard said. "Maybe I'll have Melanie give her a call and set up dinner."

"You do and you're a dead man," Mack said fiercely. He didn't want his brother, his aunt or anyone else messing with Beth's head—or his, for that matter. "Leave it alone. This is not like that. Beth and I chat from time to time. We have coffee. It's no big deal, and I don't want to turn it into one."

Richard's gaze narrowed. "You really mean that, don't you?"

"What was your first clue?" Mack retorted.

To his consternation, Richard burst out laughing. "I'll be damned," he said. "Destiny's done it again."

"Destiny hasn't done a thing," Mack shouted after him as Richard strolled off.

Unfortunately, it was evident that his protest hadn't done a thing to convince his brother. Heck, he wasn't so sure he was buying it himself anymore.

# 4

After his disconcerting encounter with his brother, Mack realized that he hadn't been out on anything that qualified as a real date in several weeks. Maybe that was why he was feeling so edgy and out of sorts. Maybe that was why he was spending so much time seeking out Beth for a few minutes of female companionship at the end of the day.

Beth was quiet and undemanding and most definitely female. Seeing her casually at the hospital was a comfortable pattern to have fallen into. In fact, her total lack of personal interest in him was a relief after the pressure of too many feminine expectations and after his own misguided attempts to live up to the public perception that he was some sort of football-celebrity playboy. There had been a time when he hadn't minded being labeled that way, but it had grown old recently. Very recently. In fact, it had happened when he'd realized it had shaped Beth's view of him.

Consoled by the notion that his attentions toward Beth had nothing to do with an interest in the doctor herself, he vowed to rectify the situation as quickly as possible before anyone other than Richard started getting ideas. It would be especially bad if Destiny got wind of his nightly chats with the doc.

Rather than going directly back inside the hospital, Mack pulled out his cell phone in the parking lot and called an attractive stockbroker with whom he'd done a little professional business and a whole lot of off-the-clock deal-making of a personal nature.

Ten minutes later he'd scheduled a dinner date for later in the evening at her place. Given their usual pattern, they'd spend most of their time concentrating on dessert.

Satisfied with the proof that Richard was dead wrong about Mack's interest in Beth, he went back to Tony's room to play a few quick video games before his date. When he opened the door, though, he caught Beth with the hand-held computer, a little furrow of concentration on her brow as she tried to master the fast-paced game. His heart seemed to do an odd little stutter at the sight. He had no idea why.

"Come on, Dr. Beth," Tony encouraged. "It's not that hard."

"Tell it to someone who'll buy it," she grumbled, not taking her eyes off of the small screen. "You hustled me, kid. You told me this was easy."

Tony laughed. "It is," he insisted, his gaze moving to Mack, who stood frozen in the doorway still trying to understand his unexpected reaction. "Show her, Mack."

"I don't need his help," Beth retorted.

Tony rolled his eyes. "She keeps getting killed at level one."

"Uh-oh, that's not good," Mack said, shaking off the

disconcerting mood and moving across the room to stand behind her.

He leaned down to whisper a few tips in her ear, but the scent of a faintly sexy, musky perfume caught him by surprise. He was pretty sure she usually smelled of antiseptic and something vaguely flowery. This was something new. He wasn't sure he liked it. It made his thoughts stray directly toward rumpled sheets and pillow talk. He mentally cursed his brother for planting that idea in his head.

"Go away," Beth said, not even glancing at him. "I can do this."

Mack chuckled at the display of independence. "If you say so," he said, moving to sit on the edge of Tony's bed. He glanced at the boy, who was grinning broadly.

"Women," Mack said with a hint of exasperation. "You can't tell them anything. That's a lesson you need to learn at an early age, Tony."

Beth did look up then, and the hand-held computer beeped and whistled as she went down in an apparent burst of video flames. She glared at it, then scowled at Mack.

"Tony, do not listen to a thing this man tells you about women," she lectured primly.

"How come?" Tony asked. "Have you seen the babes he dates?"

At Beth's sour expression, Mack bit back the chuckle that crept up his throat. He sensed that now was not a good time to reinforce Tony's enthusiasm for Mack's well-publicized social life. Nor was a denial that he had a stable of "babes" likely to be believed by either of them.

"I think what the doctor is trying to say is that I might

not be the best example for you to follow when it comes to matters of the heart," Mack said.

Tony stared at him. "Huh?"

Mack tried to control a grin and failed. "Yeah, I don't get it, either, but women are funny about things like this. We'll have a man-to-man talk on the subject another time."

"Not on my watch," Beth said grimly. "Tony, you need to get some rest."

"But I'm not tired," Tony protested.

"I think she wants to get me alone," Mack explained to him. "She probably wants to chew me out for being a bad influence."

"Oh, give it a rest," Beth muttered. "This isn't about you. It's about Tony not getting overly tired."

"Hey, Doc, you were the one in here playing video games. I just got here," Mack reminded her.

Frowning at him, Beth marched to the door and held it open, giving Mack a pointed look until he finally shrugged. He bent down to ruffle Tony's hair, promised he'd be back tomorrow, then followed her from the room.

"Mind telling me what that was all about?" he inquired, regarding her with amusement. "Are you just a sore loser?"

"Don't be ridiculous."

"Jealous?" he suggested, surprisingly intrigued by that particular scenario.

She gave him a look that could have melted steel. "I don't think so."

"There must be some reason you don't want me talking to Tony about women."

"How about the fact that it's inappropriate? It's not your place. Besides that, he's twelve, for goodness' sakes. He doesn't need to start thinking about girls in that way for a while."

"I had a girlfriend when I was twelve," Mack said, recalling the blue-eyed imp with curly hair rather fondly.

"Why doesn't that surprise me?" Beth responded irritably.

Mack smothered a laugh. "Something tells me you were not dating at twelve."

"I wasn't dating at twenty," she snapped. "That's hardly the point."

"Then what is the point?" He studied her closely. "And why did you wait so long to date? You're not bad-looking." He deliberately chose the massive understatement just to see the flags of color brighten her pale-as-cream cheeks.

She opened her mouth to respond, then snapped it shut again.

"Not sure?" he taunted.

The fire in her eyes died slowly. She regarded him with a vaguely chagrined expression. "Not entirely, no."

"Yeah, that happens to me sometimes, too. I lose track of what point I was trying to make. Of course, it usually only happens when a really sexy woman catches me off guard. Is that what happened here? I got to you in there, the adrenaline started rushing around, and you kinda lost track of things?"

The fire came back with a vengeance then. "In your dreams, bud."

She whirled around and stalked off, leaving Mack to stare after, oddly aroused by the whole exchange.

"Hey, you didn't tell me why you were such a late bloomer," he called after her.

She pointedly ignored him, her spine rigid as she

rounded a corner and disappeared from view. Only when she was out of sight did he stop and question exactly which one of them had actually won this latest little skirmish. Since he was standing here all hot and bothered, he had a feeling Beth had triumphed without even realizing the game they were playing.

Every positive point Mack had accumulated in recent days flew out the window as Beth walked away from his taunting gaze. The man was maddening. He was an immature, skirt-chasing rogue. Worse, he prided himself on it.

Giving Tony advice on women? Please! What was he thinking? If Maria Vitale heard about that, she'd probably ban Mack from ever seeing her son again.

Then, again, maybe she wouldn't, Beth concluded with a sigh. Mack was good for Tony, inappropriate remarks and all. He made the boy laugh, and under current circumstances, even Beth could forgive him a lot for accomplishing that miracle.

That didn't mean she had to like Mack or spend another minute in his company. She'd simply steer clear of him. It shouldn't be that difficult. It wasn't as if he was underfoot at the hospital all day long.

He had a job, an important job in the view of some people, even if she wasn't among them. He had a family, even if at least one member of that family was in part responsible for pushing Mack into Beth's life. He had a lot of community obligations. And, goodness knows, he had a social life. Given all that, it was astonishing that he spent any time at all at the hospital. Avoiding him should be a breeze.

Satisfied with her plan, Beth had barely made it back to her office when Mack appeared in the doorway.

"You!" she muttered, not sure whether she was more annoyed at him or at herself for not anticipating that he'd be right on her heels.

Mack chuckled. "You didn't actually think we'd finished talking, did you?"

"I had high hopes that we had," she told him. "Don't you have a date or something?"

"As a matter of fact, I do," he responded. "But I have time for this."

"For what?" Beth asked warily as he strode across her office.

"This," he said, lowering his head to touch his lips to hers.

It began as a gentle, exploratory kiss, maybe meant to tease, maybe to shock. Beth reached up to shove him away, but instead found herself clutching his jacket just to hold herself upright. Her knees were suddenly unsteady, her heartbeat frantic. In some distant part of her brain, she heard herself saying that this was crazy, that it was stupid, that it was dangerous. The litany of warnings went on and on, as did the kiss until her brain shut off and her senses took over.

She heard a soft moan of pleasure and realized it came from her as Mack's mouth plundered hers, making her blood sing and her head reel. This was bad. Really, really bad.

But oh, so good, she thought with a whimper of dismay as he slowly pulled away, one arm still firmly behind her back, one hand gently cupping her chin.

As her eyes fluttered open, she was looking into his

steady, turbulent gaze. She couldn't have looked away if her life depended on it.

"What the hell just happened here?" Mack murmured under his breath.

Beth had a hunch he was asking the question more of himself than of her. Even so, she was tempted to offer Destiny's explanation of chemistry, which she was pretty sure she totally understood for the first time in her life. She wondered how Mack would react to the idea that she and his aunt had had a little tête-à-tête about sexual attraction. She had a hunch he'd be more stunned and exasperated than he already seemed to be.

"I'm actually asking," he said, when Beth remained silent. "What just happened here?"

Something in his tone irked her even more than his assumption that he could walk into her office and kiss her senseless. "I would think a man of your worldliness and sophistication would recognize a kiss that got out of hand better than most," she snapped, jerking away and moving to stand behind her desk. It wasn't much of a defense, but she'd take anything she could get. "I think you should leave now."

To her annoyance, Mack seemed vaguely amused by her response, or maybe by her actions.

"Retreating to a neutral corner, Doc?"

"No, trying to get some work done. I've already wasted enough time on you for one day."

"A great kiss is never a waste of time," he told her, his lips curving into a smile. "Especially for a woman who didn't start dating till after she turned twenty. You have a lot of time to make up for."

Great? He thought the kiss was *great?* Beth had certainly thought so herself, but as he'd just reminded her, she sure as heck didn't have his level of expertise on the subject. How flattering was that? One of the region's most eligible, sought-after bachelors thought she was a great kisser. It almost made her exasperation with him fade.

"Go away," she said, because she was pretty certain that letting him stay another second was a bad idea. She just might be tempted to throw herself at him to see if the kissing could get even better.

Suddenly she recalled what Mack had said when he'd first entered her office. He had a date. The man had a date and he'd been kissing her. Maybe that was par for the course in his life, but not in hers. It seemed a little sleazy, in fact. No, a *lot* sleazy. She frowned at him.

"Go away," she repeated more emphatically. "I wouldn't want you to be late for your date."

"Date?" he echoed blankly.

"You told me you had a date," she said tightly.

He muttered an expletive and got out his cell phone.

"You can't use that in the hospital," she told him.

He muttered something else, then picked up her phone and dialed, punching in the numbers so hard the phone practically bounced on her desk.

With his gaze locked with Beth's, he offered some sort of halfhearted excuse to whoever was on the other end of the line, then hung up.

Beth stared at him. "You broke your date?" she asked incredulously.

"I broke the damn date," he said, not sounding especially happy about it.

"Why?"

"Because I'm taking you to dinner instead."

She bristled at the assumption. "I don't think so."

"Oh, yes," he said. "I just broke a date for you. The least you can do is have dinner with me. You don't want me to spend the evening alone, do you?"

Beth couldn't decide which part of his recitation to react to first. "Okay, let's get something straight," she began. "You did not break that date for me. I didn't ask you to do it."

"No, but after that kiss we shared, you'd have been furious if I'd gone through with it," he said.

"Furious? I don't think so. I might have thought you a little sleazy," she admitted, "but then I don't have a very high opinion of you to begin with, so that shouldn't be too worrisome for you."

"Cute."

"I'm not finished," she said. "Whether or not you spend the evening alone or with a steady stream of willing women has nothing whatsoever to do with me."

"I didn't think so, either, at least not until a few minutes ago," he agreed pleasantly.

"What happened a few minutes ago?" she asked cautiously.

"I kissed you and decided I'd rather take a chance on getting to do that again instead of going out with a sure thing." He settled down in the chair beside her desk. "If you have things to do, I can wait."

Beth sorted through his latest outrageous claim and tried to decide whether to be flattered. Since listening to flattery was dangerous around Mack, she concluded it was smarter to ignore it.

"I could be a long while," she told him to test his determination. "A really long while."

He picked up a medical journal from the corner of her

desk. "Take your time. This doesn't look like fast reading. It ought to keep me occupied for hours."

She stared at him, thoroughly bemused. "You're really not going to leave, are you?"

"Not without you," he said, already flipping through the journal.

"I don't understand you," she said plaintively.

Mack looked up and met her gaze, looking almost as bemused as she felt. "To tell you the honest truth, Doc, I'm not real sure I understand what's going on here, either."

Beth's pulse did a crazy little lurch. "I suppose I can spare an hour for dinner," she said ungraciously. "Not one second more."

Mack dropped the journal on her desk, his eyes filled with something that might have been relief. "Let's go, then."

He steered her out of her office, a hand possessively placed in the center of her back. Beth liked the touch more than she cared to admit.

When they turned toward the front of the building, rather than toward the cafeteria, she regarded him curiously. "I thought we were going to the cafeteria."

"Not tonight," he said tightly.

"We only have an hour," she reminded him.

"Believe me, you have made the timetable abundantly clear. It may take a little finesse, but I will have you back at your desk in an hour."

A few minutes later they pulled up in front of one of the hottest new restaurants in Washington. The gossip columns were filled with lists of society bigshots and power brokers who'd been turned away each evening. Mack had barely stopped the car, however, when the valet parkers converged, gave him a ticket and ushered Beth to the curb.

"I'll need the car back here in front in fifty-five minutes," Mack told the valet.

The man checked his watch, made a note on the ticket, then said, "No problem, Mr. Carlton. It'll be here when you're ready to leave."

Inside the crowded foyer, Mack spoke to the maître d' in a hushed tone that Beth couldn't hear. Two minutes later they were seated and practically no time after that two steaming meals were placed in front of them, along with a chilled bottle of sparkling water.

"Since you're going back to the hospital, I took a chance that you wouldn't want champagne," Mack said.

Beth nodded slowly. "The water's perfect." She looked at the grilled salmon on her plate, the tiny Red Bliss potatoes with parsley, the perfectly steamed green beans, then lifted her gaze to Mack's. "So is the meal. How did you manage this in…?" She glanced at her watch. "Less than five minutes."

Mack shrugged. "No big deal. In a place like this, it's all about who you know."

"And you know the maître d'?"

"Among others," he said.

"The owner?"

"Yes."

Beth shook her head in amazement. "Given that crush of people out there waiting to get in, I know we took someone else's reserved table. Are there other diners in here who are still waiting for these particular meals to appear?" she asked, glancing around worriedly.

He grinned. "Don't feel guilty, sweetheart. They're probably having wine to tide them over."

"Probably?" She regarded him incredulously as the reality of the extremes to which he'd gone sank in. She wasn't sure whether to laugh or cry at the absurdity of it. "You really did steal someone else's dinners? And you bribed them with a bottle of wine?"

"Not me," he claimed with suitable indignation. "I never left your side."

"You know what I mean."

"Eat up, Doc," he encouraged, clearly unwilling to be drawn into the discussion. "That clock of yours is ticking and I, for one, intend to have the crème brulée for dessert. I'd recommend the chocolate soufflé, but we're a little short on time for that."

"Unless, of course, some unwary couple already happens to have their order in," Beth teased, not sure how she felt about a man who could snap his fingers and make this happen, apparently without offending anyone. In some ways, that was the most astonishing thing of all.

"Good point," Mack said, and immediately beckoned for their waiter.

"Mack, don't you dare," Beth said.

"You'll settle for the crème brulée?"

"I think that's best," she said, even though she was sorely tempted to throw caution to the wind and opt for the chocolate soufflé. "Otherwise we're liable to start a riot."

Mack grinned. "I guess it will be the crème brulée for dessert, John. Give us about twenty minutes, though, okay?"

"Sure thing, Mr. Carlton." He leaned down to whisper conspiratorially. "Of course, if you're on a tight timetable, there's a soufflé that should be ready in a half hour.

I could put in another order for those diners and put this one in one of our takeout containers. Would that work?"

Mack glanced at Beth. "What do you say? Dessert at your desk?"

There were a lot of things in life that Beth could resist. Chocolate wasn't one of them, and a warm chocolate soufflé just out of the oven had the power to smash her resistance to smithereens. There were many things she might not like about Mack, many more things about which she had serious reservations, but if he could get her that dessert, she was willing to forgive a lot.

Giving in to temptation, she said, "The chocolate, definitely."

Mack regarded her with fascination as the waiter walked away. "Good to know," he murmured, his gaze on her filled with heat.

"What?" she asked, her voice surprisingly shaky.

"That your weak spot is chocolate."

"That's one of them," Beth agreed, since there seemed little point in denying the obvious, not when she'd just caved and renounced several of her scruples to get a soufflé for dessert.

Mack lifted his glass of water. "To discovering the rest," he said, his tone soft and his gaze serious.

Beth returned his gaze and tried not to notice that her heart and her stomach were turning cartwheels. Sweet heaven, was there any female on the face of the earth who could remain immune to this man once he set out to be charming? She certainly prayed she'd turn out to be one of the rare ones, but right at this moment she didn't give herself a chance in hell.

# 5

Mack had absolutely no idea how his evening had taken such an unexpected shift the night before. One minute he'd been looking forward to his date with a woman who undoubtedly would never speak to him again now. The next minute he'd been irresistibly drawn to Beth's office just for the simple pleasure of stealing a kiss. It didn't make a lick of sense.

Something about her revelation that she'd hardly dated as a teenager had stirred some kind of purely male reaction in him. If he hadn't known himself better, he might have thought it was some sort of weird attraction to the virginal nature of the admission, which was ridiculous. Not only had Beth not said anything at all about *still* being innocent, he definitely preferred women who knew the score.

But that hadn't stopped him from hightailing it after her like some sort of overheated jerk intent on making a conquest. He was damn lucky she hadn't guessed all of the undercurrents behind that kiss and leveled him with some sort of sedative, the way a vet took care of an unruly animal.

Okay, he thought as he unintentionally snapped a pencil in two, that explained the kiss. The assessment wasn't pretty, nor did it speak well of him, but it was honest. It did not, however, give him a clue about what had happened during and after the kiss.

The woman had made his supposedly rehabilitated knees weak. When in hell was the last time that had happened? Maybe never. He never lost control of a situation the way he had last night. From the minute his lips had touched Beth's, he'd been transported to some other dimension, a place where he wanted to take risks and give pleasure, not in some casual, meaningless way, but something real and lasting.

Which was absurd. Totally and utterly absurd, he decided as another pencil broke in two in his grip. He stared at the little pile of wood and lead and concluded he needed to get out of his office and away from all this unfamiliar introspection before it led him down a dangerous path or at least before he destroyed most of his office supplies. Wasn't he the one who was always going on and on around here about wasting everything from bandages to paper clips?

Outside and in his car, a recently developed habit made him turn in the direction of the hospital, but he overrode the instinct and headed instead to Virginia. He hadn't been out to Ben's farm in a while. Being around his artistic brother was usually soothing. Ben was an accepting guy. He took people as they came. He didn't ask a lot of probing questions, especially since his own life was such a mess. Nor was he the least bit inclined to meddle. Yep, visiting Ben was definitely a good choice. Mack would be able to chill out for a couple of hours and forget all about that disconcerting encounter with Beth.

As Mack approached the farm, the rolling Virginia countryside slowly began to work its magic. Mack found himself unwinding and understanding for the first time what had drawn Ben out here after the tragedy that had shaken him to his core. It was hard to feel anything here except for an appreciation of nature's beauty in the distant purple haze of the Blue Ridge Mountains, the soft green of the grass, the canopy of towering oaks and the majestic stature of the horses grazing behind pristine white fences.

Because Ben was always hungry, rarely paused to eat and never stocked his refrigerator with any decent junk food, Mack stopped at a coffee shop in town and picked up sandwiches, sodas and chips to take along as a peace offering for interrupting his brother's work. He grabbed a few freshly baked chocolate-chip cookies while he was at it. Those would go a long way in diverting Ben's attention away from the reason for Mack's unexpected visit.

By the time he finally reached the gate to his brother's place, Mack had pushed aside all thoughts of his own tumultuous emotions, if not the image of Beth herself.

Mack parked in the shade of an oak tree and headed directly to Ben's studio in the converted old red barn. No one responded to his knock, but that was fairly common. Ben wouldn't hear a herd of Black Angus cattle approaching if he was absorbed in one of his paintings.

As he stepped into the barn, Mack noted it was a good ten degrees cooler inside, despite the sun shining through a skylight overhead. As Mack had expected, Ben was staring at a half-finished canvas, his brush poised in midair, a faraway look in his eyes. Something told Mack that look had less to do with the work on his easel than with a sad memory of the tragedy that had sent him scurrying to the country in the first place.

"Hey, bro," Mack said, startling Ben, who took a long moment to shake off his mood before he finally met Mack's gaze.

"Has the sky started to fall?" Ben inquired. "Surely that must be the case for you to drive all the way out here on a weekday."

"Nope. As far as I know, the sky's still in place. I'm here on an impulse." He performed a visual search of the studio, then gave an exaggerated sigh of disappointment. "I was hoping you'd have a naked model in your studio."

His brother grinned, the last shadows finally disappearing from his eyes. "I paint landscapes," Ben reminded him. "Which you would know if you weren't such a culturally deprived human being."

"Hey, I appreciate art," Mack objected. "Especially yours. I have a sketch you did of me on my refrigerator door."

"How flattering! I believe I was six when I did that."

"Yes, but you showed promise even then," Mack said with total sincerity, then had to ruin it by adding, "And I'm sure when you're really, really famous that little scrap of paper will be worth a fortune."

"Not if you get mustard and ketchup all over it," Ben retorted, then caught sight of the bag in Mack's hand. "You brought food. I take back every mean thing I said to you, if that's lunch for me. I had an idea when I woke up this morning and skipped breakfast to come straight out here."

Mack glanced at the canvas. As Ben had said, he was no expert, but this didn't look like his brother's usual style. "How's the idea working out?" he inquired carefully.

"Not quite the way I envisioned it," Ben admitted. "Now hand over the food. If one of those sandwiches is roast beef, it's mine."

"Which is why I got two roast beef," Mack said. "I'm tired of you stealing mine."

Ben chuckled. "Took you long enough to catch on. Did you get orange soda?"

Mack regarded him innocently. "I thought you liked grape."

"Very funny. Hand it over."

"Damn, but you're greedy. What happened to the whole starving artist thing?"

"I was never a starving artist. I can thank our parents for that. I'm famished. There's a difference." Ben took a bite out of the thick roast beef, lettuce and tomato sandwich and sighed with obvious pleasure. "Nothing on earth better than a fresh tomato in midsummer."

"Unless it's corn on the cob," Mack countered, falling into the familiar debate. "Dripping with butter."

"Or summer squash cooked with onion and browned."

Mack regarded his brother wistfully. "Do you suppose we could plant an idea in Destiny's head and get her to cook all our favorites this Sunday?"

"You mean, could *I* plant the idea in her head?" Ben guessed.

"You are the one she loves best," Mack pointed out, drawing a sour look. Ben refused to admit that their aunt was partial to him, and Destiny would deny it with her dying breath. "Besides, she thinks you don't eat enough. She'd have pity on you. It would just take one little word."

Ben regarded him curiously. "Since when has the cat got your tongue? Nothing's ever stopped you from pleading with our aunt to fix you something special."

"Truthfully, I'm trying to avoid Destiny these days," Mack said casually.

"Won't that make eating all these goodies you want a bit tricky?"

"I was kinda hoping you'd pack up some leftovers and bring 'em to me," Mack admitted.

Ben chuckled. "Don't tell me. She's found a woman for you. What's wrong with Destiny's selection? Does she have buckteeth and wear glasses? Or is she simply not up to a ten on the Mack-o-meter for beauty?"

"I am not that shallow," Mack protested. "And there's nothing wrong with the woman. Nothing at all."

Ben studied him quietly. "I see," he said slowly, fighting a grin. "In other words, Destiny got it just right and you're running scared."

"Go suck an egg," Mack suggested mildly.

"Want to talk about it?"

"Nope."

"But panic is what brought you flying out here bearing gifts," Ben surmised.

"Can't a guy go visit his brother without getting cross-examined about ulterior motives?"

"Sure, but since you haven't been here in weeks, you'll have to excuse me for being a little suspicious."

Mack frowned at him. "We could talk about your social life."

Ben's expression immediately shut down. "No, we couldn't," he said tightly.

Mack instantly felt guilty for turning the tables on

Ben. "I'm sorry. I was only teasing, but I should know better. The wound's still too raw, isn't it?"

"Drop it," Ben said, his tone angry, his eyes dull.

Mack regarded his brother helplessly. "Maybe I shouldn't. Maybe it would help if we all made you talk about it."

"Graciela's dead, dammit! What's to talk about?" Ben all but shouted in a fierce tone rarely used by Mack's soft-spoken brother. "Why the hell doesn't anyone get that?"

Mack barely resisted the urge to go to his brother, but Ben wouldn't appreciate any gesture of sympathy. Ben still blamed himself for Graciela's death and was convinced he wasn't deserving of sympathy. He only resented anyone's attempt to assuage his grief or his guilt.

"I'm sorry," Mack said again quietly. "I didn't mean to stir up the pain. That was the very last thing I wanted when I came out here."

Ben gave him a haunted look. "You didn't stir up anything," he told him. "It never goes away."

Telling Ben that Graciela wasn't worthy of the kind of guilt or misery Ben heaped on himself wouldn't help. Mack knew that much by now. He wasn't sure what it would take to finally shake Ben out of the dark, brooding mood which kept him isolated out here at his farm, but he prayed it would happen soon. Ben's ongoing despondency worried the whole family. Once in a while they caught glimmers of the old, easygoing Ben, but those reminders were all too rare.

Mack studied his brother. "Anything I can do?"

"Nah," Ben said, obviously fighting to shake off his mood before Mack could make too much more of it. "Just keep coming around despite my general crankiness."

"That's a promise," Mack assured him.

Ben glanced across the table and his expression brightened. "You gonna finish that sandwich?"

Mack chuckled. "I thought the big, hulking football player in the family was supposed to be the one with the insatiable appetite," he grumbled even as he shoved the other half of his sandwich toward his brother. "Take the chips, too. I have to hit the road."

"Big date tonight?"

"No."

"Damn. You know I live vicariously through what I read about you in the papers."

"Sorry to disappoint you, but I'm living life in the slow lane right now."

"There has to be a story there," Ben guessed.

"None I intend to share."

"But it does have to do with that woman Destiny picked out for you, right?" Ben prodded.

"I came out here because you never pry," Mack grumbled.

"But this news is too good to pass up," Ben told him.

Mack frowned at him. "Get back to your canvas. Right now it looks a lot like a squashed pumpkin. Is that what you were going for?"

Ben groaned. "Heathen!"

"Hey, I have a good eye."

"For women, maybe."

Mack deliberately squinted intently at the half-finished painting. "The very large rear of a woman in an orange two-piece bathing suit?"

Ben laughed. "You were closer with the pumpkin."

"Well, what the hell is it?"

"Since you're having so much fun guessing, I think I'll let you wait till it's finished. Then you can try again."

"I'm usually better at this," Mack said. "Then again, you usually paint recognizable fields and trees and streams."

"This was an experiment," Ben reminded him.

Mack regarded him seriously. "A word of advice?"

Ben nodded, his expression wary.

"Stick to what you know," Mack said, then dodged when Ben tossed his empty soda bottle straight at his head. For an artsy kind of a guy, his brother had dead-accurate aim.

Better yet, for most of an entire hour, Ben had kept Mack's mind off one very disconcerting lady doctor.

"I'm not happy with Tony Vitale's blood count," the hematologist sitting across from Beth said. "He's not responding the way I'd hoped. I think we ought to consider a transfusion before he gets any weaker."

Beth bit back a sigh. She didn't have a good argument against that, but she was afraid that scheduling a transfusion would be demoralizing for Tony and for his mom. They would both know that all the other steps being taken weren't working. Transfusions were commonplace enough with kids in Tony's situation, but none of them were crazy about the process, even if they felt temporarily better in the end.

"Do you disagree?" Peyton Lang asked.

"Not really, but I know how discouraged Tony and his mother will be. I was really hoping that this last medicine and the food Mack's been bringing by for him would do the trick and get his blood count back up again, at least for the short term."

"Believe me, so was I," Peyton said. "We're running out of options."

"We can't give up on him," Beth said, unable to keep the frantic note out of her voice.

Peyton gave her a sharp look. "We may not win this one. You know that, Beth. It's time you started accepting the possibility. Maybe you need to pull back a little, let someone else step in as Tony's attending physician."

"Absolutely not. Besides, losing Tony is just a possibility," Beth said fiercely. "And I refuse to accept it until there are no other options. He's such a brave kid. He doesn't deserve this."

Peyton gave her a sad look. "None of them do."

"No, they don't, do they?" she said wearily. "Okay, then. Schedule the transfusion for first thing in the morning. I'll talk to Tony's mom tonight."

The hematologist looked as if he wanted to say more, but he finally shrugged and left without another word. Some things just couldn't be said aloud, even though they both might be thinking them. And no doctor ever wanted to acknowledge that a fight might be nearing an end.

A once-familiar sense of outrage and anger stirred in Beth's chest. She needed to get back in the lab and look over the latest test results from her current research one more time. The first batch hadn't held much promise, but this recent round was looking more hopeful. She needed more time, dammit. More time to get it right, so she could help Tony and some of the other kids who were at the end of the line with current treatments.

She was at the door, about to open it, when Mack appeared. He took one look at her and steered her right back inside her office.

"What's wrong?" he demanded at once. "Sit down. You look like hell."

"Just what every woman wants to hear," she muttered, even as she gratefully sank back onto her chair. The longer she could postpone seeing Maria and Tony, the better.

"I'm not here to flatter you."

"Obviously not. Why are you here?"

"I just saw Tony. He's not looking so good."

Beth nodded. If it was apparent even to a layman, then her decision a few minutes ago was the right one. "He needs a transfusion to buy him a little time," she admitted bleakly.

Mack looked stunned by the blunt assessment. "A little time?" he echoed warily. "What are we talking here, Beth? Days? Weeks?"

"No more than that."

"What about the bone marrow transplant?"

"He's not a candidate right now. It would be too risky."

"You just said he's only got a few days or weeks. Isn't it about time to start taking a few risks?"

"There's protocol," she began, only to have him cut her off with a curse. She looked into his eyes and saw the same torment she'd been feeling before his arrival. "I'm sorry, Mack."

"I won't accept this."

"We don't have a choice."

"I have a choice," he all but shouted. "We'll find another doctor, another treatment. That boy is not dying unless we've exhausted everything available."

Beth tried not to feel hurt that Mack didn't think she knew what was best, that he didn't think she was up to the task of saving Tony. She understood the kind of powerless rage he was feeling all too well. If she'd thought for a second that another doctor or another course of treatment might improve Tony's odds, she would have called for the consultation herself.

"Mack, right here at this hospital, we are his best hope," she said quietly.

"But you're giving up," he protested.

*"No,"* she said vehemently. "Never. I'm just trying to be realistic."

"Damn being realistic," he said heatedly, then sighed and gave her an apologetic look. "I'm sorry. I know I shouldn't take this out on you. I know how hard you're working on his behalf. I know how much he matters to you."

"It's okay. Believe me, I understand your frustration."

"And I see now why you looked so beat when I got here." He met her gaze. "What's the plan?"

"A transfusion in the morning and then we wait to see if it helps," Beth explained. "A little prayer wouldn't be misplaced, either."

Mack nodded. "Okay, then." He held out his hand. "Want to go with me to pay Tony a visit?"

"I was on my way when you got here," she said, taking his hand because right now she desperately needed the contact with someone who shared her dismay. She also needed the little spark that came with it, the reminder that no matter what happened with Tony she was alive, that she would still be here fighting for other kids down the road.

Mack gave her hand a squeeze. "How about we take a little detour to the chapel on the way?"

She met his gaze. "You read my mind."

It was a habit of his that she was starting to take for granted. Moreover, instead of making her uncomfortable, it was beginning to feel very, very good to have that kind of connection with someone.

"Dr. Beth's really pretty, don't you think so, Mack?" Tony's huge eyes were focused intently on Mack's face.

Mack tried to ignore the question. He wasn't getting drawn into that discussion with yet another matchmaker. Instead he held up the assortment of comic books he'd brought with him. "Look at these, Tony. I had no idea there were so many cool new superheroes out there."

Tony's gaze remained unrelenting. "You didn't answer my question, Mack. Don't you think Dr. Beth is really pretty?"

Mack sighed. "Yes, she is."

"Maybe you should ask her on a date or something. I'll bet she'd go."

Mack had enough trouble convincing Beth to slip out of the hospital for an occasional meal on the run. An actual honest-to-goodness date was probably out of the question. He didn't want to ruin his image with Tony by admitting that, though.

Tony studied him worriedly. "She didn't turn you down already, did she? Did you say something to make her mad?"

"No, kid, I haven't bombed out entirely with the doc, but she's pretty busy, you know. She has a lot of responsibilities around here."

"I know. That's why I think she needs a date, to get her mind off things, you know what I mean? Sometimes she seems real sad."

"I've noticed," Mack said. In fact, some days he wondered how she stood it. Today had to be one of the worst since they'd met. Even he was shaken by the grim outlook for Tony's future.

Earlier, when they'd been on their way from the chapel to Tony's room, she'd gotten a beep and had taken off at a run with a terse apology and no explanation. He was dawdling in Tony's room now, hoping she'd eventually turn up. If that beep meant the kind of emergency he suspected, he thought she might be in need of some company this evening, maybe even another dinner someplace that wouldn't remind her of the hospital.

He turned his attention back to Tony, whose energy had obviously faded. He was resting against the pillows, which were barely a shade whiter than his pale complexion.

"How are you feeling, pal?"

"Kinda tired," Tony confessed.

Mack was taken aback by the rare admission. Usually Tony was all bluster when it came to his health. For him to admit that he was feeling tired meant he had to be exhausted. Mack recalled what Beth had said about a transfusion, but he knew the word on that hadn't gotten to Tony yet.

"Get some sleep. You want to be rested when your mom gets here after work," Mack told him.

"But you just got here," Tony protested weakly. "And you brought all those awesome comics."

"They'll be here when you wake up, and so will I," Mack promised. "Now close your eyes and take a nap."

Tony struggled to keep his eyes open. "Hey, Mack."

"What, pal?"

"Could you maybe sit here next to me?"

"Sure," he said, lowering himself carefully to the edge

of the bed. He'd noticed that too much movement seemed to make the boy wince. It was yet another sign that his condition was worsening.

Mack was barely seated when he felt Tony's hand slip into his and hang on tight. Tears immediately stung the backs of his eyes.

"It's okay," he said softly. "You can sleep. I'm right here."

"Can I tell you something?" Tony asked sleepily.

"Anything, pal."

"You won't tell my mom or Dr. Beth?"

"No," Mack promised.

"Sometimes I'm scared to close my eyes," Tony whispered. "'Cause I'm afraid I won't wake up."

Ah, hell, Mack thought, blinking back tears.

"You don't need to worry about that now," Mack said, his voice choked. "Nothing's going to happen while I'm here with you."

Tony's eyes blinked open and his expression turned serious. "It could, Mack. So if it does, will you tell my mom I love her?"

Mack struggled to maintain his composure. If this boy could lie here so bravely facing death, then surely he could give Tony the reassurance he needed to hear. "I think your mom already knows that," he told Tony. "But I'll tell her."

Tony sighed then and finally allowed himself to fall asleep, his hand still clinging to Mack's.

And somewhere deep inside, Mack's heart broke.

# 6

When Beth finally finished dealing with the emergency that had sent her racing away from Mack, she felt as if she'd been through an emotional wringer. The young patient who'd come in with a severe reaction to her chemotherapy had finally been stabilized and sent to a room. Beth would have given just about anything to go home to her own room, to spend an hour soaking in a hot bath and then to crawl beneath the covers and sleep for a month.

Instead, she drew in a deep breath, steadied her nerves and headed to Tony's room to break the news about the transfusion scheduled for morning. She was not looking forward to the meeting with Mrs. Vitale. Maria had had just about all the bad news she could handle lately.

As Beth turned the corner toward Tony's room, she spotted Mack in the hall, shoulders slumped, eyes closed. He was leaning against a wall, looking about as wiped-out as she felt.

"You okay?" she asked.

He blinked as if he'd been a million miles away, then

smiled weakly. "How the hell do you do this every day?" he asked, his voice filled with respect.

Beth instinctively glanced at the door to Tony's room. "A tough night in there?"

Mack nodded, his expression bleak. "You could say that. Tony asked me to tell his mom he loved her if he died during his nap."

"Oh, no," Beth whispered, her heart aching for him and for Tony. "I'm so sorry, Mack."

"Don't be sorry for me," he said fiercely. "Be sorry for Tony. No kid should ever have to say something like that. He shouldn't have that kind of weight on his shoulders. My God, how does he bear it?"

Beth put her hand on his arm, felt the muscle jerk beneath her touch. "I couldn't agree with you more, but sometimes life simply isn't fair or just. If you can't accept that, then you'd better not choose medicine as a career."

"Then you accept it?" he asked skeptically.

"I have to," she said. "It's not easy, but what else can I do? I have to focus on the times we win, not on the times we lose."

"I don't envy you. Compared to this, getting pummeled on a football field on Sundays was a piece of cake."

She managed a weak smile. "Maybe I should give that a try sometime."

He grinned. "I imagine you have some pretty tricky moves, Doc. How's your throwing arm?"

"Like a girl's."

"Yeah, it figures." His expression sobered and his gaze sought hers. "You know what else was on Tony's mind tonight?"

She was almost afraid to ask. "What?"

"He thought I should ask you on a date." Mack shook his head. "The kid is sick as a dog and he's matchmaking."

Beth grinned, despite the sorrow eating at her. "More proof that life goes on. Even a kid like Tony sees that." She studied Mack's tense expression and decided he'd gotten a whole lot more than he'd bargained for when he'd befriended Tony. "Tell you what. I'm going to break a vow and ask you on a date."

Mack regarded her with surprise. "You made a vow never to ask me out?"

"I made a vow never to ask any man out," she corrected.

"Any particular reason?"

"It tends to give a man the illusion that he has the upper hand," she explained.

"And you don't like relinquishing control?"

"Not especially."

"But you're willing to make an exception for me?"

"Yes, and don't make me regret it by reacting predictably and letting your ego get out of hand. It's dinner, Mack. Nothing more."

Mack chuckled. "I think I can control my ego." He gave her a thorough once-over with a devilish twinkle in his eye. "And my hormones, if it comes to that."

She gave him a stern look. "You're determined to cross a line, aren't you? I could take back the invitation."

"You won't, though. You're feeling sorry for me. Besides, I'm not determined to cross any lines, just considering the possibilities," he replied. "Especially since mentioning them has put some color back in your cheeks."

Beth frowned at him, and he managed to look suitably chastened. It was probably an act, but she let it pass. "Okay, then. Can you stick around while I speak to Mrs. Vitale? Then I'll take you someplace for dinner."

He regarded her with a hopeful expression. "Home?" he inquired. "That's where I feel like being tonight. Yours. Mine. It doesn't matter. I just don't feel like being around a lot of people."

Beth totally understood what he was saying. Being under a microscope must be hard enough when life was perfect. Being subjected to scrutiny when you'd been through an emotional wringer as Mack had been tonight would be unbearable.

She tried to imagine what in her kitchen might be edible, given the way she tended to ignore things like grocery shopping, then nodded. "There's bound to be something I can throw together that won't kill us both."

"Works for me," he said.

"I'll just be a few minutes."

"Take your time." He gave her a faint smile. "If you want to make Tony's day, tell him you're taking me home with you."

Beth laughed despite the somber mood and her exhaustion. "I think that might encourage his matchmaking efforts a little too much."

Mack was still a little stunned that Beth had invited him to her place. He must have looked like the emotional wreck he was if she'd felt the need to take pity on him. Despite the obvious reason for the invitation, he couldn't help looking forward to the opportunity to get a look at where she lived and maybe discover a few more details that would tell him what made her tick. His curiosity about her seemed to deepen with each encounter.

A woman with Beth's sort of dedication and commitment to her work, with the compassion to treat kids in Tony's dire straits, was a rarity in his world. His admiration for her grew with every minute he spent around her and the kids to whom she'd devoted her life. He'd done his share of good deeds and small kindnesses in his time, but Beth did Herculean good deeds every day.

When she finally emerged from Tony's room, she gave him a distracted look and beckoned for him to follow her. "We can get out of here as soon as I get my purse and keys," she told him. "I'll jot down my address for you."

A few minutes later she gave him an address on the fringes of Georgetown. He had a hunch she'd chosen it less for the prestige of the neighborhood than for its proximity to the hospital and the short commute required in an emergency.

"See you there in ten minutes," she told him when they'd reached her car in the hospital parking lot. Mack had insisted on walking her there, though his own car was in the visitor's lot. She seemed about to say something more, then hesitated, her expression thoughtful.

"What?" Mack prodded.

"Just trying to remember if there's any wine in the house. Probably not. If you want some, you'll need to stop and pick up a bottle," she said as she got behind the wheel of her small SUV.

"I'm too wiped-out for wine," he told her. "Unless you want some?"

She shook her head. "Not unless you don't mind me falling sound asleep in whatever pot of food I'm fixing."

He studied her weary, fragile features. "Look, Beth, I really appreciate the invitation, but we don't have to do this tonight."

"We both need to eat," she said, sounding exactly like the dictatorial doctor he knew her capable of being. "Don't dawdle along the way or I'll make you eat spinach."

Mack laughed. "I happen to love spinach."

"Oh, my, your aunt really did train you well, didn't she?"

"Let's leave Destiny out of this. See you in a few," he said, dropping a quick kiss on her forehead before closing the door of her car. "Drive safely."

He loped out of the employee parking lot toward his own car half a block away feeling surprisingly energized all of a sudden, enough to motivate him to make a quick stop by the florist's so that when he showed up on Beth's doorstep he was carrying a huge bouquet of flowers.

As he rang the doorbell of her small brick town house, he realized he was anticipating the rest of the evening in a way he hadn't looked forward to a date in a very long time. The knowledge that this impromptu date had been initiated by a woman to whom he supposedly wasn't the least bit attracted didn't seem to matter. Nor did the fact that sex clearly wasn't on the agenda. He was content with the prospect of food and some intelligent conversation, anything that might delay going home, where he was certain to be plagued by dreams about Tony's sad situation.

When Beth opened the door, her eyes widening in delight at the sight of the flowers, Mack felt something shift inside him. He had the funniest feeling that few men had ever bestowed such a simple gift on her before, probably because they mistook her cool, professional demeanor to mean that she didn't appreciate the more feminine pleasures in life.

"Oh, Mack," she said softly, burying her nose in the flowers. "What on earth made you think to do this?"

"A gentleman caller always brings something for his hostess," he recited, grinning at her.

"Remind me to thank your aunt for drilling those manners into you," she said. "I hope I have a vase big enough for all these. Did you buy out the shop?"

Actually he had. The man had been ready to close and had given him a deal on all of the bunches that remained in the cooler. There had been lilies and roses, baby's breath, snapdragons and some other colorful, fragrant blooms he couldn't identify. Impulse had made him take them all. If anyone on earth deserved to be pampered a bit, it was Beth after a day like today. He only wished flowers could brighten his mood as easily. Better to concentrate on Beth.

He could think of all sorts of ways she ought to be indulged. Maybe he'd get her one of those spa days he'd heard women talking about, one with a facial, massages, wraps and who knew what else went on behind those discreet doors.

"Mack?"

"Hmm?"

"Where'd you go just then?" she asked.

"I got a little lost envisioning you in a seaweed wrap," he said just to watch the color in her cheeks deepen.

"What an odd imagination you have," she said, leading the way into the kitchen.

"Have you ever had one?" he asked.

"My time and my budget don't really run to seaweed wraps," she said, clearly amused. "Have you had one?"

He shuddered. "Hell, no, but I hear women talking about that kind of stuff. I thought you might like it."

"Who knows? Maybe one of these years, if I ever get a whole day off, I'll try one," she said. "Seems like a waste of money to me."

"Being pampered is never a waste of money, especially not with the kind of work you do. You need to take better care of yourself."

She regarded him curiously. "Is this some new mission you're on? It's not enough that you cheer up Tony, now you're intent on cheering me up, too?"

He thought about it and decided it was. It didn't have to mean he was falling for her or anything. It was just common decency to worry about someone who spent her life worrying about others. "Yep," he said. "I'm making you my project."

"Don't you have an entire football team to worry about? That's what? Eleven men?"

He chuckled. "On the field at any given moment. There are a lot more on the bench. Remind me to get you a manual explaining the basics."

"It would be wasted. Besides, you're missing my point that you have your own responsibilities. Those should keep you busy enough."

"Not the same thing," he told her. "Besides, those guys have trainers who worry about whether they're eating properly, getting enough exercise and generally staying fit. Who worries about you?"

She shook her head as she poured him a glass of iced tea. "I'm an adult and a doctor. I can pretty much look after myself."

"But do you?"

"Of course I do."

"When was the last time you took a day off?"

She hesitated so long, he knew she was having to really think about it. *"Ding,"* he said as if calling time in a game. "Too long. That must mean it's been weeks, if not months."

She frowned. "Actually I was off last Saturday," she retorted, then sighed. "But I got called in around eleven-thirty and never got away."

"That's exactly what I'm talking about. You're not invincible. What happens if you get so worn down, you get sick?"

"I don't get sick." She gave him an exasperated look. "I appreciate your concern. I really do, but it's misguided." She poked her head in the refrigerator. "Your choices are scrambled eggs or…" Her voice became muffled until she withdrew and gave him a chagrined look. "Or poached eggs or an omelet, assuming this cheddar isn't too hard to grate." She held up a pitiful-looking block of cheese.

Mack shook his head. "Where's your phone?"

"Right behind you on the wall," she said. "Why?"

He was already punching in a familiar number. "Do you have some sort of aversion to meat?" he asked her as the phone rang.

"No," she said, regarding him curiously. "What are you doing?"

"Isn't it obvious? How about baked potatoes?"

"Love them."

Mack nodded. "Hey, William, can you throw together a couple of filet mignons, baked potatoes with sour cream and butter, caesar salads and something decadently chocolate?"

"Absolutely, Mr. Carlton," the chef at one of the Carlton Industries steak-house restaurants in Georgetown said at once. "Is this for your house?"

"No." He gave the man Beth's address. "Will a half hour be too much of a rush?"

"Of course not. I'll send it right over."

"Thanks, William. You're a lifesaver."

"It's my pleasure, sir."

"Oh, and one more thing, William."

"Yes, sir."

"Could you at least wait till morning before you call Destiny and tell her about this?"

"Sir, I do not report to your aunt," the chef said indignantly.

"Not officially, no," Mack said. "But she does have a way of wheedling information out of you, doesn't she?"

William chuckled. "Your aunt is a very clever woman," he admitted. "She does have a way of getting whatever information she wants. Most men find her irresistible."

"Irresistible or not, try not to let her get hold of this little tidbit to chew on, okay? She'll make my life a living nightmare."

"Only because she cares about you and your brothers," William said. "You're very lucky to have such a fine woman in your lives. I'm not sure any of you appreciate that."

"Your scolding is duly noted, William."

"As it should be, sir. I'll have your dinner there shortly."

Mack sighed, almost regretting the can of worms he'd

opened by making that particular call. Unfortunately, despite his tendency to blab what he knew to Destiny, William served the best steaks in town.

As he hung up, he saw Beth studying him with a bemused expression. "Was that William of William's Steak House?"

Mack nodded.

"And he's going to send over takeout in thirty minutes?"

"Yes."

"And then, most likely, report back to your aunt?"

Mack nodded again.

"You live in a very fascinating world."

He grinned. "It has its moments." He regarded her with interest. "I suppose your family is totally normal."

An odd look that Mack couldn't quite interpret passed across Beth's face. "Not so normal?" he pressed.

"I guess that depends on your view of normal," she hedged.

"I mostly grew up with an aunt who regards life as one gigantic adventure and who has turned meddling into a fine art," he said. "Believe me, I have a very loose definition of what constitutes normal. Do you have brothers and sisters?"

A shadow darkened her eyes and he immediately recalled the brother who'd died during a childhood bout with leukemia. "I'm sorry. I forgot about your brother."

"That's okay. Sometimes it feels as if it happened several lifetimes ago."

"Because every time you face losing a patient, it's like going through it all over again," Mack guessed.

"In a way, though at the time I was so young, I was only aware that someone I loved very much was really,

really sick and then he died. It left this huge void in my life, because Tommy was all I had in some ways."

"You mean because he was your only sibling?" Mack asked.

Beth shook her head. "Because after he died, my parents retreated even more deeply into their work. They were research scientists, too. They were never very outgoing, demonstrative people, but after Tommy died, it got worse. They were driven to find answers. Most nights they got home long after I'd gone to bed, and they were usually gone when I got up in the morning. I rarely saw them."

Mack heard the hurt behind the factual recitation, and another piece of the puzzle clicked into place. "So your work isn't really all about your brother, is it? It's also a connection to your parents."

She seemed startled by the comment, then relieved when the doorbell rang to prevent her from having to answer.

Mack looked her in the eye as he stood up to go to the door. "I'm not forgetting about this conversation," he warned as he left the kitchen.

When he returned a moment later, Beth was busy setting the table. She never even looked up to meet his gaze until after he'd set out the dishes from the restaurant.

"It smells heavenly," she said a little too brightly, taking her place at the table. "You must order from William a lot to get such incredible service."

"I do, but it's also a company restaurant in some division or another."

She studied him curiously. "You really don't care about all that, do you?"

"Only when it's convenient, like tonight," he admitted. "Thank God I don't need to think about it. The company is totally and completely Richard's bailiwick."

"You never had the slightest inclination to claim your part of the family legacy?"

"Nope," he said readily. "I made my own money playing football, even though my career was brief. I made some sound investments, then used those to buy a share of the team. I love football. I get it. When I was on the field, I enjoyed the competitiveness, the physical demands of the game. I still like the strategy involved. I don't care about manufacturing widgets or running restaurants or whatever else Carlton Industries is into."

He waved a finger under her nose. "And don't try to get me off track. I haven't forgotten that we were talking about your family."

Her expression immediately closed down. "There's not much more to say."

"Are you trying to prove something to them? Maybe finally earn the attention they denied you growing up?"

She deliberately put a bite of meat in her mouth and chewed slowly, her expression thoughtful. "Probably," she said at last, surprising him with the admission.

"But didn't you learn anything from them?" he asked.

"Sure," she said at once. "I learned all about dedication and focus."

Mack regarded her impatiently. "But they hurt you, Beth. Call it benign neglect, if you want to be generous, but it was neglect. Is that how you want to live your life, being oblivious to the people around you, not having any sort of personal life?"

She stared at him in shock. "Is that what you think? Do you think I don't date much, because I'm trying to emulate my parents?"

"It looks plain as day to me."

"Well, who died and named you Freud?" she inquired tartly.

"Are you denying it?"

"Of course I'm denying it. I work hard because I love what I do, because it matters."

"I'm sure your folks thought the same thing. Did that make you cry any less when you went to bed at night without them there to read you a story or tuck you in?"

"You don't know what you're talking about," she insisted stubbornly. "I was ten when my brother died, much too old for stories."

"But not for a kiss before bed," Mack said, recalling how Destiny had insisted on tucking them all in, even when they protested that they were much too old. He and Ben had loved it. Richard had grumbled loudest of all, but Mack realized now that he'd needed Destiny's attention most of all, and she had instinctively known that and ignored all their complaints.

"It wasn't important," Beth insisted.

Mack shrugged. "If you say so." He met her gaze and saw the confusion and vulnerability she was trying so hard not to let him see. "You know, Beth, when you look at my life, you see a life of privilege, right?"

She nodded.

"Because my family has money?"

"Of course."

He shook his head. "The money's there, no question about it. And it's made a lot of things easier, there's no doubt about that, either. But you know what really made our lives rich?"

"What?"

"Having an aunt who was willing to give up a life she

loved, even a man she loved, to come back to the States to take care of three little boys she barely knew just because they needed her. After our folks died, Destiny was there every single night to tuck us in and reassure us that we'd be okay. She taught us by example that there was still joy to be had in living life to its fullest. She didn't retreat into some other place and hide out, leaving us to struggle to figure out how the hell to heal from the hurt."

Beth carefully put her fork down and met his gaze. "Your aunt sounds remarkable, but my parents did the best they could," she claimed, though there wasn't much conviction behind her defense of them.

"Well, if you ask me, it sure as hell wasn't good enough," he said angrily, thinking about how terrified and lonely she must have been after her brother died, how she must have feared the same thing could happen to her. Had they reassured her about that much, at least? Probably not. In their self-absorbed world, they'd probably never even noticed she needed the reassurance, or maybe they'd even dismissed it as a weakness in a way that had stopped her from even voicing her fears.

"You don't have any right to say that," she said, her lower lip quivering. "None. You weren't there. You don't know what it was like for any of us."

Mack sighed. "No, I don't suppose I do, but imagining what it must have been like for you kills me."

"I was okay," she said, but the tears welling up in the corners of her eyes said otherwise.

"Ah, Beth," Mack whispered, standing up and pulling her into his arms. "I'm sorry. I may hate what they did to you, but I never meant to make you cry."

"I'm not crying," she insisted, sniffing, her face pressed against his chest.

"If you say so," he said, even though he could feel the dampness of tears through his shirt.

"I *never* cry," she said staunchly.

He had a feeling she'd spent a lifetime trying to get the lie to come out so adamantly. "I know," he said, holding her tight and wondering how someone so emotionally fragile ever managed to get through the kind of days she had to endure. She had more real strength than some of the three-hundred-pound players on his team, certainly more than he had.

When she lifted her gaze to his, the tears were still shimmering in her eyes and clinging to her dark lashes. Mack couldn't seem to help himself. He leaned down to kiss a streak of dampness on first one cheek and then the other. The salty tears, the petal-soft skin were wildly intoxicating, far more so than any wine might have been. He needed to resist the temptation, needed to release her before the evening took a turn neither of them had anticipated.

But then with the tiniest shift of her head, Beth's mouth found his, and he was lost.

# 7

Beth had never been so hungry for a man's touch. That it was Mack's touch she craved was a shock, but right now all she could think about was the way his mouth felt on hers, about the way his hands covered her breasts and stroked the sensitive peaks into tight buds of exquisite pleasure.

"Don't stop," she pleaded when he pulled back, his breath ragged. He looked as stunned as she was feeling, maybe more so.

"Beth, are you sure about this?" he asked with obvious worry. "It's been a long, stressful day, and I've just put you through an emotional wringer. I don't want to take advantage of you. I don't want us to do something you'll be sorry about in the morning. Hell, up until a few minutes ago, I wasn't even sure you liked me very much."

"Guess we both know better than that now," she said wryly.

Thanks to the unmistakable concern she heard in his voice, Beth felt more certain than ever that this was right. What Mack had said was true. He had put her through hell with all his questions about her uneasy relationship with her parents. He'd managed to open up too many old wounds and leave them raw.

But no one else had ever cared deeply enough to dig past the facade she put on for the world. She felt connected to Mack in some weird way that didn't bear close scrutiny. And tonight, most of all, she needed to go with her senses for once, and not her head. Her senses were practically screaming for more of Mack's touches.

She looked deep into his eyes. "I want this," she reassured him, reveling in the sandpapery feel of his cheek beneath her lips. "I need to feel alive, Mack. I know you do, too. Please give that to me, to *us*."

She saw by the sudden spark of heat in his eyes that she'd said exactly the right thing. After the turmoil of the day, after listening to Tony's sad request that Mack relay his love to Maria, Mack understood better than most the need to feel excitement and anticipation, rather than dread and despair, to revel in the here and now and tomorrow be damned.

His answer was in the touch of his lips against hers, tender for an instant and then greedy, his tongue plunging deep in her mouth in a dark, sensual assault that filled her body with heat and made her senses spin.

Beth had known he would be good at this—the media made him out to be some sort of expert, after all—but she hadn't expected him to know just how to move her. It was as if their bodies knew something their brains did not, as if there was a mystical connection that ran so deep that one touch was all it took to unlock it.

"Bedroom?" he murmured, his breath ragged.

"No, now," she said, the urgency of her need stunning her as it must be shocking him. She wanted to forget the world and this was the way, the only way. She was already tugging at the buckle of his belt, fumbling for his zipper. She didn't want time to think, time to reconsider, not so much as a second to wonder if this was an act of desperation she would live to regret.

Mack caught her frenzy. Buttons flew as he pushed aside her blouse, then caught the peak of her breast in his mouth, sucking, using lips, tongue and teeth until she was writhing against him, certain that she would fly apart from that touch alone.

With a clever flick, her bra disappeared and then her skirt was hiked up to her waist, her panties stripped away. His fingers found her moist heat and dove inside, making her cry out with the sheer wonder of it as wave after wave of pulsing pleasure washed over her.

That quick, violent release should have been enough to slake the need, but she wanted more, so much more. She tugged at the zipper she'd forgotten in the swirl of wild sensations he'd stirred in her. There was something wild and totally uninhibited in control of her now, a need so great, so demanding that she couldn't have turned away from it even if the thought had crossed her mind. Not that it did. Stopping wasn't an option.

She looked deep into Mack's eyes and saw the answering hunger, the same desperate need even as he rolled on a condom, then lifted her and drove himself into her, filling her, taking her right here, right now with her back pressed against the kitchen wall, her legs wrapped tightly around him as he thrust into her. Her last conscious thought was that she was just beginning to fully appreciate the advantages of a man with the well-toned body and strength of an athlete.

Sensations ripped through her—the cool hardness

of the wall at her back, Mack's rough breathing in her ear, the slick slip-slide of him inside her, the rigid tension of his muscles where she clung to him, the scent of aftershave and sex. It was all so sweet, so powerful, so amazing...and shocking in its unexpected intensity.

When the hard, throbbing waves of a second release finally crashed over her, Beth felt as weak as if she'd been thrown on shore after a storm at sea. But she was exhilarated, too, as if she'd had one exquisite chance to touch the sky.

Slowly, oh, so slowly, she fought her way back to earth, back to the here and now, back to her own kitchen, which would never, ever feel the same again. There were clothes strewn everywhere, a plate had somehow ended up on the floor, a glass of tea had toppled over leaving melting ice cubes sitting in puddles on the table.

Before she realized his intention, Mack reached for one of the cubes of ice and lightly swirled it across the tip of her breast, then lower, his clever mouth following the same intimate path. The shock of cold, the heat of Mack against her still-sensitive skin sent her off into another totally unexpected whirl of mind-blowing sensation. Shattered, all she could do was cling to him and let the ride take her where it would.

Afterward, she struggled with embarrassment, looking everywhere except at Mack until he touched a finger to her chin and forced her to meet his gaze.

"You know, Doc, if I'd just hit that many highs with anyone else, I'd worry about dying on the spot."

Relieved by the flash of humor in his eyes, she said, "But not with me?"

"Nope. I figure you know CPR and you'd be highly motivated to save me so we can do this again."

Her lips curved at the purely male arrogance of the suggestion. "Again?"

"Definitely again." He grinned sheepishly as he tugged up the briefs and pants pooled at his ankles. "Maybe not in the next ten minutes," he conceded, "but most definitely again."

Her own grin spread, along with a heady dose of feminine satisfaction. "In that case, maybe I'd better tell you where the bedroom is, after all."

Lying next to Beth in the middle of the night, Mack was pretty sure he wouldn't have been more stunned by the way the night had unfolded if Beth had stripped naked and run through the hospital. Under all that starch and propriety, the woman had a wild streak. Since she seemed almost as shocked as he did, he couldn't help wondering if she'd known about it all along or if this was something he'd managed to unleash in her. He rather liked that scenario, probably more than he should.

Unfortunately, he also knew that what seemed right and inevitable tonight was going to prove worrisome in the morning, most likely for both of them, no matter how many disclaimers each of them had uttered. He wondered if it wouldn't be smart to slip away before daybreak, but dismissed the idea on several counts. First, it was cowardly. Second, the image of her face when she discovered he'd run out would nag at him. And third, he was pretty sure he couldn't crawl out of her bed even if he wanted to. He might have just enough energy to make love to her one more time before morning, and that seemed infinitely preferable to wasting it sneaking out of her house as if he—as if *they*—had committed some unpardonable sin here tonight.

Right now she was plastered across his chest, exactly where she'd collapsed after riding him to another explosive climax once they'd come upstairs to her room. Mack was just as beat as she was, maybe even more so, but he was also energized in a totally unexpected way. He was filled with a whole new sense of curiosity about this woman who'd once expressed disdain for him and everything he stood for. Apparently she'd concluded he wasn't such a bad guy, after all. Either that or she'd simply been as desperate for human contact tonight as he had been.

Slamming up against the mortality wall had shaken him, especially since the person involved was a twelve-year-old boy he'd grown to love. Usually his life revolved around fun. Even work was something he enjoyed, not something with life-or-death consequences. Since meeting Tony, it had been harder and harder to maintain that devil-may-care attitude. Tonight he'd pretty much snapped.

Beth sighed and snuggled more tightly against him, her head tucked under his chin, her hand distressingly close to a part of him that he was trying hard to ignore so she could get some obviously much-needed sleep.

She shifted again, tormenting him further, but then as if the contact finally sent an electrical charge straight to her brain, her eyes snapped open. She would have scrambled away from him, if he hadn't kept his arm firmly around her waist.

"Where do you think you're going?" Mack asked lightly.

"Over…um, to my side of the bed," she mumbled finally.

"I like sharing the middle," he teased.

She finally met his gaze. "Really?" she asked, looking surprised. "I'm not bothering you?"

"Oh, you are definitely bothering me," he said. "I think that's evident."

She followed the direction of his gaze, then blushed. "I had no idea."

"That I wanted you again?"

"That it was even possible for you to want me again," she said.

Her comment told Mack all he'd wanted to know about the kind of experiences she'd had in the past. Whatever jealous twinges he might have felt about the man who'd hurt her so long ago vanished. "Not to make too big a deal about it, but a guy would have to be made of stone to get his fill of you after just a couple of tastes."

A spark of amusement lit her eyes as she glanced pointedly downward. "I'm not sure the analogy works," she said. "You're obviously rock hard at the moment. And, for the record, it was more than a couple of times."

He feigned shock at the observation. "Why, so it was and so I am. Since you're awake and counting, maybe we ought to do something about that."

"Medically speaking, that's what I'd prescribe," she said agreeably, already shifting to accommodate him.

It was no surprise to him that she was as ready and eager as he was. She'd already proved that her sexual appetite was a more than even match for his. What amazed him was her willingness to let him see this neediness in her, this slight hint of vulnerability that came from sharing something so intimate. He would have been less surprised if she'd kicked him to the curb after that first time downstairs.

The heat between them flared again, this time more

slowly, more sweetly, as if the discoveries they'd made earlier gave them the leisure to savor each touch. Instead of urgency, Mack felt his body taking an exquisitely lazy ride to the top of yet another cliff. Gazing into Beth's eyes, he saw every emotion as she made her way to the same peak.

Only when they were there together, their bodies damp with perspiration, their senses razor sharp so that the mere flick of a tongue, the sweep of a caress worked magic, did they fly over the edge.

Only then, still trembling from that incredible release of passion, did Mack close his eyes and give himself over to sleep, with Beth still cradled in his arms. For the first time in months, maybe years, he wasn't falling asleep after sex, worried that he'd just made a terrible mistake. In fact he felt as if he'd finally done something very right. He was pretty sure that this was the first time that what he'd done could only be described as making love.

Beth wasn't a morning person by nature. Only rigid self-discipline made her reach for the alarm clock to hit the off button and start to roll out of bed in the same fluid movement. When she ran smack into a hard, obviously male body as she was about to make her half-asleep flight from bed, she felt as if she'd suddenly touched a live wire.

Mack! The memory of the night before slammed into her. Every single touch, every single amazing release replayed itself, not only in her mind but in the sudden humming of the blood through her veins. She had to smother a smile. This was better than any alarm clock— bells, buzzers or cheery beeps—she'd ever tried. She was completely, totally, instantly awake. Too bad there wasn't time to do anything about it.

Filled with regrets, she found a way to extricate herself from Mack's embrace. To her astonishment he slept on. It was the dead-to-the-world sleep of the truly exhausted. She smothered another grin at the realization that she'd done that to him. Imagine that! She had left a physically fit, professional athlete—a *playboy*—too wiped out to move. She was still gloating when she climbed into the shower.

The icy water meant to revive her had barely hit her overheated skin when the shower curtain was swept aside and Mack climbed in with her.

Beth stared at him in shock, not sure she was ready for quite this much intimacy, even after the night they'd just shared. "What do you think you're doing?"

"The bed got lonely without you. Besides, I can't let you go sneaking off without so much as a morning kiss."

She gave his body a thorough once-over. "Something tells me you're after more than a kiss."

He grinned and backed her against the tile. "I'm open to negotiations."

"You're a Carlton. Negotiating is second nature to you. I'm sure you always get the terms you want." She hooked a leg around his. "Let's just cut to the chase."

He laughed. "Works for me."

Fifteen minutes later Beth's knees were wobbly and her body still sizzled with so much heat she was amazed the bathroom wasn't filled with steam despite the icy temperature of the water flowing over them. She gazed into Mack's eyes. "What have you done to me?" she asked. "I'm used to starting my day with oatmeal."

"This is healthier," Mack said.

"I'm not so sure about that. I feel a little faint."

He looked pleased with himself at her admission. "You get dressed. I'll fix breakfast. Eggs, I think. You obviously need the protein."

"I don't have time," she said as she scrambled from the shower, wrapped herself in a towel and ran into the bedroom. One frantic glance at the clock proved how true that was. She was running well behind schedule.

"Make time. Breakfast is the most important meal of the day," Mack said, wandering in after her. "You'd think a fine doctor would know that."

"I do know it. I also know I have a jam-packed day ahead of me and I'm already late."

"Then ten more minutes won't make any difference, will it?" he said.

Beth tried not to stare as he pulled on his briefs over his excellent backside, then turned his pants right side out and climbed into those. He didn't bother to button them at the waist. Since they were the only clothes that had actually made it upstairs, Beth was treated to one more excellent view of his muscles as he left her room without wasting another word arguing with her. She sighed heavily after his exit.

As soon as he was gone, she dived into her closet, dragged out the first skirt and blouse she came to, then dressed in the kind of rush with which she was all too familiar.

A quick flick of her brush through hair that had a surprising hint of curl to it—no time to tame it into submission—a touch of lipstick and she was done. By the time she walked into the kitchen, she'd figuratively drawn her protective professional cloak around her. Other than those wayward curls, there was no hint of the wanton woman she'd been during the night.

True to his word, Mack had juice on the table and a plate of perfectly scrambled eggs in his hand. He'd put on his shirt, but thankfully he hadn't buttoned it. She liked the sexily rumpled look. In fact, she was fairly certain she could become addicted to it. She'd have to remind herself later how dangerous and ill advised that would be.

"Sit," he ordered, his expression uncompromising.

The order was a bit less attractive, but the protectiveness behind it had its charm. "Five minutes," she muttered, because it was easier than arguing with him. Besides, she was starved and *her* eggs never looked that good.

The toaster popped up, and she stared at it in surprise. "You found bread?"

"In the freezer," he said, then added wryly, "you should look in there sometime." He put the buttered toast in front of her, then took his own place opposite her with only a cup of coffee in hand.

"You're not eating?" she asked.

"Not enough eggs. I'll grab something at my place when I go home to change."

"I could share," she said, shoving the plate in his direction.

"Nope. I fixed those for you with my own secret ingredient."

She frowned at the eggs. "You didn't find any poison around, did you?"

His lips twitched at the outrageous suggestion. "Why would I want to kill you?"

"So I can never tell about the night you spent in the

arms of a woman who isn't some glamorous model or sexy actress," she said, exposing a hint of vulnerability. She'd been attacked by self-doubt almost from the second he'd left her room. It was running rampant now.

Mack regarded her with disbelief. "Are you crazy? Believe me, letting the world know I slept with a brilliant, dedicated doctor would probably do more for my reputation than you can imagine. This is something worth bragging about, not hiding." He grinned. "Not that I will, of course."

Beth faltered at his acknowledgment that he wasn't ashamed of the time they'd spent together. She hadn't gone looking for any kind of compliment, but she was ridiculously pleased that he'd offered one.

"How?" she asked, unable to resist pursuing it.

"People might finally accept that I have half a brain."

She'd never considered that one aspect of his football and playboy celebrity might mean that people didn't take him seriously. She should have, too. Until she'd gotten to know him, wasn't that how she'd seen him, as a mental lightweight with few scruples? Not even his law degree was that impressive, since he wasn't using it. On some level she'd wondered if he hadn't cruised through law school simply because of who he was. Thankfully she'd never said such a thing. Her cheeks still burned when she thought of the comments he'd overheard her making the first time he'd come to the hospital to meet Tony.

"I'm sorry," she said. "I never looked at all the gossip from your point of view."

He shrugged. "Why would you? It's not as if I ever shied away from it. The image worked for me."

"How so?"

"Because if I ever let anyone take me too seriously—

any woman, that is—I might have to deal with real emotions," he said easily.

The comment and his tone were fair warning. Beth couldn't mistake the message he was sending. "Last night didn't give me any expectations where you're concerned," she reassured him, surprised by just how empty those words made her feel. "It was nothing more than two people who were hurting reaching out for each other."

Mack's gaze lingered on hers, his expression wary. "And you don't have a problem with that?"

She forced herself to shrug. "Why would I?"

"I just thought you might," he said.

"Hey, it was no big deal, Mack. Nothing you need to worry about."

He nodded slowly. "Good to know."

Beth expected to see relief in his eyes, to hear it in his voice, but it wasn't there. In fact, if her imagination wasn't playing tricks on her, what she heard instead was disappointment.

Or maybe she was merely projecting, because right this second she felt more of an emotional letdown than she'd ever felt in her life. If she weren't so late, she'd sit right here and try to figure out why.

Then again, the prospect of spending one more second with Mack right now, when she was feeling totally vulnerable and exposed, was too much to bear.

"Gotta run," she said, taking one last bite of toast, then standing up. "Lock up when you leave."

Before Mack could even react, she grabbed her purse and keys and tore out the door. She wanted to be safely in her car and on the road before the first traitorous tear fell.

# 8

Mack sat at Beth's kitchen table for a very long time after she'd gone, staring into space, trying to figure out why, after such an incredible night, he felt so damned lousy. Surely it wasn't because he'd been honest with her, warned her not to make too much of what had happened between them. He'd had the same conversation dozens of times with dozens of women. It was a part of his spiel, as routine as the flirting that came second nature to him. It usually filled him with relief to know that things had been clarified.

But Beth was not in the same sophisticated, blasé league as all those women. They knew the score from the moment Mack met them, understood the rules going in and accepted them. In fact, they had rules of their own about the level of emotional attachment they were interested in pursuing…or not pursuing.

With Beth, despite that brave, nonchalant front she'd put on, he felt as if he'd just kicked a friendly puppy. There had been a brittle edge to her voice, the slightest hint that she might suddenly shatter if pushed. And in those expressive eyes of hers, he'd seen the faint shadow of genuine hurt.

For the first time in a very long time, Mack wasn't proud of himself and his brand of so-called honesty. He saw it as the cop-out it was, a way to extricate himself from guilt over doing whatever the hell he wanted to do. Something told him if his aunt ever found out about this encounter, she'd tear a strip out of his hide for treating Beth in such a cavalier way. Not that Destiny was likely to berate him any more than he was berating himself at the moment.

Sure, he and Beth were consenting adults. Sure, she'd wanted last night to happen every bit as much as he had. But looking into her eyes this morning, he couldn't help but conclude that it had really meant something to her. Hell, it had meant something to him, too, but he wasn't about to acknowledge that to her or to act on it in the future. At the first warning sign that he might become emotionally involved with someone, he generally took off without a backward glance.

In fact, his usual panic was already telling him that if he had half a brain, he'd immediately start making himself scarce around the hospital. He wouldn't stop seeing Tony, but he was familiar enough with Beth's routine to avoid running into her. No more casual little drop-ins at her office just to catch a glimpse of her. No more coffee breaks in the cafeteria. No more dinners just to get her away from the hospital for a bit. He was pretty sure she'd gotten the message this morning, but just in case, his actions would reinforce it. That was what he *should* do, what he always did.

And, he realized with a sinking sensation, if he followed his usual pattern, he would feel like an even worse heel than he felt like right at this moment. He wasn't sure he had it in him to do the smart thing this time.

When Beth's phone rang, Mack stared at it. With her running late, it could be the hospital calling. It could be an emergency, and at least he could alert whoever was on the other end that Beth was on her way in. Did that outweigh whatever gossip might arise from having a man answer her phone? How would she see it?

With the phone still ringing insistently, he finally grabbed it. "Hello, Dr. Browning's residence."

His greeting was met with silence.

"Hello," he prompted.

"Who the hell is this and why are you answering Beth's phone?" a very possessive-sounding male voice demanded with open hostility.

Now there was a question that could lead down a path Mack didn't want to travel, especially with some stranger who hadn't even bothered identifying himself.

"I'm a friend of Dr. Browning's," he said cautiously. "She just left for the hospital. Can I take a message for her?"

His reply was greeted by another hesitation.

"Well?" Mack prodded.

"No. I'll speak to her when she gets here," the man said. "I intend to tell her I spoke to you."

Mack grinned despite himself at the tattle-tale tenor of the warning. "You do that," he said, then hung up.

He wasn't entirely sure whether to be amused or worried by the threat. He'd know soon enough. His intention to avoid Beth had flown right out the window the instant he'd heard that trace of possessiveness in the caller's voice. If some other man had the right to think of Beth as his, then what the devil had she been doing

in Mack's arms the night before? He wasn't crazy about
the streak of jealousy that had shot through him. He did
know that since it was a first in his life, he had no intention of ignoring it.

Beth spent her first two hours at the hospital racing
from one crisis to another. She was beginning to wonder
if she'd ever get another minute to spend in her lab with
the research that was so important to her. She was also
having trouble staying focused, which wasn't like her
at all. When it came to medicine and her patients, she
rarely allowed anything to distract her. Today, though,
images of Mack and the way they'd parted this morning kept intruding.

At eleven-thirty she'd finally had enough of fighting
the distraction. She needed a break. She needed caffeine.
Caffeine *and* chocolate, she decided en route to the cafeteria. Maybe a lot of chocolate.

After loading up on candy bars and a large takeout
coffee, she found a quiet table, spread her loot out on
the table and debated about which chocolate to eat first.
Snickers had nuts and caramel, but a chunk of plain old
Hershey bar melting on her tongue had its own allure.
Then there was the Kit Kat or the Peanut M&M's or
maybe the Milky Way.

"Boy, your diet really has taken a turn right off the
nutritional charts, hasn't it?" Jason commented, sliding
into the chair opposite her.

Beth glared at the radiologist. "Keep your snide comments to yourself."

"Tough morning?" he asked, then struggled with a
grin as he added, "Or a tough night?"

She stared at him trying to gauge what on earth he

knew or thought he knew. "If you have something on your mind, just spit it out. I'm in no mood for games."

"Yes, I can see that," Jason said, his grin spreading. "The chocolate's a dead giveaway, especially before lunch. Usually you don't have one of these attacks till around four, right after rounds." He gestured toward the little pile of candy. "Even for you this is a bit over the top."

Beth was not half as amused by his observations as he clearly was. "Did you come over here to hassle me or is something else on your mind?"

The radiologist regarded her innocently. "Can't I do both?"

"Not if you expect to live," Beth said sourly, tearing open the M&M candies and popping several into her mouth.

Unfortunately, Jason didn't look daunted. If anything, the level of amusement in his eyes increased. "Called your house looking for you earlier," he said. "You were running late. I got worried. Beth Browning is never late. She never misses an important meeting."

Her gaze flew to his. "What meeting?"

"Peyton called one to talk about Tony. He wanted to go over a few things with our entire oncology team before Tony's transfusion this morning. You didn't know?"

"Oh, hell," Beth moaned. "Yes, I knew. It completely slipped my mind. Was he furious?"

"Actually, I think he was relieved. It was the first sign any of us have ever had that you're human and fallible."

Beth covered her face with her hands. "What is wrong with me? How could I forget a meeting like that?"

"Maybe it had something to do with that man who

answered the phone at your house when I called," Jason suggested mildly. "Could that be?"

Beth had honestly thought it impossible to be any more embarrassed, but with her cheeks burning and her stomach churning, she discovered she'd been wrong. This was a thousand times worse.

"You, um…" She gazed into Jason's laughing eyes, then sucked in a breath. "You spoke to my houseguest?" There, that was a good, safe, anonymous description of Mack, though she intended to be sure that he was never her guest again.

"That I did," Jason said gleefully. "Funny thing, too. He wasn't much more communicative about his identity than you're being."

"Maybe because it's none of your business who he is," she replied testily.

"My money's on Mack Carlton," Jason responded.

Beth fought the panic creeping up the back of her throat. "Why on earth would you think that?"

"Informed guess," Jason told her. "And the fact that I recognized his voice."

"From meeting him once?" she asked incredulously.

Jason laughed. "For the moment I'll ignore the fact that you as much as admitted it was Mack and say that his voice is familiar because he's interviewed on TV about every ten seconds during football season." His expression suddenly sobered. "You sure you know what you're doing, Beth? This guy has a reputation, you know."

"Tell me about it," she said glumly.

"Don't get in over your head."

Because she desperately needed someone to talk to, because she could use a male point of view and because she trusted Jason to keep his mouth shut, she muttered, "Too late for that, I'm afraid."

Jason regarded her with shock. "You're not actually falling for him, are you?"

*"No!"* she said so fiercely that Jason whistled in disbelief. She scowled at him. "Oh, shove a sock in it."

"That will severely limit my attempt to give you some well-meaning advice."

Beth sighed heavily. "Okay, then, talk, but try not to sound smug or disgustingly macho. Remember, I'm your friend and your colleague. Mack's just some football idol you met once."

Jason opened his mouth, then clamped it shut again, his expression going blank.

"Jason?" Beth prodded.

"I think the cat's got Jason's tongue," Mack said, pulling up a chair to join them. "Isn't that right, Jason?"

"Pretty much," Jason said. "I think I'll go take some X rays or do some radiation treatments or maybe lock myself in a convenient closet."

Mack gave him an approving look. "Thanks. Nice talking to you earlier. That was you on the phone, I assume."

"Yep," Jason said.

Then he took off like the little weasel he was. Beth had expected better of him. Hadn't he just warned her about Mack? Then why would Jason turn right around and leave her alone with the man? It must be some tacit, male, nonpoaching, noninterference agreement that women weren't privy to.

"You answered my phone this morning," she said accusingly, frowning at Mack. "What possessed you to do that?"

He shrugged. "It was ringing. I thought it might be important."

He sounded so blasted reasonable, she wanted to strangle him. "And it never occurred to you that it could prove embarrassing for me?"

"I thought it would be more embarrassing if you missed being notified of an emergency."

"If it had been an emergency, someone would have beeped me," she said.

"Never thought of that." He nodded in the direction in which Jason had gone. "He sounded a little miffed to find me there. Something going on between you two that I should know about? Until this morning I had the impression you were just friends."

She could claim there was and put an end to things with Mack right here and now, but then he'd wonder about what kind of woman she was to sleep with him while she had some sort of relationship with Jason. She might accept that there wasn't ever going to be anything more between her and Mack, but she didn't want him to think badly of her. She had too much self-respect to leave him with an impression like that, as convenient as it might be at the moment.

"Jason is a friend," she confirmed finally. "If he implied it was anything more, it was only because he's worried that I'm in over my head with you."

"It wasn't anything he said," Mack admitted. "Just something in his tone. He sounded possessive."

Something in *Mack's* tone sounded a wee bit possessive, as well. Beth studied his expression for a minute before it sank in what was going on in his head. He was jealous. At least for one tiny fraction of a second Mighty Mack Carlton, of the date-a-night gossip, was actually jealous that there might be another man in her life. She had to fight to keep from chuckling aloud. This was definitely a twist she hadn't anticipated.

Unfortunately, the twist felt a little too welcome, especially after she had spent most of the morning warning herself to cut Mack out of her life before she got burned. Heck, she was sitting here downing chocolate before lunch to forget about him.

"Jason and I have known each other since med school. He's protective, not possessive. There's a difference."

"He thinks you need protection from me?"

She grinned at his vaguely incredulous expression. "Don't you?"

"I'm not going to hurt you," he said sharply.

Beth leveled a look straight into his eyes. "Too late," she said quietly.

Then, before he could react, she stood up and headed for the nearest exit at a clip that few people could keep up with. Mack, of course, could have caught her in a few long strides had he wanted to. That he didn't even try told her all she needed to know.

Or at least she thought the message was pretty plain, until she walked into her office an hour later and found a little mound of candy bars in the middle of her desk. She recognized them as the ones she'd left behind in her haste to leave the cafeteria. More disconcerting was the sight of Mack sprawled out on the sofa where she caught catnaps on the nights she couldn't get away from the hospital. He had an open medical journal on his chest, but his eyes were shut tight. The steady rise and fall of his chest suggested he was sound asleep.

Beth stood there staring at him in consternation. The memory of waking in his arms just a few hours ago was still a little too fresh in her mind. A part of her wanted to crawl onto that sofa with him and recapture that amazing feeling.

Because of that, she deliberately walked behind her desk and sat down, cursing the loud creaking in her old chair. Mack's eyes promptly snapped open.

"Ah, you're back," he said, "I figured you'd turn up here sooner or later."

"Good guess, since it *is* my office," she said tartly. "What are you doing here?"

He gave her an oddly bemused look that made her heart flip over.

"Not sure entirely," he admitted.

"That must be a first."

"It is," he said. He met her gaze. "You confuse me."

She found his honesty a little *too* charming. Maybe it was part of some game he played. "I'm a fairly straightforward kind of woman."

"I get that," he said.

"You are not a straightforward kind of man," she added bluntly.

"I'm trying to be, at least with you."

"Why?" she asked.

"I wish to hell I knew. I sat there after you'd left the house this morning and tried to figure it out, but I still don't entirely get it."

Beth lost patience. She was in over her head with Mack and she didn't like it. That she'd slept with him at all was probably a huge mistake. That she wanted to do it again was pure insanity. Hearing that he was beset with uncertainties was not reassuring. One of them surely needed to know what the hell they were doing.

"Well, since it's such an obvious struggle for you to

figure it out, maybe you should just stop trying," she said. "We spent one night together, Mack. We didn't make a commitment. You don't do commitment. From what I've read in the paper, you don't even go out with the same woman twice. I get that. My time is up."

He frowned at her. "You're making this hard."

"What am I making hard?" she asked, unable to hide her growing exasperation. "I just let you completely off the hook. No harm, no foul. Go forth and do whatever the hell you do without giving me another thought."

"That would be the sensible thing for me to do," he agreed.

"Then do it."

He shook his head. "Can't."

"Why not? There's the door. Walk out and that's that. No big deal." She held her breath waiting for him to take her advice and go. Instead, he sat right where he was, his expression glum. Beth sighed. "Mack, what is going on?"

"Have you had lunch yet?"

"I've had coffee and candy. In my book that qualifies."

"Not in mine. Let's go."

"I don't have time."

"You do for this," he coaxed, his lips twitching when her stomach growled. "I'll have you back in an hour, like always."

"It's twelve-thirty. There's not a decent restaurant anywhere that won't be mobbed at this hour."

"I'll have you back in an hour," he repeated.

Since he'd never before broken that promise, Beth finally gave in. And since the coffee and caffeine definitely hadn't done what she'd intended—taken her mind off Mack—maybe another hour in his annoying company would do the trick. At least she'd be well fed at the end of it.

"Okay," she relented. "One hour, and we don't talk about us."

"Deal," he said.

Once again, the instant they reached the very popular crab house on the Potomac River, a table magically appeared. Their food arrived moments later—a dozen steamed and spiced crabs with coleslaw and potato salad.

Mack handed her a wooden mallet with a grin. "Pretend you're bashing me upside the head, and you'll get through these in no time."

Cracking crabs was messy work, but the succulent meat was worth the effort. And thinking of each red shell as Mack's hard head did give her a certain amount of perverse pleasure as she hammered away. She uttered a little sigh when she'd finished the last one. Only then did she realize that Mack had eaten very little.

"Weren't you hungry? This is the second time today when you've sat there and watched me eat."

"I'm trying to fatten you up," he said.

"Planning to have me slaughtered like a pig?"

"Nope. Looking for a little more flesh to hang on to."

The comment brought an immediate flush to her cheeks. "Mack!"

"Sorry," he said at once, though he didn't look especially repentant. "I promised you we wouldn't talk about us. I suppose that precludes any talk of sex, as well."

"There is no us," she said flatly, refusing to get drawn into any discussion of sex.

"Yeah, you would have thought so, wouldn't you?"

She stared at him, not sure how to take the wry note in his voice. "Meaning?"

"We're not much alike. You're serious. I'm not. You're brilliant—"

"So are you," she said impatiently, tired of him using his own stereotypical image as some sort of cop-out. "Stop denigrating your intelligence. You have a law degree, which you earned while playing professional football. You can't juggle all that without being smart. And it must take some intelligence to run a successful football franchise, even if I don't happen to get why you'd want to."

"Thank you," he said. "I think."

"Since you're busy laying out all our differences, how about this one? I'm a struggling researcher and physician and you're very, very rich."

He grinned. "Too obvious and not that important, unless, of course, you're trying to decide whether to go after me for my money."

Beth smiled as she was struck by a brilliant idea to get her research project moving along at a swifter pace. Maybe she should test the waters and see if he was open to the idea. Hopefully he wouldn't conclude that she really was in this just for the money. "Actually I'm trying to decide whether to get you to fund a new research project," she retorted cheerfully.

"Just tell me what you need," he said matter-of-factly.

She stared at him in shock, totally unprepared for his immediate agreement. "I was joking," she protested. "Or at least half joking."

"I wasn't."

"Oh my God," she whispered, not quite daring to believe he was as serious as he sounded. She had grants, but with just a little more funding she could hire the kind of assistant who would enable her to move her research along much more quickly.

"While it's always nice to show your appreciation of a Higher Power, in this instance you should really thank football and wise investments," he teased. "Of course, if you can't bear the thought of taking any money earned playing such a stupid game…"

"I'll give it some thought," she replied oh, so seriously, then added a quick, "Yes. When it comes to saving more kids, I'm not proud. If you're really serious about this, I'll get together with my team and put a proposal together by the end of the week."

Mack nodded. "I'll be in to pick it up."

She studied him intently, then shook her head at the unexpected turn the day had taken. It was yet more proof that she had seriously misjudged Mack. If the sex had been predictably incredible, then this gesture was equally mind-boggling in its unpredictability and its generosity.

"You're not at all what I expected," she admitted.

"Not so dumb?"

She flushed. "I thought we'd already established that as a lie. More important, you're amazingly kind to Tony. And this whole playboy thing, I'm beginning to think maybe that's more an image you've created for the media than a fact."

"You think that after last night?" he asked, regarding her with evident surprise. "And all that fancy footwork I danced through this morning?"

Beth thought about it and finally nodded slowly. "Yes. Now that I look back over the last few weeks, I realize that you never seem to have a date. You've been spending every evening at the hospital."

He gave her long, simmering look that made her pulse race.

"What do you think you and I have been doing?" he asked quietly. "I mean even before last night."

"Grabbing a quick meal on the run," she said, confused by the hint of amusement in his eyes.

"You with an eligible man. Me with a beautiful, intelligent woman. In my book, those are dates." His grin spread. "And just look where they led."

She sat back, stunned. "Well, I'll be damned." Somehow she'd dismissed all that earlier stuff as casual, friendly, inconsequential get-togethers, while he'd seen it as some sort of foreplay.

"I doubt you'll be damned, unless of course you let me take advantage of you," he taunted. "Any possibility of that happening again? Not right this second, of course, but sometime when you're not due back at the hospital in less than five minutes?"

Before last night, Beth would have said there wasn't a snowball's chance in hell of her letting that happen. Even this morning, with his stinging reminder that he wasn't to be taken seriously, she would have said a flat no.

Now, seeing the faint vulnerability in his eyes as he awaited her reply, guessing that he was stepping far outside of his own relationship comfort zone to even ask such a thing, she was tempted to see where this could lead.

With her heart hammering in her chest, she met his gaze evenly. "You never know."

Mack laughed, as if he'd never expected a different answer. "I'll take that as a yes."

"Has any woman ever actually said no to you?" she asked curiously.

"More than you might imagine. Then again, I've probably asked the question a lot less than you've imagined."

To Beth's very real regret, she wanted to believe that far more than was wise. She wanted to believe that the media had gotten it all wrong, but even she was savvy enough to accept that where there was smoke, there was usually fire. Or in this case, that if gossip paired Mack with a different woman every night, then more than likely he'd done something to foster that impression.

But maybe, just maybe, he'd done it as a defense mechanism to keep from having to put his heart on the line. That was a scenario Beth very much wanted to believe. In fact, she wanted it so much it should have sent her scurrying right straight out of Mack's life before she got her own heart well and truly broken.

It should have, but she very much feared she wasn't going anywhere.

# 9

When Mack wandered into the Carlton Industries offices after dropping Beth off at the hospital, he headed straight for Destiny's office. She rarely put in an appearance there, but a few calls had assured him she was in this afternoon. He'd been drawn there because his aunt had a way of clarifying things for him when he was faced with uncertainty. Since meeting Beth, he'd spent a lot of time feeling completely off-kilter.

It had been a most enlightening lunch. He'd discovered that Beth was more of a risk taker than he'd imagined. He'd expected her to turn him down flat when he'd suggested they spend another passionate night together, especially after the way they'd parted just this morning. That she hadn't said an immediate no had left him turned on and more intrigued than ever.

He wasn't entirely sure what conclusions Beth had reached about him or about their prospects for the future. Given his confusion on that point, dropping by Destiny's office to solicit advice probably wasn't really a wise thing to do, but he was feeling a bit reckless.

He was also feeling somewhat in Destiny's debt for

steering Beth into his life. Not that he intended to tell Destiny that—in fact, he'd probably claim just the opposite, if she pressed him—but he didn't doubt for a second that she was smart enough to read between the lines of whatever he did say. He doubted his aunt would be the least bit surprised that he was finding himself more than a little conflicted where Beth Browning was concerned.

"I haven't seen much of you lately, Mack," Destiny scolded, after he'd dropped a kiss on her smooth cheek. "Where have you been spending your evenings?"

He poured himself a cup of her special-blend coffee, then lounged in a chair opposite her while he contemplated just how much to tell her. She was bound to take a certain amount of gloating satisfaction in whatever he revealed. He decided to take the cagey route and see what she already knew.

"As if you didn't know," he said finally, regarding her with amusement. She was damned good at the innocent act, but he wasn't buying it. Getting her to confess her involvement in this matchmaking plot could be highly entertaining. Matching wits with Destiny and avoiding her romantic snares had been a lifelong challenge for him and his brothers. He was usually quite good at it. Maybe that was another reason he found Beth so fascinating. She was the first woman he'd met who challenged him mentally with the same deft skill as his aunt.

"Would I be asking if I did?" Destiny inquired tartly, sticking to the charade.

"Of course, you would. You want me to reveal all, so you'll have a reason to gloat."

Her innocent look was priceless. "I have no idea what you're talking about, Mack."

"Were you or were you not the one who insisted that

I go over to the hospital a few weeks ago to see that sick kid?" he coached, watching her carefully for any hint of a reaction. She kept her expression perfectly bland.

"Tony Vitale?" she asked after a thoughtful pause.

He grinned at the well-honed act, knowing full well that the name had been on the tip of her tongue. She probably got daily updates from the hospital. Lord knew she had sources everywhere. "Precisely."

"Then you have continued to visit him? That's wonderful," she said, regarding him with evident approval. "I'm sure that's helped his morale considerably. Darling, I'm so proud of you for taking an interest in him."

"He's having a rough time," Mack said, momentarily distracted from his mission to exasperate his aunt. "He's such a tough kid. It breaks my heart to see him so sick."

"When I first spoke to his doctor, she said things hadn't been going well. Has there been any change at all?"

"Only for the worse," Mack said.

"Oh, I'm so sorry," Destiny said with genuine sympathy. "His mother must be completely distraught. Surely they'll be able to turn things around."

"I hope so." He met her gaze with an innocent look of his own. "Since you've shown such an interest in his case, I imagine you'll be willing to match the research donation I'm making in his name," he said.

His aunt's eyebrows rose, suggesting that he really had caught her by surprise this time.

"You're funding a research project?" she asked. "Mack, that's wonderful! What a generous thing for you to do. Of course, I'll match it. Which doctor is in charge?"

Mack laughed. "I suspect you can pull that name out of thin air in another second or two."

She looked momentarily perplexed. "I'm sure I have no idea," she claimed. "There are many fine doctors there."

"Try," he pressed.

She appeared to give it some thought. "It wouldn't be that lovely Beth Browning, would it?"

He lifted his coffee cup in a congratulatory toast. "Bingo."

"I understand she's very dedicated," Destiny said smoothly, not giving away by so much as the blink of an eyelash that she'd all but hand picked the woman for Mack, most likely because of Beth's dedication and brilliance.

"And very beautiful and very available, but then that never crossed your mind when you sent me scampering over there, did it?" he asked.

Destiny looked for a moment as if she might try to keep up the charade, but eventually she simply shrugged, conceding the game. "It might have crossed my mind," she conceded.

Mack laughed at her total lack of chagrin. "Oh, give it up, Destiny. You've been meddling again, and you're damned proud of it."

She leveled a look directly into his eyes. "Do you honestly have a problem with that, Mack? It worked rather well with Richard, didn't it? He and Melanie are deliriously happy."

"But I'm not in the market for a wife," Mack pointed out, though with considerably less vehemence than he might have a few short weeks ago.

"Neither was Richard," she reminded him.

"Why are you so blasted anxious to marry us all off?" he asked curiously. "Do you have someplace you'd like to be besides here? Are you thinking of going back to France and taking up your Bohemian lifestyle once we're all settled? Is that what the rush is all about?"

"This isn't about me," she said. "It's about you. Not a one of you has learned the first thing about love. I simply can't understand how I failed so abysmally at teaching you the most important lesson of all. I decided it was past time I did something about it."

Mack heard the genuine frustration in her voice and regretted that he couldn't give her what she wanted. "I know you think we won't be happy without wives and children, but there are other measures of happiness, Destiny."

"Name one," she challenged.

"I can do better than that," he claimed, then ticked them off for her. "Success, friendships, family."

"Family is exactly what I'm talking about," she retorted impatiently.

"We have each other and we have you." He gave her a penetrating look. "Unless, as I said, you're anxious to leave after all these years and want to be sure we have someone in our lives to take your place."

"Don't be ridiculous," she snapped. "I'm perfectly content with my life just the way it is."

He gave her a wide-eyed look. "How can that be? There's no man in your life."

She frowned at having her own argument tossed back in her face. "There is no need to be snide, Mack."

"Just pointing out the obvious flaw in your case for marrying us off."

"If you are so fiercely determined never to marry, why are you still seeing Beth?" she asked.

He honestly didn't have an answer for that. As they'd discussed at lunch, Beth wasn't at all like the women he usually dated. She wasn't wild or carefree. She was serious and thoughtful and took far too many of her patients' problems to heart.

In recent weeks he'd often felt ashamed at how little he took seriously and how easy his life was. He'd always been conscientious about good deeds—Destiny has raised him and his brothers with a strong sense of their obligation to give back to the community—but he hadn't taken it to heart the way Beth did. She genuinely cared about people. She had a passion for her work. More important, it was work that truly mattered. What he did was frivolous by comparison. Even his visits to Tony were window dressing. They weren't the thing that would ultimately save the boy. Only Beth and her team could do that.

Mack cared about his brothers and his aunt. He even cared about Tony Vitale and other kids like him. But in general he'd learned to keep the world at a distance. Losing his parents so young had made him wary about loving anyone too much. It was too hard to tell when fate might snatch them away. He was terrified that the simple act of loving someone might doom them in some weird way. He knew it was a kid's reaction to loss, but more and more lately he'd come to realize that he'd never entirely gotten past it. Faced with his growing feelings for Beth and his attachment to Tony and the fears they'd stirred in him, he was coming to accept that he was as haunted by it as his other brothers had been.

"Mack," Destiny coaxed gently. "You don't go out

with a woman like Beth Browning unless you're serious about her. She's not one of those clever, worldly women you can toss aside with no harm done."

Mack nodded, accepting the truth of that despite Beth's own claims to the contrary. "I know that."

Acknowledging that meant he ought to give Beth up now. It was the right thing to do, the noble, self-sacrificing thing to do. He'd been telling himself that all day. It hadn't kept him from making another date with her.

The sad truth was, when he thought about how empty his life would be without her, he couldn't begin to contemplate doing the right thing.

"Well, then?" Destiny prodded.

He met his aunt's gaze and made a decision. "I'd like to bring her to dinner one of these days. How would you feel about that?"

Destiny's eyes glowed with immediate excitement. "I'd be delighted. You know that I love meeting your friends. I'm free tonight. Will that work?"

He concluded he might as well get it over with. Maybe after seeing him and Beth together, Destiny could help him sort out his feelings. "Tonight's fine for me. I'll check with Beth and get back to you in an hour or so."

"Perfect."

He studied the glint of anticipation in her eyes warily. "You won't make too much of it?" he asked. "I rarely bring a woman to dinner, because you always get this gleam in your eyes—the one that's there right now, by the way—and start imagining wedding bells."

"I will make Beth feel welcome, and I will not bring out a single bridal magazine," Destiny promised. "I won't even leave one conspicuously lying around the living room."

He knew there were a million other sneaky ways to get the same message across. "And you won't drag out Richard's wedding pictures?" he asked, naming one of them.

"Heavens, no," she said with suitable indignation. "I certainly know better than to force someone to look at family photos. That can be so tedious." She grinned. "Though there is one of you in the bathtub at two that I think is awfully cute. Few women could resist it. In fact, it might plant a few ideas about how absolutely adorable your babies will be."

Mack gave her a genuinely horrified look. "I just changed my mind. I'm not bringing Beth anywhere near you."

Destiny laughed merrily. "I was teasing, darling. I won't embarrass you."

"You swear?"

Destiny sketched a cross over her heart. "Not one inappropriate word," she vowed.

Mack frowned. "Why doesn't that reassure me?"

"Because you have a cynical nature," she told him. "Anything in particular you'd like me to cook? One of my Provençal specialties perhaps?"

"Anything," he said, wondering if he was making a huge mistake in exposing Beth to Destiny's probing gaze and clever questions. "Just keep in mind that I'm lucky to steal her away from the hospital for an hour. This can't be one of your long, drawn-out, five-course meals."

"Fine dining can't be rushed, darling. You know that."

"I also know that Beth will refuse to come if she thinks this is going to be some sort of formal occasion. It has to be just the three of us, and it can't be one of your dressed-to-the-nines nights. She'll probably have to come straight from the hospital and then go right back there."

His aunt scowled at that. "If you insist. Would you like hot dogs and baked beans? Those are quick and easy," Destiny said tartly.

Mack knew she wasn't entirely kidding. She had her standards when it came to the way someone in their position should entertain. "I think you can do better than that," he told her. "In fact, I'm counting on it."

She studied him intently, then finally nodded. "Okay then, but may I ask one thing?"

"Sure."

"Why does this dinner mean so much, Mack, if Beth's not becoming important to you?"

"Can't we just have a nice meal together without turning it into a precursor to an engagement?" he asked plaintively.

"I can do that," Destiny agreed readily, then gave him a far too knowing look. "Can you?"

Because he didn't have a ready answer to that, Mack merely frowned and headed for the door. "See you tonight."

"I'm looking forward to it, darling," Destiny said cheerfully.

"Yeah, I'll bet," Mack muttered, already regretting the impulse that had caused him to make the arrangements for this little get-together.

He'd told himself that he wanted Destiny's insights and impressions of the relationship, but maybe the truth was something else entirely. Maybe he was hoping that exposing sensible, down-to-earth Beth to the realities of life with a Carlton would scare her off and he'd never have to break her heart by doing what he always did...walking away.

Beth's day had gone from bad to worse. A patient had swatted away a bottle of bright-orange antiseptic, sending most of it cascading over Beth's blouse. Though there had been a faint hint of amusement lurking in his eyes, Peyton had soundly scolded her for missing the morning meeting. And Tony had regarded her with a hurt expression for not being there for his transfusion.

"You know it hurts less when you're the one who has to stick me with a needle," Tony said accusingly. "I was counting on you."

"Oh, sweetie, I know and I'm sorry," she said, although somewhat relieved to hear the feistiness in his voice and to finally see some color in his cheeks.

"Where were you?" Tony asked.

"I've had one crisis after another today," she told him. "But that's no excuse. I should have been here."

"Mack wasn't here, either."

She regarded Tony with surprise. Since she had seen Mack, she'd assumed Tony would have, too. "Mack hasn't been by all day?"

"Not once," Tony confirmed. "He said he'd be here, too."

That made no sense at all. Mack had been in the hospital most of the morning. She sighed as she realized that he'd spent the better part of that time with her. "If Mack said he'd be here, then he'll be here," she reassured Tony. "He's never once broken his word to you, has he?"

"No." Tony gave her a curious look. "Do you like Mack?"

"He's been a wonderful friend to you," she responded carefully.

"But do *you* like him?" Tony pressed. Before she could respond, he added, "I think maybe he likes you."

Beth had to fight a grin at the latest round of matchmaking. She'd been warned about Tony's interest in her relationship with Mack, but even so, the questions surprised her.

"I was kinda hoping he'd fall for my mom," Tony admitted. "That would be so awesome, but he hardly gives her a second look. If he can't be my stepdad, then it would be really great if he was with you, Dr. Beth. You're way prettier than those flashy babes with him in those pictures in the paper. You're real, you know what I mean?"

She laughed at the compliment. "Thanks, Tony. I appreciate the loyalty, but I don't think I can compete with a supermodel."

"Sure you can," a much deeper voice chimed in.

Beth whirled around to find Mack in the doorway, a grin on his face. "How long have you been eavesdropping?" she asked testily.

"Long enough to hear my pal Tony here trying to set us up again." He gave her an impudent look. "So, how about it, Doc? You want to have dinner tonight with my aunt?"

Beth gaped at him. He was inviting her to Destiny's? "Maybe we should discuss this outside."

"Just say yes, Dr. Beth," Tony encouraged. "It's not every day you get asked out by a guy like Mighty Mack."

"I'll say," she muttered, then forced a smile for Tony's benefit. "Could I see you in the hallway for a moment, Mack?"

Mack winked at Tony. "I hope she's not going to turn me down. Rejection really sucks, you know."

Tony nodded knowingly.

Beth rolled her eyes at the pair of them. In the hallway, she frowned at Mack. "Why did you put me on the spot in front of Tony?"

"Because Destiny invited us for tonight, and I told her I'd have an answer for her in an hour. I wasn't sure I'd be able to track you down once you got away from Tony's room. Besides, what's the big deal? Hearing me ask you out obviously made his day."

"That's what worries me. Tony has expectations for us now. And your aunt?" She shook her head. "Are you really sure you want to do this?"

"Truthfully, it was my idea," he admitted.

She regarded him with surprise. "You're willingly going to subject yourself and me to your aunt's matchmaking? I thought you said she was like some sort of grand master manipulator. Why would you want to put ideas into her head?"

"The ideas are already there," Mack pointed out.

Beth thought back to her private dinner with Destiny and knew he was right. "Then how do you see this helping?"

"It might not. It might be a terrible mistake."

"Well, that makes me feel all warm and fuzzy about tonight," she said irritably. "I think I'll pass."

"And let Destiny think you're a coward? Or worse, convince her that you're already emotionally involved with me and trying to fight it?"

She regarded him blankly. "Huh? That's too convoluted even for me."

"Not for Destiny." Mack insisted. "I'm telling you,

if you say no, it will open up a huge can of worms. This way we get the dreaded meeting over with. She might even conclude that we're a very bad match."

Suddenly Beth got it. She wasn't sure she liked it, but she understood exactly what Mack was up to. He was looking for an out, and he was hoping his beloved aunt would provide it by finding fault with Beth after all. If Destiny found Beth to be an unsuitable match for a Carlton, Mack would use that valued opinion to let himself off the hook.

She looked Mack directly in the eye. "Okay, here's what I'm hearing. You want Destiny to decide I'm wrong for you, so you can give yourself permission to stop seeing me," she said.

"You're crazy," he said just a little too quickly and vehemently.

"Am I?" she asked doubtfully. "Mack, if you're scared, I understand. If you want to call it quits, the way you're used to doing about now in a relationship, I understand that, too. Nobody's forcing you to be with me, certainly not me. I'm not exactly deliriously jumping up and down with joy at what's going on between us, either."

Mack frowned at that. "I'm not looking for an easy out," he claimed again.

"Aren't you? There's an attraction going on here, but attractions come and go. They're not necessarily permanent. Instead of getting all panicky about the future, we both need to go with the flow or just get out now before things get complicated. I'm not going to freak out on you. I have enough self-confidence to weather your rejection. Heck, I won't even lump myself in with all those other women you dumped when you got scared."

She was about to go on, doing her best to let him off the hook and avoid the impending disaster, when he leaned down and covered her mouth with his own. Her words immediately died in her throat, and every sensible thought flew from her head.

When he finally pulled away, she stared at him through dazed eyes. "What was that for?"

"It was the only way I could think of to shut you up. You were thinking too much. Stop trying to guess what I'm feeling. If I don't know, you can't possibly know. We're still at the early stages of this thing."

Beth couldn't seem to drag herself back from the impact of that kiss to absorb what he was saying. Instead, she told him stiffly, "Kissing me outside of my patient's room where anyone could be passing by is inappropriate."

"Sorry."

She studied his expression for so much as a hint of sincere regret, but there was nothing. If anything, he looked a little smug at having rattled her.

His attitude, the conversation, the whole stupid dinner—it was all too much. She whirled around. "I have to go," she said, already striding away.

"Pick you up at six-thirty," he called after her.

"No."

"Be ready."

"I am not going to dinner."

"Sure you are."

She turned around and marched right back until she was in his face. If necessary, she would shout and make a total scene until he got the message.

"I am not going to dinner at your aunt's," she announced very firmly.

He studied her intently, then nodded. "Okay."

She faltered at his acquiescence. For some reason that irked her even more than his assumption that she would fall in with his plans. "Maybe I will go, after all."

"Okay." He looked as if he was struggling to bite back a grin.

"But I'll meet you there."

He frowned, but nodded. "Okay. I'll give you the address."

"No need," she said blithely, beaming at him. "I've been there."

He stared at her as if she'd announced a familiarity with the direct route to Mars. "When in the hell did you visit my aunt?"

"Weeks ago," she said.

"Before she sent me over here to meet Tony?" he asked suspiciously.

"No, after. Well, later that same day, to be precise. Your aunt has impeccable timing. She called me minutes after you left."

"She never said anything," he said, half to himself. He stared at Beth. "Neither did you."

"I'm sure your aunt doesn't run all of her social engagements past you," Beth told him. "And just so you know, I have no intention of doing that, either."

He shook his head. "Good to know."

"See you at seven," Beth told him. "Maybe I'll call Destiny and see if she'd mind if I bring a date."

"You do and he's a dead man," Mack said grimly.

Beth laughed. Once again she had made Mighty Mack Carlton jealous. Damn, but that felt good. She glanced at his fierce expression and concluded it might be wise not to test him too often, though.

She reached up and patted his cheek. "Okay then, it's just you and me, pal."

"I am not your *pal*. You can get over that idea right now."

"Oh? Then how would you describe yourself?"

"I'm the man you're currently driving stark raving mad," he said. Suddenly a grin spread across his face. "Of course, if you play your cards right over dinner, I can be driving you a little crazy by ten."

She nodded slowly. "A fascinating prospect," she noted. "I'll definitely keep it in mind."

He pressed another hard, sizzling kiss to her mouth, then released her. "Just a little something to tide you over," he said.

He was whistling when he walked back into Tony's room. Beth waited until the door was firmly shut behind him before sagging against the wall. The arrogant, impossible man had once again made her knees weak. She could only pray he never figured out just how easily he could accomplish that. Then again, given how well he understood women, he probably already knew.

# *10*

Mack paced around Destiny's den like a caged tiger. Where the devil was Beth? He'd called the hospital an hour ago and been told that she'd left at five-thirty. He'd assumed she'd gone home to change, especially since her blouse had been stained with some god-awful orange stuff, but how long did it take for a woman to put on a new outfit and drive across the bridge into Alexandria? He was surprisingly inexperienced when it came to knowing such things, which just proved how little he'd ever discovered about the personal habits and idiosyncrasies of the many women he'd dated.

It was nearly seven-thirty now. For a woman as punctual as Beth tried to be, running a half hour late or more was totally out of character.

"Will you sit down, please?" Destiny said, her exasperation evident. "You're giving me a headache. Beth said she'll be here, and I'm sure she will be."

"She was supposed to be here thirty minutes ago."

"Darling, I'm sure she wouldn't stand you up."

Mack took note of the distinction, implying that *he* was the only one with any cause for worry. Besides, he wasn't so sure Destiny was right about Beth not ditching him at the last minute. It would be just like her to do something so completely unpredictable to annoy him. He hadn't guessed about that perverse streak in her until that conversation they'd had in the hallway this afternoon. He was still trying to decide how he felt about it, especially that belated revelation about her prior meeting with Destiny.

"She wasn't that enthused about coming," he admitted in what had to be the most massive understatement he'd ever uttered.

Destiny regarded him solemnly. "But she has very lovely manners, Mack. She might not contact you if you've somehow offended her, but she would call me if she intended to cancel."

He scowled at the suggestion that he was somehow at fault. "I didn't offend her. And how would you know about her manners?" he asked. Then, without waiting for a response he added, "Oh, yes, that would be because of the cozy little dinner you two shared not long ago, the dinner you neglected to mention when we spoke earlier today."

Destiny regarded him with surprise. "She told you about that?"

"Gloated about it, in fact," he said, then added sourly, "I thought it was great that someone finally thought to bring me into the loop."

Destiny's expression grew thoughtful. "Isn't that interesting?"

"What's so blasted interesting about her finally 'fessing up to the fact that the two of you were sneaking around behind my back? For all I know, you've been in cahoots with her for months. This little admission could be the tip of the iceberg."

His aunt frowned at him. "Don't be melodramatic, darling. It was dinner, nothing more. It's not as if we hatched some plot to reel you in. You're obviously a man who makes up his own mind about these things. You don't believe I would set a trap for you, do you?"

He scowled right back at her. "Oh, please. I learned a long time ago never to underestimate you. You might not be successful at setting me up with a woman I'd walk down the aisle, but you're not above trying."

"Do you think Beth is so spineless that she would go along with a scheme of mine?"

He considered that and knew it was unlikely. If there was one thing he was certain of it was that Beth had a very strong sense of herself. Spineless was the last thing she was. Heaven knew, she didn't hesitate to tell him what was on her mind. He doubted she'd be any less forthcoming with Destiny. If his aunt had approached her about Mack, Beth most likely would have laughed in her face.

"No," he finally conceded to Destiny.

"You know, Mack, I'm a little surprised you decided to go through with dinner tonight once you found out about my previous meeting with Beth. Since you obviously see a conspiracy around every corner where I'm concerned, is there some particular reason you chose not to back out?"

He had a pretty good idea what she was driving at, but he decided to give her the satisfaction of making her point. "Such as?"

"Are you looking for some evidence that Beth doesn't fit in here?"

He started to deny it, but Destiny knew him too well. Besides, Beth had had the exact same suspicion. Obviously, these two people, who knew him better than most, could see straight through him.

"It crossed my mind that she might come to that conclusion," he conceded eventually.

"And then what?" Destiny kept her gaze on his face while she awaited his reply. When he said nothing, she asked, "Surely you weren't hoping that she'd dump you?" At his continued silence, she regarded him incredulously. "That's exactly what you were hoping, isn't it?"

"It's not like I'm this incredible prize," he said defensively, "especially for a woman who hopes to marry and have a family."

"Oh, please, this is no time for false modesty," his aunt said, dismissing the comment as ridiculous. "Besides, has Beth said anything about getting married?"

"No."

"Is she ready to start a family?"

"She hasn't mentioned it, no."

"Then aren't you jumping ahead a bit prematurely?" She regarded him intently. "Or is that the point? Are you the one who's beginning to think about marriage?" Amusement sparkled in her eyes. "Oh my," she said happily. "No wonder you're terrified and looking for the fastest exit. Even worse, since you're not sure you'll take it, you're obviously hoping to push Beth through it."

Mack's head was spinning from Destiny's convoluted logic. He couldn't cope with that and his concern over Beth's whereabouts at the same time. "Maybe I should call her cell phone. She could be stuck in traffic."

"Avoiding the question won't make it go away," Destiny chided. "And if she were stuck in traffic, don't you think she'd call?"

"Do you have an answer for everything?" he grumbled.

Destiny smiled happily. "I like to think so," she said as the doorbell rang. "Why don't you get that, Mack? And try to wipe that scowl off your face before you get there. You don't want to scare the woman to death before she even crosses the threshold." Her smile spread. "Or do you?"

When he reached the front door, his temper was still simmering, though whether his irritation was directed toward his impossible aunt or Beth was hard to say. He flung open the door, took one look at Beth's disheveled appearance and immediately forgot all about his lousy mood.

"What on earth happened to you?" he demanded, noting that before she'd ruined them, her clothes were very feminine and flattering compared to the tailored look he'd grown accustomed to. She'd really made an effort for tonight's dinner.

"Flat tire," she said succinctly.

Judging from the grease all over her, she had changed it herself. "Didn't it occur to you to call a garage or me?"

She gave him an impatient look. "I know how to change a tire. I figured it would be faster to do it myself than to wait for a tow truck to get there in the middle of rush hour. I should have gone back home to change again, but I was already so late, I decided I'd better come on over."

Still not reassured, he studied her from head to toe. "You didn't hurt yourself, did you?"

She rolled her eyes and held out her arms for his inspection. "See, no blood. No bruises. Just grease. Do you suppose I could use a bathroom to clean up?"

"Come with me," he said, and led the way toward the kitchen instead. "The soap in the bathroom isn't going to do it. Ben used to have a snazzy little car he worked on in the garage. Believe me, this house is no stranger to grease and oil. There's bound to be something in the garage we can use to get off the worst of this, though I'm not sure anything will help with the clothes."

She glanced down at her flowery silk dress and groaned. "This was brand-new."

Mack shook his head. She could have seriously injured herself wrestling with the damn tire and she was worried about her dress. "I'll buy you another one," he said impatiently.

She regarded him with a withering glance. "I can buy another dress myself."

"But that doesn't solve the immediate problem." He handed her some rags and a can of cleanser. "You get started on the grease and oil and I'll speak to Destiny. I'm sure she has something you can put on. You're about the same size. I'll be right back to show you where the downstairs powder room is."

Once he'd explained the problem to his aunt, Destiny immediately hurried off to find something suitable in her closet. When she returned, Mack started to take the clothes from her, but she brushed him off. "You don't get to help her undress in my house."

He chuckled at the unexpected display of propriety. "I would have thought you'd be inclined to encourage me to do just that."

She frowned at him. "You can check the oven and make sure dinner isn't burning. Turn it down to low."

"Yes, ma'am."

"And Mack..."

"Yes?"

She gave him a warm, reassuring smile. "I told you she wouldn't stand you up."

He sighed, not even attempting to hide how relieved he'd been to realize that for himself.

Beth kept touching the fine fabric of the cardigan Destiny had given her to slip on over a sleeveless silk top. She was amazed at what a difference there was in the quality from her usual wardrobe. She'd always believed it was ridiculous to spend a fortune on clothes, but now she understood why people who had the money did just that. She was fairly certain she never wanted to take this off.

"I think you should keep the sweater," Destiny said, regarding her with amusement. "That soft pink color is very becoming on you. Don't you agree, Mack?"

Mack nodded distractedly. He'd been in an odd mood ever since Beth's arrival. She couldn't quite pin down what was wrong. He'd been so anxious for her to come tonight and he'd looked so relieved when he'd opened the door. He'd looked even more relieved when he'd assured himself that she wasn't hurt. It had been some time, though, since he'd entered into the dinner conversation.

Not that it had made things awkward. Destiny was perfectly capable of keeping the talk lively. She had a million and one questions about Tony and about Beth's work.

"Mack tells me he's going to fund a research project," Destiny said eventually. "I hope you'll accept a donation from me, as well."

Beth stared at her, overcome with gratitude. "That's very generous of you," she said when she'd gathered her composure. "I know you already give quite a bit to the hospital. Are you sure you want to do more?"

"Absolutely. As soon as you have your proposal put together, Mack and I will sit down and discuss the details with our attorneys. Carlton Industries will participate, as well. Your research should be quite adequately funded."

"Did I hear some mention of the family company in connection with giving away money?" Richard asked, walking into the dining room with his wife just as it was time for dessert.

"Yes," Destiny said. "And no penny-pinching, either. Beth's work is important."

"Are you sure you're not just trying to buy her for Mack?" he teased.

The comment drew an immediate rebuke from the petite woman accompanying him.

"What?" Richard asked. "It's not as if Destiny is above such a thing."

"I don't need anyone buying a woman for me," Mack countered indignantly. "If anything I usually have more than I can handle."

"None of them appropriate," Destiny retorted.

Richard's wife gave Beth a commiserating look. "Don't mind them. I've been really looking forward to meeting you," Melanie said.

Surprised that Melanie Carlton even knew about her, Beth merely said, "Oh?"

"I wanted to express my heartfelt sympathy."

"Sympathy?" Beth asked, puzzled.

Melanie directed an impudent look toward Destiny. "If I'm not mistaken, you're the latest target of the Carlton steamroller. If it gets to be too much for you, give me a call. I'll be sure to give you my number. I may not be able to save you, but we can discuss a few evasive maneuvers."

Beth regarded Richard's wife with an immediate sense of camaraderie. "Been there, done that?" she inquired.

"In spades," Melanie said, casting another pointed look toward Destiny.

"I really don't see that you have a thing to complain about," Destiny said, a glint of amusement in her eyes proving that Melanie's teasing hadn't offended her.

"Not now," Melanie agreed, linking her arm through Richard's. "It all turned out rather well in the end, once we caved in and did what Destiny had wanted all along."

Mack had remained silent, his expression gloomy, during most of this exchange, but he finally frowned at his brother. "So, what brings you by tonight? Did you just have a sudden impulse while driving by?"

Richard grinned. "Actually we were invited for dessert."

"Really?" Mack said, frowning at his aunt. "Which part of just the three of us did you not understand, Destiny?"

"It's my home," she chided. "I'm entitled to include your brother and his wife, if I so choose. I thought it was time they had a chance to meet Beth."

Mack gave her a wry look. "Then Richard didn't mention that he'd taken the bait you tossed out weeks ago? He came scurrying right over to the hospital to meet her. I would have thought he'd give you a full report long before now."

Destiny looked genuinely surprised. "Really? What

brought that on? Surely not some casual remark I might have made."

"He came to gloat," Mack said before his brother could speak. "Seems he'd figured out you were up to your eyeballs in planning my life and wanted to see for himself how it was working out."

Beth turned to Melanie. "Was it this bad with you?"

"Worse," Melanie said with heartfelt sincerity. "Richard was the first part of Destiny's grand scheme. She really had something to prove with us."

Beth buried her face in her hands. She'd had no idea things were going to spin this far out of control so quickly. She finally drew in a deep breath and looked up. "I think it's time for me to get back to the hospital."

"I agree," Mack said at once, practically knocking over his chair in his eagerness.

"You don't need to come," she told him. "I have my own car, remember?"

"It's got a spare tire on, probably one of those little doughnut things. At the very least, you need to let me follow you to make sure you don't have another problem."

Beth's chin set stubbornly. "It's not necessary."

Mack's set just as firmly. "Yes, it is."

She realized he wasn't going to bend on this, either, out of a real sense of protectiveness toward her or out of desperation to make his own escape. She might as well give in gracefully.

"Fine, then," she relented. She faced Destiny. "Thanks so much for a lovely dinner. And I apologize again for being so late. I'll get your clothes back to you."

"I still think you should keep them," Destiny said. "They're very becoming."

Beth shook her head. She wasn't about to owe this clever woman for another thing. "I couldn't."

"Your decision, of course," Destiny said, giving in. "I do wish you wouldn't run off, though. I made something chocolate for dessert. I understand you're partial to it."

"So am I," Melanie said, then added eagerly, "I'll eat her share."

"And probably Mack's as well," Richard said, regarding her indulgently. "Before you two leave, you should know that Melanie and I have an announcement to make."

Everyone turned to stare at them expectantly.

Eyes shining, Melanie said, "We're going to have a baby."

"Well, I'll be damned," Mack said, grabbing his brother and enthusiastically slapping him on the back. "Congratulations!"

Tears spilled down Destiny's cheeks as she embraced first Melanie and then her nephew.

Melanie winked at Beth. "There, that should take the heat off you for a bit. Run now, while you have the chance."

"Not until we drink a toast," Destiny insisted. "Let me get some sparkling cider for Melanie and the rest of us can have champagne."

Not willing to spoil Melanie and Richard's moment, Beth nodded. "We can wait just a minute, but make mine sparkling cider as well, since I'm heading back to work."

"What the heck," Mack told his aunt. "Make it sparkling cider all around. I'm getting behind the wheel, so it's best if I don't have anything more to drink."

"Richard, darling, why don't you come into the kitchen with me?" Destiny suggested. "You can help me carry the glasses. And, Mack, you can clear the table and bring in dessert." She glanced toward Beth. "You might as well have that chocolate mousse now, too, don't you think?"

The temptation was too great to resist. Beth nodded. "Sure."

Destiny beamed. "I knew you could be tempted."

After they'd all disappeared into the kitchen, Melanie turned to Beth. "So, tell me, just how pressured are you feeling?"

Beth thought about it. She'd really only experienced one panicky moment earlier. "Actually it's not so bad. Mack and I are in the same place, I think. He's no more interested in marriage than I am."

Melanie chuckled. "Is that what you think?"

"It's the truth," Beth insisted.

"I'm sure he thinks it is," Melanie said agreeably. "And I know it's what you want to believe, but I just caught a glimpse of the way he looks at you. The man is head-over-heels in love with you."

"Mack? Don't be ridiculous." Beth retorted. "In lust, maybe."

"With the Carlton men, it's sometimes the same thing. I'm not talking about the casual kind of lust-at-first-sight business. I'm talking about the can't-keep-his-hands-off-you lust that doesn't quit and gets more intense with every day that passes."

Beth was embarrassed by Melanie's frankness and by her ability to see the desire that Beth had been trying very hard to conceal all night. Even when Mack had been at his most exasperating, all she'd been able to think about was his earlier promise to take her home tonight and drive her a little crazy. When she'd announced her intention to return to work, she'd half expected never to make it there.

"Are you denying that that's what is going on with you two?" Melanie asked.

"I really don't think we should be discussing this," Beth said, uncomfortable not only with the topic, but with Melanie's accurate assessment of the situation.

"I've embarrassed you, haven't I? I'm sorry," Melanie apologized. "It's just that I've been down this road, and I can see all the signs. When the Carlton men finally fall, they fall hard. If you ever decide you do want to talk about it, give me a call." She pulled a Carlton Industries business card from her purse and jotted a number on the back. "There. Now you have my number at the office and at home. I mean it, Beth. The only way for us to hold our own when the Carlton steamroller gets into high gear is to stick together. I know I'd have been happy to have the moral support when I was in the same place you're in now."

Beth laughed. "Yes, I can see how that might help," she said, tucking the card into her pocket. She could also imagine being friends with this open, energetic woman who saw the Carltons so clearly. It had been years and years since she'd had a woman friend to confide in, years since she'd had anything to confide, for that matter.

Before either of them could say more, Destiny, Richard and Mack came back with the drinks and dessert.

During the toast, Mack's gaze caught Beth's, and she felt herself responding to the barely banked heat in his eyes. Okay, she admitted, her hand trembling slightly, she was a little bit past being in lust herself.

But in love with the region's consummate playboy? No way. She simply couldn't allow it to happen.

\* \* \*

Mack rolled over and stared down into Beth's face. She looked so peaceful, so beautiful with her cheeks still flushed from sex, her skin still glowing with a soft sheen of perspiration. He wondered if he'd ever get his fill of moments like this.

"Do you intend to spend the night watching me sleep?" she murmured.

"I didn't think you'd catch me. I thought you were actually asleep, rather than playing possum," Mack said, daring to reach out and tuck a curl behind her ear now that he knew he wouldn't be waking her. He let his fingers linger against her petal-soft skin.

"Faking it," she teased. "You wore me out. I needed a breather."

Mack laughed. "If anyone needs a breather, it should be me. I thought I was going to follow you back to work and leave you there, then go home and spend a quiet night all alone in my own bed. I still have a lot of recovering to do from the last night we spent together. It's a good thing I'm not in training any more. The coaches would have a lot to say about me being this wiped out."

"Ha!" she muttered. "You knew exactly where we were heading the instant we left your aunt's. In fact, you were leading the way."

He grinned. "Well, I was hopeful," he admitted. "I kept watching in my rearview mirror to see if you were going to turn off and head straight for the hospital, after all."

"I thought about it," Beth said. "Then I thought about this. It was no contest."

"Glad to know you find me more fascinating than your paperwork," he groused.

She regarded him with an impish expression. "Definitely better than paperwork, though my research might give you a run for your money."

"Want to tell me about what you're working on?" he asked, realizing that he truly did want to understand every single thing that was important to her. He couldn't recall another time when he'd cared about anything more than the moment, when it came to a woman who was in his bed.

"It'll be in the grant proposal," she said. "Do you really want to hear me go on and on about it now?"

"I could listen to you go on and on about most anything," he said honestly, no less surprised than she was by that. "You're so passionate about what you do."

"And you're not?"

"You said it yourself," he reminded her. "Football is just a game."

She winced. "That was a really lousy thing for me to say. The important thing for anyone is to do work that they love. You're doing that. Who knows, maybe one of these days I'll even let you take me to a game and try to explain why all those huge, hulking men are running up and down the field."

Mack stared at her, certain he couldn't be understanding her correctly. "You've *never* been to a football game?"

"Never."

"Watched one on TV?"

"Not if I could help it."

"So all that dismissive talk was based on absolutely no firsthand experience whatsoever?" he asked incredulously.

"Afraid so."

He shook his head. "If there's a football-for-complete-novices book, I'm buying it and giving it to you. Once you've learned a few things and been to a few games, we'll discuss this gap in your education again."

Beth chuckled. "Will there be a test? I'm very good at tests."

He heard the low, taunting note in her voice and his body immediately responded to the unspoken challenge. He reached for her.

"How about this test?" he murmured. "Are you ready for this?"

"Oh, yes," she said fervently,

And for the rest of the night, football, his meddling aunt and the future were the very last things on Mack's mind.

# *11*

When Beth walked into the hospital cafeteria at lunch-time the next day, she was greeted by an unexpected sea of guilty expressions. Jason immediately tried his best to slide a newspaper out of sight under the table. Three people rose, nodded a greeting and suddenly took off, leaving her with Jason and Peyton.

Since their odd reactions seemed to have something to do with that newspaper, Beth walked right up to Jason and plucked it out of his hand before he could safely stash it somewhere. "Something interesting in here?" she asked, holding it aloft and attempting to skim the headlines, a task made more difficult by Jason's urgent attempts to snatch it back. She gave him a withering look that finally caused him to retreat, albeit with obvious reluctance.

"It's no big deal," he muttered defensively. "It's just some silly item. Nothing important."

Unfortunately, he had the kind of open face that told Beth he was lying.

"Then why don't you want me to see it?" she asked

reasonably. "Or is it some girlie club ad or an ad to end sexual dysfunction that you think will embarrass me?"

"Come on, Beth," Jason protested, his cheeks now flaming. "You know we wouldn't be looking at anything like that."

"What then?"

When he tried once again to make a grab for the newspaper, she held it out of his reach and glanced more thoroughly at the page that her colleagues had been so absorbed in reading. All she spotted was the daily gossip column by that sleazy tabloid-style reporter Pete Forsythe.

"You guys were reading the local gossip?" she asked incredulously. "I thought you were above such things. Don't you have all sorts of lofty medical journals you could be reading instead?"

"But this is lots more interesting and hits closer to home," Peyton said, a definite twinkle in his eyes.

It was so rare to see the serious-minded hematologist with a smile tugging at his lips, that Beth almost didn't care what was in the paper as long as it was responsible for that smile. Unfortunately, she had a hunch she couldn't dismiss it so lightly. She took a second look at the headline: Man-About-Town Missing In Action. She still didn't get the fascination. She gave the men a curious look. "So?"

"Did you read the first paragraph?" Jason finally asked, his expression resigned.

Beth scanned the beginning of the article, her jaw dropping as she read on.

Playboy jock Mack Carlton, who can normally be spotted in every hot spot in town, always with a glamorous beauty by his side, has vanished from view lately. The lonely women are starting to ask questions. Has some secret gal-pal snagged his attention and taken him out of the social whirl?

Well, we can answer that. Mighty Mack has been spending a lot of time at a local hospital lately, and the word is that he's not there for medical tests. A brilliant doc has caught his eye, and he's been wooing her far from the prying eyes of the local media.

Stay tuned, Mack watchers. We'll be the first to report when the ex-quarterback and current team owner scores his first marital touchdown. Based on what we've heard, we'll give you odds that it's going to happen before the football season starts.

Beth reread the entire item again, her cheeks burning. Even though her name wasn't mentioned, the men gathered around this table—including those who had taken off at her arrival—all knew the article referred to her. Otherwise they wouldn't have reacted so guiltily or tried to keep it from her.

"Sorry," Jason said. "I was hoping you wouldn't see it. It's just a silly little item, Beth. Not anything to get upset about."

"Hardly anybody reads that junk," Peyton chimed in.

"Oh, please. If you guys—who are oblivious to most of this so-called junk—read it, then obviously the entire metropolitan Washington region has seen it by now," Beth said grimly. "Actually, I'm glad you brought it to my attention, albeit reluctantly. Now I have time to do a little damage control."

Jason regarded her with alarm. "What are you going to do?"

"I'm not going to kill Pete Forsythe, if that's what you're worried about," she said.

"And you're not going to break up with Mack, are you?" Jason asked with evident dismay. "I've been counting on this lasting at least through football season, so maybe you can snag a pair of tickets for me."

"How thoughtful of you to put my reputation first," Beth said.

"Your reputation is just fine," Peyton pointed out. "Your name was never mentioned. Only a few people know you're the doctor in question."

"Sure. Just you guys, Mack's entire family, anyone who's seen us together around here and a half-dozen maître d's around town. How long do you think it will be before one of them fills in the blanks for Forsythe? People love to share inside information."

"What difference does it make?" Peyton persisted. "It's not as if either of you is married. You're dating. So what?"

Beth knew what he was saying was perfectly reasonable, but she wasn't feeling especially reasonable. She wanted to string up whoever had planted this item with the gossip columnist. She wanted to strangle Mack for ever giving her a second glance. And, come to think of it, she wasn't all that happy with herself at the moment.

She'd known this was one of the risks of getting involved with a high-profile playboy. But once she'd drifted into a real relationship with Mack, her concerns and good sense had flown right out the window. All she'd thought about lately was how alive she felt in his arms. She hadn't given a moment's consideration to how their relationship might blow up in her face. If she'd found the stares disconcerting before, they were going to be even more humiliating now, just as they had been after her ex-fiancé had spread his lies about her.

"I have to do something," she insisted. "I have to put an end to this before things get any worse."

"What can you do that won't make it worse?" Peyton asked.

"He's right," Jason said. "If you call Forsythe, you'll be giving him exactly the information he needs to print another item."

Because even she could see that there wasn't much she could do about any of it, Beth finally sighed heavily and sat down. Jason regarded her warily, then stood.

"Chocolate?" he asked, his expression filled with concern.

"As much as the vending machine has," she said, feeling defeated. Even if the vending machine had been filled just that morning, it probably wouldn't be enough. She reached for her purse.

"No, I'll buy," Jason said. "I feel responsible for setting off this chocolate attack."

"I'll chip in, too," Peyton said, tossing a few dollar bills to Jason.

"I'm depressed, not suicidal," Beth said, a faint flicker of amusement sneaking in at their sudden show of protectiveness. "Besides, maybe we should use some of that money to buy up all the newspapers in the machines around the hospital."

"Too late for that," Peyton said. "The way the rumor mill fires up in this place, it takes only one person with the inside scoop to have the news spread far and wide by lunchtime."

Beth scowled at his bleak outlook, but she knew he was right. The only news medium faster than the hospital grapevine was *CNN*.

Jason was already loping off toward the vending machine when she called after him. "Bring me chips, too."

Peyton regarded her worriedly. "Chips? You never eat chips."

"I'm feeling reckless."

"Junk food is not the answer," he scolded, looking more like his somber self.

"Any idea what might be?"

"That depends."

"On?"

"Whether you're in love with Mack Carlton."

Shocked that a man so totally absorbed in his work might have taken note of the attraction, she felt compelled to deny it. "Of course I'm not in love with Mack," she said, though her protest wasn't nearly as fierce as it had been the night before.

Peyton shook his head. "Not convincing, Beth. For it to be believable, you must sound certain, not miserable."

"Why do I have to convince you?"

His lips twitched. "Not me. Yourself."

Ah, Beth thought. He had a point. She wasn't buying her own protests anymore, either.

Mack was seething when he saw the gossip column that someone on the team's administrative staff had thoughtfully left on his desk first thing this morning. Beth was going to be fit to be tied. He could sympathize, but at least he was used to seeing his name in the paper. He'd become accustomed to the half-truths and innuendoes that made up a column like Pete Forsythe's.

He'd learned to shrug it off as a cost of celebrity. Beth wouldn't have any such defense mechanisms.

It didn't matter that her name hadn't been mentioned. It was only a matter of time before it would be. Too many people could fill in that particular blank. He hadn't realized how much he valued the lack of media attention vis-à-vis this relationship until now, when his peace and quiet were being threatened.

He picked up the phone and tried Beth's office. He left a voice mail on her machine, then beeped her. It was ten minutes before she finally returned his call, ten of the longest minutes of his life that left him wondering if she was too furious to ever speak to him again.

"I'm sorry," he said the instant he heard her voice and the edginess in it. "I should have warned you something like this could happen."

She sighed. "I should have known," she said. "After all, isn't that the column where I spotted your name all the time? That's how I formed my rather jaundiced view of you."

"Maybe so, but I'd thought we were being discreet. I never wanted to drag you into the spotlight."

"Not your fault," she said.

To his relief, she sounded sincere. She wasn't blaming him. "Thank you," he said.

"For?"

"Letting me off the hook. I probably don't deserve it."

"Look, Mack, I know we've been discreet, but it's not as if we've never been anywhere at all together. We've just avoided your usual haunts in prime time, so to speak. We should have expected something like this to happen sooner or later."

"I can't get over the fact that you're not more upset."

"At you? No. I'm not crazy about this, believe me. Jason and Peyton had to buy all the chocolate in the vending machine to calm me down, but they've finally convinced me it could have been much worse."

"It could still get worse," Mack warned her. "Once Forsythe's on the scent of a scoop, he can be relentless. Ask Melanie to fill you in on the role he played in her relationship with Richard."

"Actually, now that you mention it, I remember that. I wonder who put Forsythe onto this particular scent," Beth asked. "I'm a boring doctor, not your usual high-profile date."

"Which is exactly why he probably finds it so intriguing," Mack told her, then was suddenly struck by something that was so obvious, he should have suspected it right off. "Damn!"

"What?"

"Look, I'll see you later, okay? There's something I need to do right now."

"What's so important that you don't want to finish this conversation?" she asked, her voice filled with suspicion.

"I'm going to have a chat with Forsythe's informed source," he said grimly.

"You know who spilled the beans?" Beth demanded

"Not with absolutely certainty," he said. "But I'd give you Vegas odds I can name the culprit in one guess."

"Who?"

"Destiny, of course."

"She wouldn't," Beth said, sounding genuinely shocked.

"Darling, this is vintage Destiny. She's been stirring our particular pot for weeks now. After last night's dinner, she's obviously decided it needs a little something to spice it up a notch. Pete Forsythe has been her chosen messenger before. Hell, she probably has his private fax number memorized after spilling all those juicy little tidbits about Richard and Melanie to him."

"Are you serious? She was behind those?"

"Oh, yes, and proud of it," Mack said. "You know the expression 'All's fair in love and war'? Well, Destiny thinks she's fighting a war for romance. Believe me, Forsythe's column is just one of her weapons of choice."

"Are you going over there?"

"The instant we hang up."

"Pick me up on your way," she said. "I want a piece of this. I have more at stake than you do."

Mack laughed at her out-for-blood tone. "I'll be there in twenty minutes."

"I'll be out front," she said, then hung up.

"Oh, Destiny," Mack murmured, not even bothering to hide his anticipation. "You have really gone and stepped in it this time."

For once, he wasn't going to have to say a single word to his aunt about her meddling. He could sit back and let Beth do all the dirty work. Damn, this was going to be more fun than watching a couple of sexy women get down and dirty in the mud.

Unfortunately, Destiny Carlton was nowhere to be found. Beth's frustration grew with every call Mack made on his cell phone only to be told that he'd just missed his aunt.

"She's lying low," he finally concluded.

"Smart woman," Beth said with a trace of admiration. Destiny was clearly a worthy adversary. No doubt that was why her nephews hadn't succeeded in foiling her meddling yet.

"Want to have lunch?" Mack asked.

"In public?" she responded, not even attempting to hide her horror at the prospect.

He chuckled. "Oh, I think I can pull it off so that we don't get caught by the paparazzi."

"How?"

"Watch a master at work," he said, making a few calls, then heading through Washington's crowded roads at a pace few race-car drivers would have attempted. He turned into a back alley, pulled up beside an unmarked door and told her to sit tight. "I'll be right back."

Beth looked around warily. "Are you sure it's safe here?"

"From everything except rats, most likely," he said,

She shuddered. "Hurry."

"Five minutes," he promised.

The entire time he was gone—which seemed like an eternity—Beth's gaze darted in every direction, on the lookout for lurking dangers. To her relief he was back before she'd spotted so much as a rodent of any kind. The aromas drifting from the cooler he was carrying were worth all the moments of anxiety she'd suffered.

"Garlic," she whispered happily. "Tomatoes. Oh, my God, what did you get? There was no sign over that door you slipped through."

"The best pasta you will ever put in your mouth," he told her. "Your place?"

She sniffed greedily even as she nodded. "And step on it," she told him. "My mouth is watering."

Mack gave her a sideways glance. "I gather Italian

food ranks right up there with chocolate on your personal aphrodisiac scale."

"Oh, yes."

"Does this mean I'm going to get lucky this afternoon?" he inquired, his expression hopeful.

Beth considered the proposition for about fifteen seconds. "If there's time," she said conscientiously. "I do have to get back to work, you know. Peyton and Jason are covering for me now, but at some point people might start to wonder why I'm not on duty."

Mack took the corner on two wheels and was parked behind her town house in three minutes flat.

"Ever consider trying out for NASCAR?" she asked as she got out, still clutching the cooler.

"Nah, too tame," he teased. "I like the challenge of maneuvering through rush hour."

"You just like a challenge, period," she guessed.

"That, too."

Even as she put the food on the kitchen table, she studied him closely. "Is that what I am, Mack? A challenge?"

Rather than the flip response she'd anticipated, he seemed to take the question seriously. "Not the way you mean," he said eventually.

"How, then?"

"I'm not sure I can explain."

Because his serious expression and tone told her this could be really important, she met his gaze. "Try," she said.

His expression turned thoughtful, and he took his time answering. "Okay, here's what I think. It's never been about winning your heart or getting you into bed just to prove I could," he told her. His gaze met hers. "In some weird way it's been about seeing just how involved I dared to get before the panic set in."

Beth wasn't sure how to take that, wasn't even sure she fully understood it. "And?"

He regarded her with a hint of surprise in his eyes. It was there in his voice, too. "Hasn't happened yet," he admitted.

Beth's heart beat unsteadily at what he wasn't saying. "Why do you suppose that is?"

Mack sighed then and finally looked away. "I don't know, Beth. I honestly don't know, but I will tell you this." He once again looked directly into her eyes. "Considering the possibilities scares the hell out of me."

Try as she might, Beth couldn't shake that conversation as she went about her duties at the hospital that afternoon. What was Mack most afraid of? That she was winning his heart, despite all the defenses he'd erected around it? Or that even after all of the incredible sex and growing intimacy, he was incapable of feeling anything more?

Forget Mack for a minute. What did *she* want? The lines on that had blurred a lot lately, too. If only Destiny hadn't planted that stupid item with Pete Forsythe. It was going to force them out into the real world before either of them was ready. And the real world had a way of taking the edge off the excitement, a way of stripping away pretenses and forcing an examination of the core feelings behind an involvement.

Wasn't that what had happened to her before? That grant application, which had brought the real world smack into the middle of her relationship, had exposed wounds and clashing egos in a way that might otherwise never have happened. Not that she wasn't grateful now to have made the discovery about her ex-fiancé's competitiveness, insecurities and cruelty before they married, but it had been a bitter blow at the time.

She was very much afraid that her relationship with Mack wouldn't weather this current storm any more smoothly.

When she opened the door to Tony's room, she was surprised to find Mack there. She thought he'd left after dropping her off, but there he was, leafing through a comic book while Tony slept.

"Heavy reading?" she teased. "I'm beginning to think that's why you keep coming around—because it gives you an excuse to read all those comics."

"Afraid not," he said, his gaze steady on hers. "You keep me coming around, Doc. I thought you understood that after the conversation we had earlier."

She opened her mouth to respond, then caught a flicker of Tony's eyelids that suggested he was playing possum and listening to every word. "We'll finish this conversation later," she told Mack.

"Aw, come on, Dr. Beth, it was just getting good," Tony protested, opening his eyes.

Mack whirled around to stare at him. "I thought you were asleep."

"I was, but then I woke up," Tony said. He grinned impishly at Mack. "I knew you liked Dr. Beth. I could tell. I even told my mom."

"You know, kid, my love life is none of your business," Mack scolded.

"Why not?" Tony asked. "I thought we were all friends."

"We are, but most adults like to figure things out for themselves," Beth told him.

"But you guys are taking way too long," Tony said.

"Says who?" Mack asked.

Tony gave him a feisty look. "Says me. You know I don't exactly have forever."

Tony uttered the horrific words with a blithe acceptance of the reality, but Mack looked as if someone had slugged him. Even Beth was taken aback by Tony's matter-of-fact statement about his own prospects.

"You don't know that," she said fiercely, struggling against the tears stinging her eyes. She could not cry in front of Tony, or in front of Mack, for that matter. "I will not let you give up on yourself."

Tony reached her hand. "It's okay, Dr. Beth. I don't blame you."

"That's not the point. You *are* going to get better, Tony. You need to believe that."

Tony gave her a stubborn look. "It's not like I want to die," he said seriously. "But sometimes you just gotta face facts."

"And the fact is that we don't know what's going to happen," Beth said. "Only God knows that. And in the meantime, you have Peyton and me, your mom and Mack, and a whole lot of other people rooting for you." Desperate to get through to him, she gestured toward a colorful mural that had been painted by the kids at his school and which hung now on the wall across from his bed. "Look at that. All of your classmates are behind you, too."

Tony sighed wearily and lay back against the pillows. "I know, but sometimes it feels like it's time to let go." He looked plaintively at Mack. "You know what I mean?"

Though he was clearly as shaken as Beth, Mack moved to the edge of the bed and took Tony's frail hand in his big one. "It takes a very brave person to fight this illness," Mack told him quietly. "And, Tony, you're the bravest person I ever met." He glanced at Beth. "But there's no shame in saying 'enough' if it gets to be too much. No one will blame you."

Beth wanted to scream at Mack for saying such a thing, but she knew he was right, knew it was exactly what Tony needed to hear from his hero. She held her breath, praying he would say more, praying he would tell Tony that that time hadn't yet come.

Mack gave Tony's hand a squeeze and reached up to settle his cap more firmly on his bald head. "But you know what?" he said gently. "I've got to believe that Dr. Beth here knows what she's talking about. It's too soon to give up."

A faint glimmer of hope lit Tony's eyes. "You think so?"

"I really do," Mack said. "I think there's a lot more fight in you, Tony. And I promise you that I'll be right here with you every step of the way. If the day comes when you can't bear one more treatment or one more needle, you say the word. Okay?"

Tony nodded. "And you won't let my mom be too sad?"

Mack cleared his throat, carefully avoiding Beth's gaze. She could tell that he, too, was fighting tears.

"That's the thing about moms," Mack told him. "There's no way to keep them from being sad, but they always, always understand."

Tony struggled up and threw himself into Mack's arms. "I love you," he whispered.

Beth saw Mack's arms tighten around the boy, but his words were muffled when he responded. She didn't have to hear them, though, to know that he'd once more said exactly the right thing.

And in that moment of deepest despair, when her heart was breaking for Tony, she also felt it fill with something else and was finally forced to admit that she was wildly, madly—and totally unexpectedly—in love with Mack Carlton.

## 12

Mack left Tony's room half-blinded by tears he was struggling not to shed. Oblivious to everything, he strode down the hall, took the stairs two at a time and left the hospital, needing to escape from the overwhelming emotions, needing fresh air and...hell, he didn't know what else. He'd never felt like this before, completely and utterly helpless. He hated discovering such weakness in himself.

He was also shocked to discover just how cleverly Tony had slipped past all of his defenses. What had begun as a good deed, what had continued as a way to keep seeing Beth, had turned into genuine affection for the boy. No, even more than that, he loved the feisty kid with the smart mouth and the brave heart. And today he'd fully realized for the first time that he actually could lose him.

He was halfway to his car when he finally heard Beth's cries and realized she'd been chasing after him the whole way. He stood in the parking lot and waited for her to catch up.

"I can't talk about this," he said flatly when she was still several yards away.

His warning apparently fell on deaf ears, because she faced him with a stubborn set to her jaw and compassion in her eyes.

"I know you're upset by what happened in there," she began. "Who wouldn't be?"

"Beth, I told you, I am not discussing it," he said again. He didn't think he could bear it. He didn't want the raw emotions reduced to words, didn't want to hash it all out in a calm, reasonable way. Facts couldn't possibly tell the story. Nothing she said, however hopeful, could give a guaranteed future to Tony.

"Mack, I know you must have a thousand thoughts running through your head about what just happened in there, but you handled it exactly right," she continued, talking right over his objection. "You were wonderful. You were encouraging and reassuring, but you didn't sugarcoat anything. Most important, you didn't dismiss what Tony had to say. It's not easy to hear, but Tony needs someone he can be honest with, someone who won't flinch when he says what he's really feeling. He is so lucky to have you."

*Lucky?* If she thought Tony was lucky in any way at all, much less just because Mack was around, she was crazy. Tony didn't need Mack. He needed a miracle.

Trying to comprehend where she was coming from, Mack stared at her through his sunglasses. They were hardly necessary with dusk falling, but they were the only shield he had to keep her from seeing the despair that must be in his eyes. Even so, he could tell that she understood, that she was desperately trying to reassure him, when it should have been the other way around. He should be the one bolstering her up. That conversation couldn't have been easy for her to hear, either.

He drew in a deep breath and forced himself to speak. "You have no idea what it took for me not to sit there and curse God and medicine and everything else right there in front of him," he admitted finally.

"Oh, but I do," Beth said. "Don't you think I feel like that a hundred times a day, a few thousand times a year? But I can't focus on what's going on with me. It's only about the kids and what they're feeling. The worst thing anyone can do is make them feel even more isolated by refusing to listen to their fears. Often, their parents don't want to face the truth, so there's this awful silence that just builds and builds. I think it's worst of all when that silence is never broken and no one has ever had the chance to say goodbye."

Mack sighed, recognizing the sorrow and regrets she must deal with every day. "Do you have any idea how much admiration and respect I have for you?" he asked, fighting the desire to reach for her because he was one more person needing her comfort. He couldn't be sure how much strength she had to go around, and it wasn't fair for him to be one of those demanding a share of that incredible emotional resource. He was hurting, but the kids and their parents must be in far worse shape. He needed to let her conserve her strength for them.

He met her gaze. "It's not just that what you do is important, it's that you handle it with such grace, the ups and, more importantly, the downs."

"You haven't been around to count the number of mugs I go through in a year," she told him, her expression rueful. "It's a good thing my office is off the beaten path, since I break so much pottery."

He knew she was trying to lighten the mood, but he felt even sadder at the admission of her lonely battle against desolation. "Does it help?"

"Not a bit."

"Does anything?"

"The success stories," she said at once. "Every tiny victory keeps me going till the next time."

"Tony could use a victory about now," Mack said, unable to keep the wistful note out of his voice.

"He'll have it," Beth said. "I truly believe that, Mack."

"In your heart?" he asked, studying her intently. "Or because it's the only way you can get out of bed in the morning?"

She sighed. "Maybe a little of both." She searched his face. "Is there anything I can do for you? Would you like to come over for dinner? Or we could go to a movie, some action flick that will block out reality for a couple of hours."

Mack shook his head. He could have used the comfort of her presence, maybe even needed it, but that need scared him. Like Beth, he was used to dealing with his emotions on his own. Of course, that usually meant ignoring them, but she didn't need to know that.

Beth nodded, her expression filled with understanding. "Call me if you change your mind."

"Thanks," he said, then bent down to press a soft kiss to her forehead. He had to resist the urge to take more. "Get some sleep tonight. I'll speak to you in the morning."

He knew she was still there, watching him, her eyes filled with concern, when he pulled out of the parking lot a few minutes later. He was tempted to go back and get her. He knew she was hurting as badly as he was. She was simply more accustomed to covering it.

If he weakened and went back, they could cling to each other, maybe even feel a little better for it, but in the end it wouldn't be what either of them really needed tonight. What they truly needed was some glimmer of real hope for Tony.

Or the strength to bear it if they lost him.

Beth watched Mack drive off with her heart aching. She understood his need to go off by himself, but he looked so unbearably alone. On impulse, she reached in her pocket and pulled out her cell phone along with Melanie Carlton's business card.

"Beth!" Melanie said cheerfully when she took the call. "I hadn't expected to hear from you so soon."

"Actually I called because I need a favor," Beth told her. She explained what had happened with Tony and the way it had affected Mack. "Think you could get Richard to check on him? He said he wanted to be alone, but I think he could use his brother about now."

"Absolutely," Melanie said without hesitation. "Can you hold on a sec while I call Richard? Then you and I can make some plans. Something tells me you could use a friendly ear, too."

"Thanks," Beth said, grateful for the immediate understanding.

It was only a couple of minutes before Melanie came back on the line. "That's taken care of," she said briskly. "Richard's already calling Ben, and then he'll track Mack down. He won't let Mack put them off."

Beth sighed. "I knew I could count on you."

"Anytime," Melanie assured her. "And since the guys

are going to be tied up, why don't you join me for dinner? I imagine that Mack's not the only one who needs cheering up."

The invitation was unexpected and Beth was exhausted, but turning down this chance to get a better sense of the man she'd all but handed her heart to was too good to pass up. Besides, Melanie was exactly right. She was in desperate need of company. Once again she had the sense that Melanie was going to be a good friend.

"Tell me where and when," she said.

"I'll come to you. There's a place in Georgetown Richard and I love." She named a restaurant within a few blocks of Beth's town house. "I could meet you there around six. Would that work?"

"It's perfect."

"And, Beth, just so you know, I won't pry," Melanie said. "Of course, if there's anything you do want to tell me about you and Mack, I'll be happy to listen."

Beth laughed at Melanie's feeble attempt to bank her obvious curiosity. "I'll hold you to that."

"Well, hell," Melanie said. "I'll just have to ply you with alcohol till you forget my promise."

"I knew it wasn't going to last, anyway," Beth told her.

"And yet you've still agreed to meet me," Melanie retorted. "Brave woman."

"Not so brave. Just confident I can handle you. Destiny might be another story."

"Then I won't suggest we include her," Melanie teased. "Besides, just for once, it will feel good to know something that's going on in this family before she does. I swear the woman has eyes and ears everywhere."

"Speaking of that, remind me to ask you about Pete Forsythe," Beth said.

"Oh, that one's so easy, I can tell you right now. You can blame Destiny for that item," Melanie said confidently. "I'd stake my firstborn baby on that—something I don't say lightly in my current condition."

"Mack was equally sure it was Destiny. We tried to find her today, but she was cleverly absent every place we looked."

Melanie chuckled. "I doubt that. I imagine she bribed the help to say she was out. Everyone who works for her adores her. They'll all protect her with their dying breath—even from her own family. I wonder what it's like to instill that kind of loyalty in people."

"She's obviously a remarkable woman."

"Remarkable and sneaky," Melanie confirmed. "You're definitely no match for her, especially not when you're in this vulnerable condition. We'll work on toughening you up over dinner. I'll see you soon."

Feeling better than she had all day, Beth hung up and headed back to Tony's room for one last check. She always liked to make sure that Maria Vitale was there before she left the hospital for the night.

She cracked open the door to the room and saw that Maria and Tony were playing a quiet game of Scrabble. They didn't see her, so she closed the door gently and leaned against it, relieved that she could escape without another harrowing confrontation.

Tomorrow, with all of its uncertainties, would come soon enough.

The minute he heard from Richard, Mack suspected that Beth was behind it. Richard never called out of the blue to suggest a guys' night out, not since he'd gotten married, and rarely enough before that. As for Ben, it took a crisis of major proportions or a command from Destiny to get him away from the isolated farm in Middleburg where he was living these days.

Because Richard presented the evening's plans as a fait accompli, Mack accepted grudgingly and drove to the crowded chain restaurant that was partway between Alexandria and Middleburg, smack in the middle of what had once been the region's wildly successful high-tech corridor.

"Why are we here?" he asked, wincing at the noise level as he found his older brother at a table in the back. Ben hadn't yet arrived.

"Because Ben wanted Chinese and I figured he deserved some consideration for agreeing to drive in on short notice," Richard explained. "Besides, it's impossible to have a heavy conversation in a place like this. We'll be reduced to idle chitchat." He gave Mack an intense look. "I thought you might prefer that."

Mack nodded. "The more mundane, the better," he agreed, relieved that his brother knew him so well.

"Sure you don't want to tell me what's going on in your life before Ben gets here?"

"Nope," Mack said firmly. "What I want is a drink."

Richard immediately beckoned for their waitress. "Scotch?" he asked Mack.

"A double," Mack confirmed.

When the waitress had gone, Richard opened his mouth, probably to deliver a lecture about the dangers of overindulgence, but Ben arrived just then.

"The things I do for you," he muttered as he sat down.

He regarded Mack with the same intense look Richard had given him earlier. "You okay?"

Mack nodded. "And I'll make you a deal. I won't ask a single question about how you're doing if you'll drop all the questions about my life."

"Deal," Ben said at once, clearly eager to forgo an examination of his own recovery from the tragedy that had nearly destroyed him.

Richard shook his head. "I'll bet you Melanie and Beth are spilling their guts to each other by now and here we sit, reduced to talking about what? Football? Political corruption? Terrorism?"

Mack regarded him with shock. "Beth is out with your wife?"

"Oh, yes," Richard said, looking pleased as punch at having been the bearer of that news. "Melanie could hardly wait. She's anticipating great revelations."

Ben grinned at Mack. "You're doomed, bro. Just accept it and start looking at china patterns."

"Bite me," Mack retorted. "Besides, it's not as if she's out with Destiny. That would be terrifying." He suddenly recalled Beth's current anger toward their aunt. "Then again, that little stunt Destiny pulled by planting an item about us with Pete Forsythe got Beth pretty stirred up. I imagine she could more than hold her own with Destiny about now."

"I'd pay to see that," Richard said.

"If the occasion actually arises, I'll get you a seat in the front row," Mack promised him.

He was about to down the rest of his drink when he saw Ben's eyes widen and Richard's mouth drop open. He turned slowly and spotted a very buxom model he'd stopped seeing several months ago heading their way.

Cassandra was gorgeous, scantily clad and brash. She walked up and planted a kiss on him that would have melted his zipper not all that long ago.

"Hey, darlin'," she whispered huskily, ignoring his brothers as if they weren't even there. "I've missed you."

Mack tried to extricate himself from the hand that was sliding directly toward his belt buckle. "Cass, I'd like you to meet my brothers," he said pointedly. "Richard, Ben, this is Cassandra."

She blinked at the distinct lack of welcome in his tone, studied his face for a moment, then turned to his brothers. "Gentlemen, it's nice to meet you." She gave them both a considering look, then shrugged at the lack of response from either one. "See you around, Mack."

A pout on her full lips, she turned and sashayed off, her skimpy skirt barely covering her extraordinary derriere. Richard and Ben stared after her, then turned back to Mack, their eyes filled with amusement.

"It must be hell to be you," Richard said.

"The women, the attention, the media." Ben shook his head pityingly. "A curse. A definite curse."

Mack glowered at them, then lifted his glass. "You know, you two, I could drink at home and get a whole lot less attitude."

"But why would you want to?" Richard asked, grinning. "This way you get brotherly love, Chinese food and an excellent floor show."

"One woman stopping by the table does not constitute a floor show," Mack protested.

"Then how about three?" Ben asked, nodding in the direction of two more women heading their way. "Damn, but this is fun."

Mack scowled fiercely at the women and they turned away. At least those two were strangers who wouldn't go away pouting, their feelings hurt.

Mack loved his brothers. He even appreciated that this evening was meant to cheer him up, but he'd had all he could take. He should have taken Beth up on her offer of dinner or a movie. Maybe it wasn't too late. Maybe he could get Beth to send Melanie over here to her traitorous husband. Then he could meet Beth at her place.

Great plan, he concluded, but little chance of success. Beth wasn't like him. She wouldn't dump the person she was with to be with someone else. That didn't mean he had to stick around.

He pushed back his chair and stood up. "Guys, I love you both and I appreciate that you came here to cheer me up, but I've gotta go."

"Go where?" Richard demanded.

"Anyplace besides this hotbed of women on the prowl," he said bluntly.

Both men stared at him in shock.

"He really is in love," Ben concluded.

"Seems that way to me," Richard agreed sagely.

"Bite me," Mack said again.

Only when he'd made his escape did he stop long enough to admit to himself that his brothers had gotten it exactly right. He was in love with Beth. He waited after making the admission, expecting real panic to set in, but all he felt was this amazing sense of relief that he'd finally recognized the emotion for what it really was. He grinned as he got behind the wheel.

"Well, I'll be damned," he said as he headed for home. Maybe Destiny had gotten it right after all. But given how irritated he was with her at the moment, it would take a stack of snowballs in hell before he told her that.

Mack was still sound asleep when the phone beside the bed jarred him awake. "Yeah, what?" he growled.

"What on earth were you thinking?" Destiny demanded, snapping him awake with the genuine dismay in her voice.

"What?" he asked, sitting up in bed.

"You haven't seen the morning paper?"

"You woke me out of a sound sleep. What do you think?" he retorted more sharply than he should have. He might be irritated with his aunt, but she didn't deserve rudeness.

"Get your paper and call me back after you've read Pete Forsythe's column," she said, and hung up on him.

Mack stared at the phone, then finally returned it to its cradle. He couldn't recall the last time he'd heard his aunt so furious. Nor could he imagine anything he might have done to set her off.

Yanking on a pair of jeans, he went to the front door and picked up the paper, turning immediately to the gossip column.

"Mack's back!" screamed the headline, as if he'd been recovered from space aliens.

His heart thudding dully he began to read.

"Maybe reports of Mighty Mack Carlton's fascination with a prominent lady doctor were premature," Forsythe had written. "Just last night Mack was spotted by our photographer out on the town with an old flame, super-model Cassandra Wells."

Mack stared at the photo accompanying the article. Sure enough, there he was with Cassandra draped all over him. The photographer had managed to shoot from an angle that completely blocked out his brothers. He finally understood Destiny's indignation. He was pretty damn livid himself, especially since he knew what had gone on last night...and what hadn't.

He picked up the phone and dialed Destiny. "It's not what it looks like," he said at once.

"They doctored the photo?" she asked in a scathing tone. "Please, Mack, don't even try to suggest such a thing."

"No, but they managed to take the picture or crop it so that Richard and Ben weren't in it," he told her.

She paused then. "Your brothers were there?" she asked in a tone that sounded slightly less irate.

"Yes."

Instead of sounding relieved, Destiny muttered, "I think I'd better speak to both of them about appropriate behavior in a public place."

If she hadn't sounded so serious, Mack might have laughed. "Destiny, I think we're all a little too old for that particular lecture."

"Obviously not," she huffed. "How are you going to explain this to Beth? She must be devastated. You've publicly humiliated her. Just yesterday—"

Mack cut her off. "Destiny, you really don't want to go there. If anyone is responsible for Beth being humiliated, I think we can agree that it's you. Pete Forsythe wouldn't know about her at all, if you hadn't tipped him off."

She sighed heavily. "You're right," she said, giving up the fight gracefully. "It was probably a mistake to try that particular tactic."

"Probably? It *was* a mistake," Mack said emphatically.

"Darling, I'll ask you again, then. Why are you still seeing her? I was so hopeful that it was getting serious and here you are running around with an old flame."

"Didn't you hear a word I just said? I wasn't running around. Cassandra was at my table for less than a minute, long enough to plant that kiss and get her picture snapped. It had nothing to do with Beth," Mack insisted. "Though after this debacle, I'll be lucky if she ever speaks to me again."

"Can I help?"

"No. I think you've done quite enough. I'll handle this."

"Mack, before you see Beth, really think about what you want. It's not fair to lead her on, if you don't intend to truly open your heart and let her in. She'd be better off if you simply let her go now."

"You want me to break up with her?"

"No, of course that's not what I want, but it might be for the best. As for this business last night, I'm sorry if I jumped to the wrong conclusion," Destiny apologized. "It just made me so angry to see you taking up with that little nobody when you could have a woman of substance like Beth in your life. In the end, though, it is your decision."

Mack grinned at the dismissal of Cassandra as a "little nobody." She was on the cover of half the high-fashion magazines in the world.

"I appreciate your concern," Mack told his aunt. "But maybe you should let me handle this from here on out, okay?"

"Whatever you think is best," she said meekly.

"Thank you," Mack said, figuring that submissiveness would last for no more than twenty-four hours. "Love you."

"Love you, too, darling."

As soon as he'd hung up from speaking to Destiny, he called a florist and ordered a dozen white roses to be sent to Beth at the hospital. It might not be much, but as peace offerings went he figured it was a decent start.

Of course, there was always the slim possibility that Beth hadn't even seen this morning's paper and would have no idea why he felt the need to apologize in the first place. In that case, those roses might even buy him enough points to get another night in her bed, rather than the crack of a vase over his head.

## 13

Beth returned to her office from morning rounds to find a huge bouquet of perfect white roses in a crystal vase on her desk and Jason sitting in her chair with his feet propped up and a grim look on his face.

Jason's expression was somber enough, and his mere presence at this hour was sufficient to distract her momentarily from the flowers.

"What's wrong? Nothing's happened to one of the kids, has it? I just finished seeing most of them. Everyone seemed to be stable."

He shook his head. "I'm not here about the kids."

"What then?"

"I think you should sit down."

She lifted a brow and pointedly stared at him. When he didn't get the hint, she told him, "You're in my chair."

He guiltily scrambled up and moved out of her way. As he settled on the edge of the spare seat next to her desk, he cast a sour look at the flowers.

"Okay, now I'm sitting," Beth said, studying him and trying to make sense of his odd mood. "What's going on, Jason? It's not like you to be so mysterious."

"I think we need to talk about Mack," he said, regarding her seriously.

The announcement was so unexpected, so totally unlike Jason, that Beth merely stared. "You want to talk about Mack?" she repeated slowly. "Is this about those tickets you're so hot to get?"

"Forget about the damn tickets!" he said heatedly. "I think you should stop seeing him."

Beth couldn't have been more surprised if he'd announced a desire to marry her himself. "Why do you suddenly care if I continue to see Mack? In fact, I thought that was exactly what you wanted. The other day you all but begged me not to break up with him, at least not until after football season."

In the way of most males who took a contradictory position five seconds after battling over something, he shrugged. "I changed my mind."

"Are you going to tell me why?"

Like a kid being forced to tattle, he made a face. "Do I have to?"

"Yes, Jason," she said patiently. "If you want me to stop seeing Mack, you need to tell me why. Obviously you have a reason. What's the agenda here?"

"He's no good for you. You're a decent person, Beth. A great person, in fact. He's..." He seemed stuck for a suitable word. "Okay, he's a playboy, a scoundrel and... what's that other word? A rogue. That's what he is, a rogue."

Beth chuckled. "That's hardly news. I thought we were all well aware of that before he ever set foot in this hospital."

"I mean he's *still* a playboy," Jason said, looking miserable. "Even though he supposedly has something going on with you."

Her heartbeat seemed to slow down as Jason's message finally sank in. Mack was still playing around, despite how close she thought they'd gotten, despite the fact that she had feelings for him and he claimed to have feelings for her. In fact, most likely, it was precisely because he was starting to care for her that he'd started running around with another woman…assuming Jason was to be believed.

"And you know this because?" she asked.

He pulled a folded-up section of the newspaper from his pocket and handed it to her. "Something tells me this explains the flowers," he said quietly.

Beth stared at the photo, apparently taken the night before, when she'd assumed Mack was with his brothers. Apparently, he'd found a far more effective way to cheer himself up. She felt sick inside at the sight of the buxom woman draped all over him.

To cover her reaction, she immediately balled up the paper and tossed it in the trash, then regarded Jason with a bland expression. Pride demanded that she put on a very convincing act, even with this man who was a good friend.

"So?" she said, managing what she considered to be a respectably nonchalant tone.

"You don't care that he was out with some model?" Jason asked incredulously.

"He hasn't made any kind of commitment to me," she replied reasonably, even though her heart was breaking into little pieces. "Besides, there could be some perfectly innocent explanation."

"Then why send flowers? That's guilt talking, Beth. I know how men think."

She frowned at the bouquet. They *were* tantamount to an admission of some kind, no question about it. If Jason hadn't been here, she might have tossed them across the room just to hear the satisfying crash of that expensive crystal vase. Then again, it might be nice to keep it whole until she could use it on Mack's hard head.

Before she could come up with a less demonstrative response, her cell phone rang. She glanced at the display and immediately recognized Mack's number. Taking the call right now, with Jason watching her worriedly, was not an option.

"Aren't you going to get that?" Jason asked.

"No."

"It's Mack, isn't it?"

She saw little point in denying it. It was obvious if it had been another physician or a parent, she would have taken it at once. "Yes."

"Avoiding him won't help," Jason told her.

"Then what do you suggest?" she asked angrily. "That I take the call and tell him he's low-down, no-good scum, without even giving him a chance to explain? That's about the only thing I could say with you sitting here listening to every word. Anything else and you'd lose respect for me."

Jason looked shocked. "No, I wouldn't. I'm your friend, no matter what you decide to do. I hate this, in fact, because for a few weeks now you've seemed happier than I've ever seen you before. Even though you being with Mack caught me by surprise after the way things went that first day, I wanted it to work out for you."

Beth managed a shrug. "Yes, well, we all knew I wasn't exactly Mack's usual type. The fact that we had a few lovely weeks together is probably something of a miracle, but they had to end sooner or later. Unsuitable people are often drawn together during a crisis. It rarely lasts."

If only she hadn't been so sure that this would last, Beth thought wearily. She'd been so certain—especially after everything Melanie Carlton had said to her the night before—that she and Mack were starting something special.

"Can you really be that calm and accepting about this?" Jason asked skeptically.

She gave him a tired smile and the only truthful answer she could offer. "I have to be, don't I?" Killing the man would be highly unprofessional.

Mack was chomping at the bit with frustration. Beth wasn't taking his calls, which meant she'd seen the photo and that even after getting his peace offering, she was still absolutely livid. He couldn't blame her, but not being able to get away from the office to get over there and talk things out was making him a little crazy. If the attorney and agent seated across from him hadn't been there to finalize terms for a much-needed defensive player for the team, he'd have cut the meeting short and excused himself. Thankfully, they were finally down to the last few sticking points.

He glanced across the table, then looked down at the figures on the paper in front of him. He could probably bargain the numbers down a few thousand here and there, but right at this moment, he didn't care enough to bother.

Looking up, he met the agent's gaze. "Gentlemen, I think we have a deal."

Both men looked momentarily startled, then exuberant.

"Damn, I thought you were going to fight us for every penny," celebrity sports agent Lawrence Miller told him. "Nice to have you on the other side of the table. You bring a pro-player perspective to the negotiations."

"In other words, I let you put the screws to me," Mack said, chuckling. "Don't worry. It won't happen again. Now, if you'll excuse me, I have someplace I need to be."

"A pleasure doing business with you," attorney Jerry Warren said. "You just got yourself one hell of a ball-player."

"Don't think I don't recognize that," Mack told him. He winked at the agent. "In fact, before you start gloating too badly, you should know I was prepared to offer another million as a signing bonus."

Before they could react, he walked from the room and headed straight for the elevator. It was almost four. If he hurried, he could probably catch up with Beth in Tony's room, where she'd be unlikely to ask for his head on a platter.

Beth glanced up from her examination of Tony's vital signs to see Mack standing in the doorway. Her heart did a little hop, skip and jump, even though she'd been firmly telling herself all day that he'd never really mattered to her.

"You'll have to come back later," she told him stiffly.

"Aw, Dr. Beth, don't send Mack away," Tony protested weakly. "I've been waiting all day for him to get here."

"I'll be right outside," Mack promised. "I'll come in the second Doc gives me the all-clear."

Beth heard the message intended for her, as well. She wasn't going to get rid of him so easily, especially not after ducking his calls all day.

"Oh, come on in," she said grudgingly. "I'm almost finished anyway."

"Are you sure?" Mack asked, studying her intently.

"Sure, why not?" she said, hoping she sounded totally unconcerned about his presence.

The minute he stepped inside, though, her pulse rate escalated predictably. He looked so darn good. He was dressed in one of those light-gray perfectly tailored custom suits of his with a silk-blend shirt with monogrammed cuffs and a tie in a slightly darker tone of the same dusky blue. He was the epitome of the successful businessman with the well-honed body of a trained athlete. She'd never realized before meeting Mack just how incredibly sexy that combination could be. She almost sighed with regret that he was no longer hers.

Not that he'd ever been, she reminded herself sharply. That was something she shouldn't forget. Recent weeks, all that time they'd spent together, had been no more solid than an illusion.

She finished up her quick examination of Tony, made a few notes in his chart and turned to leave. Mack stood directly in her path.

"Did you get the flowers?" he asked.

"You sent flowers to Dr. Beth?" Tony asked, his eyes bright with excitement. "That is so awesome. How come you didn't tell me, Dr. Beth?"

Mack grinned at him. "Maybe she thought her personal business was none of *your* business," Mack teased.

"Or maybe I didn't think it was any big deal," she said, gazing directly into Mack's eyes.

She saw that he immediately got the message. Guilt and regret darkened his eyes.

"We need to talk," he said in a lowered voice.

"I don't think there's anything left to say," she replied.

"Beth, don't do this," he said with surprising urgency. "You owe me a chance to explain."

She regarded him quizzically. "I *owe* you a chance to explain?"

"Yes. You owe it to both of us. How about if I come over in an hour or so? I'll bring dinner. We can talk privately and get this settled, before the whole ridiculous thing gets out of hand."

Beth wanted to turn him down flat. She wanted to protect what was left of her tattered pride, but fairness dictated that she needed to hear him out, even if she couldn't imagine that he had anything to say worth hearing.

"Forget dinner, but you can come by," she said eventually. "I don't expect it to change anything, though."

"Maybe not, but I have to try." Mack tucked a finger under her chin and met her gaze. "This is important, Beth. Really important."

Her skin tingled at the innocent touch, proving that even as hurt and angry as she was, he still had the power to get to her. She should have told him no, should have protected her heart better. The only problem with that was that it was already way too late.

Mack had been talking nonstop since he walked through the door. Beth had heard every word he said, but she was trying so damn hard to fight the desire to give in and accept his apology. It didn't help that he kept touching her—casual, innocent touches it was impossible to protest but that managed to inflame.

"Is any of this getting through to you?" he asked eventually. "What happened last night was totally innocent. I was not out with Cassandra. She was barely at the table more than a minute, and Ben and Richard were right there. They'll back me up."

"You've explained that," she said, trying not to take too much comfort from it. "But it's going to happen again, Mack. This Cassandra person is just the tip of the iceberg when it comes to your past. I'm not sure I can live with that kind of attention. I don't want to wake up every morning and wonder what I'm going to see in some newspaper gossip column."

He nodded slowly. "I can understand how that would get old," he admitted. "Even if it's not through any wrongdoing on my part." He regarded her with obvious misery. "Maybe Destiny was right."

"About?"

"I spoke to her earlier today after she saw that picture. She was furious. She knew you would be upset. As a result there's been an unexpected shift in her position."

"Regarding?"

"Us."

"What kind of shift?" Beth asked, feeling a faint chill stir inside her. Destiny had been the staunchest supporter of their relationship. Heck, she'd been the primary instigator behind that first meeting. If she'd had second thoughts, then there really was little hope. No one knew Mack better than Destiny did, not even Beth.

"Basically she reminded me that I shouldn't be playing games with you, that you're not like the other women I've dated, all things she'd said before," Mack said. "But this time she seems genuinely concerned that I'm going to break your heart. She doesn't want that to happen. Obviously, she's concluded that I'm a bad risk in the romance department, after all."

Beth's muscles grew even tighter, despite Mack's deft touch. She was less interested in Destiny's concern for her than she was in Mack's intentions now that his aunt had shifted positions on their relationship. She met his gaze directly. "Leaving the incident last night aside, what do you think? Have you been playing games? I thought we'd clarified that, but maybe something's changed."

He abandoned the massage to come around and hunker down in front of her, taking her hands in his, his expression serious. "I honestly don't think so, but I probably need to make my position really clear in case I haven't done that before. I don't do the long haul, Beth. I can't. Not even for you, and, believe me, I am tempted to try."

She fought the dismay that crawled up the back of her throat. "That's hardly a shock," she admitted, forcing out the calm, measured words. "Your track record alone would give anyone that impression, wouldn't it?" She'd been wondering for some time now, though, if impressions were to be believed. Now she had her answer. In Mack's case, they were dead-on accurate.

"It's the truth, not just an impression," he said flatly, confirming her conclusion.

Beth stared straight into his eyes and saw the real torment there. Ironically now, with everything out on the table, she wasn't sure that letting go to avoid more hurt was the right choice for either of them.

"This is all because you lost your parents and you're afraid if you care too much about someone else, you'll lose them, too," she said quietly. "That's why you won't take a chance."

He didn't seem surprised that she'd put the pieces of the puzzle together. He merely nodded.

"I always thought I was immune to whatever damage their deaths had caused, but I guess I'm not," Mack said. "Lord knows, I've always found some reason to move on every time a relationship started to get serious. I thought it was different with you. I know how I feel about you. This morning when I thought I might lose you over that stupid photo in the paper, I panicked, but at the same time I can't see myself taking the next step."

"Meaning what? Marriage?"

He nodded. "My stomach starts churning just hearing you say the word," he admitted. "How can I not consider the probability that it's because of that early loss?"

Beth struggled with the dismay spreading through her, but no one knew better than she did the hole that was left in a heart after losing someone. Hers had healed, but that didn't mean Mack had to recover on the same kind of timetable. At least he was trying desperately to be honest with her. She had to respect him for that.

"Fair enough," she said, making up her mind not to let this matter. She'd known all along that their match wasn't made in heaven, even though it had begun to feel so right. She'd been taken by surprise from the moment they met. It struck her as a little sad that this was the one time he hadn't surprised her, but rather acted totally predictably—reaching out only to yank his hand back before it could get burned.

"We should stop seeing each other," he said when she remained silent. "Now, before I can hurt you any more than I already have."

"Is that what you want?" she asked dully, her heart in her throat. If it was, she would have to accept it and move on. She had too much pride to do anything less.

"No," he admitted.

Relief nearly overwhelmed her. Sometime soon she would have to examine why that was, but not tonight. Tonight she needed to feel Mack's arms around her again. She needed the connection to him that had made her feel alive these past few weeks. In time she might have to let go but not yet.

"Okay then," she said briskly, to cover her emotional reaction. "Neither do I. And you seem to have forgotten that I've lost someone I loved, too—my brother. I know exactly how devastating and life-

altering that experience can be."

"But—"

Beth cut him off. "You've been honest with me, Mack. That's all you owe me. I'm a grown woman. I can decide when the risk is too high. It's not your decision to make, at least not on my behalf, only for yourself."

His expression still troubled, he touched her cheek. "But I couldn't bear it if I hurt you or let you down. You don't deserve that."

"You might do both," she told him, then slid out of the chair to wrap her arms around him and rest her cheek against his. "But not tonight. Not unless you go away without making love to me."

He studied her intently, then a smile tugged at his lips. "Guess there's no chance of that, darlin'. No chance at all."

* * *

A few days later Mack sat in his office contemplating the turn of events that had kept Beth in his life. For a few minutes he'd thought it was all over, thought it needed to be over. It had stunned him how much that had dismayed him.

Until Destiny had spilled the beans to Pete Forsythe, Beth had been the first woman that the media hadn't caught on to in Mack's life. Now that the days of being out of the limelight were pretty much over, Mack appreciated them more than ever. It had been surprisingly nice to actually have a private life that was his alone.

At least so far, his warnings to his aunt had kept Beth's identity a secret. He'd thought maybe that photo had been a boon, after all, that it would throw Forsythe off the scent, but he'd been mistaken about that. In fact, according to the indignant call he'd received a half hour ago from Jason, the columnist had been poking around at the hospital this morning.

Fortunately, most of those who knew about the two of them were as interested in protecting Beth as Mack was. Jason had reassured him that he, Peyton and the other doctors and nurses who worked around Tony would never say a word. Tony might happily give away the secret, but so far the hospital public relations department had been dedicated to protecting the identity of the sick child Mack came to visit so regularly.

Yesterday, when a reporter had caught up with Mack outside the hospital, he'd uttered nothing more than "No comment," then hurried inside, beyond the reach of the reporters and photographers who were staking out the public areas outside hoping for details of the secret romance in his life. He knew that the terse reply would only stir curiosity. Until now he'd been well-known for cooperating with the media. Until now he hadn't even viewed them as adversaries, but rather as a condition of celebrity.

Of course, until now, the women he'd been with had sought the spotlight that shone on them because of him. Maybe that's why he felt so completely off-kilter. Beth didn't crave the media attention. She was with him despite it, in fact.

Just as important, his relationship with Beth was his alone, not the media's and not his fans'. He was stunned to discover he could be with a woman out of the spotlight for weeks on end without growing bored or restless. They had an endless supply of things to talk about besides football, and that was a relief, too. His brain was getting a workout keeping up with Beth, and rather than being intimidated by that, he was delighting in it.

He was pondering the meaning of all that when his secretary buzzed him.

"Dr. Browning on line one. She says it's urgent."

Heart pounding, he picked up the phone. "Beth? What is it? Are you okay?"

"It's Tony," she said, her voice oddly cool and detached. "He's taken a turn for the worse."

When? How? Was this it, then, after all that struggle? A million and one questions nagged at him, but he could tell from Beth's tone that now was not the time to ask them.

"I'm on my way," Mack promised, his heart pounding. "Hang in there, sweetheart. And tell Tony to hang on, too."

"Hurry, Mack."

# 14

"Without that donor marrow, he doesn't stand a chance," an unfamiliar doctor was telling Beth when Mack arrived. Peyton and Jason were beside her, their expressions equally bleak. "If we could get that transplant lined up, we could go ahead with the high-dose chemo and prep him. It's our only shot at this point."

"No hits on the donor list?" Beth asked in that same detached tone she'd used on the phone. She could have been talking about someone she'd barely met rather than a boy that Mack knew she loved as much as he did.

Mack studied her worriedly. There was no color in her cheeks, and her eyes were dulled by fatigue and anguish. Her demeanor might be calm and professional, but he didn't think it could possibly be healthy. She had to be as torn up by the news as he was.

Jason caught his eye and gestured for him to join them. Mack walked up beside Beth, put a reassuring hand on her shoulder and squeezed. She gave him a quick, grateful glance, but her eyes were haunted.

When Beth went back to her consultation with the other doctors, Mack looked down the hall and spotted

Maria Vitale outside of Tony's door, her shoulders shaking with silent sobs, her forehead resting against the cool tiles on the wall. He'd never seen anyone look so utterly sad and alone. Because there was nothing he could do here at the moment, he decided to go offer his support to Maria.

He leaned down and whispered to Beth that he was going to speak to Maria. "I'll be right there if you need me."

Again she regarded him with gratitude, but her focus remained with the other doctors.

Reluctantly Mack left her and went to Tony's mother. He spoke softly. "Maria?"

She looked up at him, tears streaming down her face. "Oh, Mack, I'm so glad you're here. I don't think I can bear it. He's giving up. He told me you would understand, that you would make me see that it's time for him to let go, but I can't let him do that. He's my baby. How can I let him go?"

Mack hadn't spent nearly enough time in church, had never had a reason to bargain with God. It had been too late when news of his parents' plane crash had been delivered. Prayers had been useless then. He searched his heart for the right words now, trying to balance comfort against hope.

"Maria, it's out of your hands," he reminded her gently. "Maybe it's always been out of your hands. God has a plan for Tony. He's the only one who'll decide this."

"How could God want my boy?" she demanded angrily, choking back another sob. "Tony is all I have."

Mack was helpless to answer that. "What did Dr. Browning tell you?"

"That without a bone marrow transplant very soon,

there is no hope." She gave him an anguished look. "There is no donor. I would give my boy my own life, but they say the match is not good enough. His father…" She gestured dismissively. "He's given Tony nothing, not since the day he was born. I don't even know where he is."

"Are there other family members?"

"None close enough to help," she said bleakly.

Mack finally saw the one thing he could do. He should have thought of it weeks ago, but for some reason it had never struck him that he could help in this way. He gave Maria's hand a squeeze. "Then let me see if I can buy Tony a little hope. Go back in there, Maria. Talk to him. Tell him you love him. Tell him I'll be in soon, too. He needs to know you're there beside him and that there are a lot of people around who care about him."

She nodded and wiped her tears. Her shoulders squared. "I left because I didn't want him to see me crying. He asked me not to cry for him. That's the kind of boy he is, concerned for me and not himself."

"Then, no more tears," Mack said. "Not until all hope is gone."

Maria regarded him with a sad smile. "You've been a good friend, Mack. I will never forget that you've been here for him every day. It has been like the fulfillment of a dream for him. If these are his last days, you've made them happy ones."

Mack shrugged off his effort. "Let me see if I can't do something for him that really matters."

When Maria had stepped back inside the room, Mack ducked in behind her for just a glimpse of Tony. He was paler than ever, his eyes closed. He looked so frail it didn't seem possible that there was even a breath of life left in him. Mack's heart ached, but his resolve strengthened.

Closing the door quietly behind him, he headed for an exit so he could use his cell phone. Maybe it was too late, but he had to do something. This wasn't happening to just any kid. It was happening to Tony, and over the past weeks, Mack had come to love that boy as if he were his own son. He couldn't lose him. It simply wasn't an option.

Mack was suddenly a boy again, listening to a stranger tell him, Richard and Ben that their parents were dead. The housekeeper had stood silently weeping at the stark recitation of the facts about the plane crash in the fog-shrouded mountains. Ben had cried with her, but Richard had stood stoically silent, looking dazed. Mack knew about death, but he'd never experienced its finality. He hadn't really understood what the full implications were at the time. He'd had no idea how horribly alone they were.

Only after the funeral had it begun to sink in that his mother and father would never be there with them again. Only when Destiny had moved into the house, trying in her own unexpected way to make things normal, had he fully grasped that things had changed forever. His aunt was such a dramatic change from their parents, and in some ways a welcome one. She was always laughing, always unpredictable, always ready for a new experience. It had been easier after a while to simply pretend that his world was okay.

But it hadn't been. He could see now that it had never been okay, that the scar from losing his folks ran deep, shaping him in ways he hadn't had to confront until he contemplated losing first Beth over something foolish and now Tony through a ravaging illness. He was terrified right down to his soul that he would never recover from this loss, that he would never dare to risk his heart again.

He wasn't thinking just of himself now, either. He didn't want Maria Vitale to have to face the feelings that had shaped his life. Nor could he handle watching Beth struggle so hard to bear that loss, that stark reminder of another boy—her beloved brother—who had died of the same devastating illness.

Filled with a sense of urgency, he made a mental checklist as he went down the hall. As he passed Beth, she gave him a questioning look. He mouthed that he would be outside, and she nodded. Then she and the other doctors kept on talking, struggling for answers that could buy Tony a few more days, or even a few more hours.

It was a half hour later and Mack was still on the phone when Beth finally broke free and came outside looking for him. He reached for her hand and gave her a tired smile as he wrapped up this one last call. She looked as wiped out as he felt.

"You okay?" she asked when he'd finished and stuck the cell phone back in his pocket.

"How could I be?" he asked, astounded that she had enough strength to worry about him, when she so clearly needed comfort herself.

She raised a hand, rested it against his cheek. "Don't take it so hard, Mack. We knew this could happen."

Her quiet acceptance, her defeatist attitude, grated. "We can't let it happen," he said angrily, shrugging off her touch and her words. "I won't listen to you give up on him."

"Sometimes you do everything you can and it's not enough," she said pragmatically.

"I can't accept that," he stated flatly. "I've made some calls."

"To?"

"The team."

She gave him a bewildered look. "Why?"

"He needs a bone marrow transplant, right? That's his only hope?"

She nodded. "But the chances—"

He cut her off. He wouldn't listen to any more doubts. "I've got just about everyone I know coming in here to be tested as potential donors. Can the lab handle that?"

She stared at him, her expression filled with disbelief and maybe just a tiny hint of hope. "Yes," she said at once. "I'll alert them right away, but are you sure? Did you explain to them that it's not just a simple little blood test?"

"They get it," Mack assured her. "They understand the important part, that it's a chance to save a boy's life." He met her gaze. "You can start right now with me. I should have done it weeks ago. It never even occurred to me that it was the one thing I should do that might really make a difference."

Sudden tears welled up in her eyes. "Oh, Mack."

He squeezed her hand. "Let's get started. That boy has to live, Beth. He has to."

What he couldn't say was how terrified he was of losing not only Tony but Beth. The two were so connected by now, he didn't think he could bear it if he lost either one.

Beth would have sworn that she'd already shed all the tears she possibly could, way back when her brother had died. Since then she'd maintained a stoic kind of calm in the face of each and every loss that had come her way. She might be shaken when she lost a patient, she might feel like a failure, but she never shed a tear. Even today, when she'd been forced to accept that the end was all but inevitable for Tony, her eyes had remained dry.

Now, though, as she watched one brawny football player after another appear to be tested as a prospective bone marrow donor, she kept bursting into tears. Mack had finally gone to the gift shop and brought back the biggest box of tissues the store offered.

She blinked away a fresh batch of tears when she spotted Mack's brother Richard, accompanied by a man who could only be another Carlton, the reclusive artist, Ben. Her eyes grew even mistier when she saw that Destiny was with them.

Mack opened his arms to his aunt. "You didn't have to come. I just wanted you to get in touch with Richard and Ben for me."

"Of course I had to come," Destiny insisted, reaching for Beth's hand and giving it a squeeze. "I intend to be tested, too."

"Destiny, no," Beth protested.

"Why on earth not? Is there some reason I should be disqualified?" Destiny inquired.

"No, but no one would expect you to do this."

"Then isn't it a good thing that I expect it of myself," Destiny said briskly. "Where do we need to go?"

Beth looked up at Mack, expecting him to protest, but he merely gave his aunt another fierce hug.

"Have I ever told you how much I admire you?" he asked her quietly.

"You've never had to say the words," she told him.

"None of you have. I know you think I'm impossible sometimes, that I'm annoying, that I'm a romantic meddler, but I also know that you love me."

"This isn't just about loving you," Mack said. "That's a given. Admiration and respect are something you've earned quite aside from that."

"He's right," Ben said. "You're a remarkable woman, Destiny."

"Oh, stop it," she said, clearly flustered. She grabbed one of Beth's tissues and dabbed at her eyes. "See what you've gone and made me do? I'm crying."

"And we know how you hate to spoil your makeup," Richard teased.

"Especially in a place like this," Destiny responded tartly. "With all these handsome doctors around, I want to look my best."

Beth chuckled. "Shall I take you someplace to powder your nose on the way to the lab?" She leaned in to confide, "Peyton Lang is quite something and he's single."

Destiny's eyes immediately brightened. "Really?" She winked at Mack. "See, darling, this isn't nearly the unselfish act you were making it out to be."

"You can't fool me, Destiny," he countered. "This is not about meeting a doctor. You already have half the available men in Washington falling at your feet and you never give most of them a second glance."

"Politicians and bankers," she said dismissively. "There is something so impressive about a man in a white coat, don't you think so?" she asked, linking her arm through Beth's. "It's reassuring."

To Beth's amusement, Mack rolled his eyes.

"I think I'll wait here," Mack said. "I'm not sure I

can bear to watch my aunt in there batting her eyelashes at Peyton."

"Neither can I," Ben said. "I'll wait with Mack till they're ready for me." He glanced up at Richard. "And before you say one single word, big brother, no, I'm not trying to back out. I said I'd do this and I will."

"Never doubted it," Richard said. He turned to Mack. "Just in case, be prepared to escort him down there. You know how Ben is about needles."

Ben feigned a horrified expression. "There are needles involved in this test?"

"Big ones," Mack confirmed.

Beth laughed, despite the dire situation that had brought them all here. "Ben, don't let them get to you. Mack's acting all brave and superior now, but even he turned pea-green during the procedure."

"Oh, that's reassuring," Ben said dryly, then squared his shoulders. "Hell, I might as well get this over with. Come on, Beth, lead the way. If a wuss like Mack can do this, then anybody can."

"Hey, I'll do just about anything for a lollipop and one of Beth's kisses," Mack said. "The rest of you will have to content yourselves with the candy."

Beth grinned at him. "Not necessarily. Right now I'm in the mood to dispense a lot of very grateful kisses."

Mack shook his head. "Then isn't it a damn good thing that most of the team has come and gone?" he grumbled.

"Jealous, bro?" Ben taunted.

"Damn straight," Mack shot back without hesitation.

Beth's heart filled with unexpected joy. Life was an amazing thing, she concluded. Just when you were very near the depths of despair, it could turn around.

Maybe they would find a match from today's testing or maybe not, but she doubted she would ever forget the astonishing parade of people who had come here at Mack's request. Only an incredible man could garner such an outpouring of generosity with a few phone calls.

Whatever happened with Tony, however heartbreaking the outcome might be, she would always think of this as the precise moment when she'd realized that she could never let Mack go, not without a fight.

After the last of the volunteers had gone, after his family had said goodbye and left for home, Mack paced the halls of the hospital waiting for word on the test results. Surely someone would be a match. Granted, the odds weren't in their favor—Beth and Peyton had made that clear—but Mack couldn't stop himself from hoping and praying that the news would be good.

"You should go home," Beth told him. "It could be a while before we know anything for certain."

"Are you leaving?" he'd asked.

"No."

"Then neither am I. How about some coffee?"

"I don't think I could drink one more cup," she told him honestly. "I'm jittery enough. But some chocolate would be good. I'll come to the cafeteria with you."

"You need something more substantial than chocolate," Mack coaxed when they were in the cafeteria. "How about a salad? Or some soup?"

"Something tells me you got me down here under false pretenses," she teased with feigned indignation. "You never wanted coffee at all, did you? You wanted to get me to eat."

He shrugged, not even trying to deny it. "It's been a long day and I know you haven't eaten anything."

"I'm used to that," she insisted.

"Well, you shouldn't be," he said, piling food onto a tray as she trailed along beside him. "The pie looks good. What do you think? Blueberry or lemon meringue?"

"Mack, if I eat all that, I'll be up half the night."

"Something tells me we're going to be up half the night anyway," he said, undaunted by her protest. "I'll get both. You can try some of each."

He put both pieces of pie on the already loaded tray, then carried it to the cashier, who beamed at him.

"I heard what you did for that boy today, Mr. Carlton." The woman regarded Beth with a more serious expression. "I hope there's a match, Dr. Browning. If not, maybe there will be one tomorrow."

"Tomorrow?" Beth repeated, looking confused.

"Didn't you see the news tonight?" the cashier asked. "It was all over about how Mack got the whole team over here to be tested. The news guys are challenging the community to come in, too. One of the operators told me the phone lines have been lit up all night with volunteers calling for information. The bone marrow registry is going to be flooded with new people."

Beth gazed up at Mack, her eyes shimmering with tears. "I had no idea."

"Neither did I," he said honestly. "But that's a good thing, right? There are other people waiting for marrow donors, too, aren't there?"

"Yes."

Suddenly, before he realized what she intended, she stood on tiptoe and kissed him—a hard, breath-stealing kiss that drew cheers from the few people in the cafeteria at that hour.

When she finally released him, Mack regarded her with surprise. "What was that for?"

"For doing something so incredible. I will never complain about all the media that circles around you again."

Mack thought about it and realized that for once his celebrity had been a good thing, giving Tony and maybe even others a fighting chance.

"Neither will I," he said. "Heck, maybe I'll even send a bottle of scotch to Pete Forsythe as a peace offering."

Beth frowned at that. "Don't get *too* carried away."

Mack led the way to a table across the cafeteria, then sat back and watched to make sure that Beth actually ate something, instead of just moving the food around on the plate. She was almost finished with her pie when Peyton walked in, his expression elated.

"We have a match," he called out from halfway across the cafeteria.

The announcement drew cheers. Mack felt his eyes fill with tears and saw that Beth's cheeks were damp, as well.

"Who?" she said.

"Me? One of the players?" Mack asked, hoping in a way that he could be the one, not because he wanted credit for the heroics, but because it would give him a permanent link to Tony.

Peyton shook his head, his gaze on Mack. "It's your aunt, Mack. Destiny is the match."

# 15

Mack was still in shock at the unexpected twist fate had taken. Destiny—the woman who had saved him and his brothers from despair after the loss of their parents—was in a position to save another little boy, this time from almost certain death. He should have guessed that his aunt would be the one to keep Tony alive.

He couldn't help worrying, though, whether she was physically up to it. Destiny would laugh in his face at any hint that she was old, and, truthfully, in her early fifties, she was in better health than many women much younger. Still, he was concerned.

"Peyton, are you sure this won't be too much for her?" he asked.

"We'll have to do a more complete assessment, of course, but I see no reason why she won't be able to do this," Peyton told him. "If she's willing, of course. Is there some reason why she might not be?"

"Absolutely not," Mack said with total confidence. "She'll want to go ahead. There's no doubt about that. I just need to be sure there's no risk."

"Any risk is minimal," Peyton reassured him. "Do

you want to call and tell her or should I? We'll have to get her back in here as soon as possible for a complete physical before we can go ahead with Tony's intensive chemotherapy and schedule the transplant."

"I'll go over there and tell her tonight," Mack said. He glanced at Beth. "Do you want to come? It'll probably take both of us to keep her from running straight back over here the second she hears."

Beth nodded at once. "I'm sure we can convince her that tomorrow morning will be soon enough." She turned to her colleague. "What about Mrs. Vitale? Have you told her the good news yet?"

Peyton shook his head. "I thought you two might want to come along. It's because of you that we have a real hope of saving Tony now."

"Oh, yes," Beth said fervently. "Mack?"

Suddenly it was all too much. Mack felt this overwhelming desire to shout with joy and at the same time he wanted to cry. He was ecstatic at the promise of a future for Tony, yet fearful for his aunt. "Maybe you should go without me," he said. "I'm not sure I can hold it together in there."

Beth reached for his hand. "You don't have to. This is a miracle, Mack. Even hardened football players are allowed to cry over miracles."

"Doctors, too," Peyton said, his gaze on Beth filled with understanding.

"Later, when Tony is out of the woods. Besides, I've shed more than my share of tears today," she said, avoiding his gaze. "Now I just want to get on with things."

Peyton gave her a knowing look that only another physician could fully understand. Mack wasn't entirely sure how to interpret it.

"Is there something you two aren't telling me?" he asked.

"No," Beth assured him at once. "There's every reason to believe Tony is finally going to turn the corner. The bone marrow transplant should put him into remission, and with luck he'll stay there. He'll be watched closely and given frequent blood tests to make sure his white count stays up, but this is absolutely his best shot at a normal future."

Mack wasn't sure whether to believe her, but he had little choice. Besides, he'd endured about all the doubts and fears he could handle for one day.

Upstairs, he hung back while Beth and Peyton broke the news to Maria Vitale. When it finally sank in that her son truly had hope, she ran to Mack and clung to him. He hadn't expected the emotional outburst, and once again he found himself fighting tears. After a moment, though, he let them fall unashamedly.

"Maria, don't thank me," he pleaded, uncomfortable with the outpouring of gratitude. "I didn't do anything."

"You got those people to come here," she insisted fiercely. "And it is your aunt who is the one who will save my boy. With my dying breath, I will thank her and you."

"The important thing is that now Tony has a fighting chance," Mack said. "I couldn't be happier about that."

"What will happen now?" Maria asked Beth.

"I think I'll let Dr. Lang explain that to you. Mack and I are going to go to see Destiny and tell her the good news, then prepare her for what happens next."

As they were about to leave, Maria came to Mack and met his gaze. "Please tell her for me that I will ask God to bless her."

"I will, Maria."

Mack was silent on the drive to Destiny's. Beth kept making halfhearted attempts at conversation, but he was too drained to respond until she finally asked, "Mack, are you having second thoughts about this?"

He stared at her in shock. "Why would I have second thoughts? Besides, it's not my call. It's in Destiny's hands now."

"It's just that you're not saying anything. I was afraid you might be worrying that something will happen to her and it will be your fault. No one would blame you for feeling that way. I feel scared every time I recommend a risky treatment to someone, even if it's their only hope. It's a perfectly natural reaction."

"I can't tell you that I'm not concerned, but I don't doubt that it's the right thing to do," Mack said. "If Destiny wants to go ahead, I'm behind her one hundred percent."

"Nothing's going to go wrong," Beth told him.

"Sweetheart, we both know there are no guarantees, but I can't look back. I won't. Tony has to have his chance to live."

Beth tucked her hand in his. "Can I tell you something without you getting all crazy?"

Mack fought a grin. "Try me."

"I love you, Mack. If I hadn't before today, I would now," she said quietly.

Mack wanted to say the words back. They were on the very tip of his tongue, but somehow he couldn't get them out.

Beth met his gaze and smiled. "It's okay. I know."

He studied her face for a minute, then nodded. She did know. That was the remarkable thing about Beth.

She seemed to know what was in his heart, even when he couldn't explain it.

One of these days, though, he was going to have to find the words. She deserved to hear them.

And their future depended on them.


"I simply don't understand why there's so much commotion over this," Destiny said when the entire family had gathered for dinner a few nights later. "It's a simple, uncomplicated procedure. That handsome Dr. Lang explained that to all of us at the hospital today."

"It's simple and uncomplicated if you're a doctor who does it routinely," Mack said dryly. "*You've* never done it before."

"Well, fortunately I'll have very experienced doctors doing the hard part," Destiny told him. "Now stop it, all of you. I've made up my mind. If I hadn't before, that visit to Tony today would have clinched it. What an amazing boy he is. I look forward to having him in my life after this."

"I'm glad you're looking ahead," Richard said, "but I don't think any of us could live with ourselves if something happened to you."

"Then we'll make sure that nothing does," Destiny told him firmly. She looked pointedly toward Melanie. "How are you feeling? Any morning sickness?"

Mack sat back and sighed. So did Ben and Richard. It was evident that the topic of the transplant was over and done with for the evening. Destiny had made up her mind days ago as soon as she'd been told that she was a good match. She intended to be at the hospital at 6:00 a.m., no matter what any of them said. The wheels had been put into motion. Tony had received the high-dose chemo and was pronounced ready for the procedure. There would be no turning back now. A part of Mack was relieved, a part of him still terrified.

"I'm feeling fit as a fiddle," Melanie said, going along with Destiny's attempt to change the subject. "Of course, maybe that's because Richard hasn't let me pick up anything heavier than a glass since we got the news."

"Enjoy it while you can," Destiny told her. "Once the baby comes, Richard will fall back into his old workaholic patterns, and you'll be left to fend for yourself."

Destiny pushed aside her plate. "I want you all to know that I appreciate you coming over tonight, but I need to get my beauty sleep if I'm going to be up before dawn. I'll say good-night now. I'll see you at the hospital in the morning."

"I'm staying," Ben said, regarding her defiantly.

"So are we," Richard added.

Destiny returned their stubborn expressions with an impatient look, then finally uttered a sigh of her own. "Whatever makes you happy." She gazed at Mack. "Since I'm going to be so well looked after, why don't you go on over to Beth's? I'm sure she could use some company tonight. I'm still not sure I understand why she turned down my dinner invitation."

"She thought you should concentrate on family tonight," Mack said.

"She's family, too," Destiny replied. "Or she will be if someone we know doesn't blow it."

Mack shook his head. "Stop with the matchmaking, Destiny. It's already worked."

Her expression brightened. "Really?"

"As if you would have allowed it to turn out any other way," Ben remarked.

Mack bent down and kissed his aunt's cheek. "I owe you one."

She grinned at him. "You usually do. Good night, darling. Give Beth my love and tell her I'm counting on her bringing both Tony and me through all of this with flying colors."

"How would you like to have that pressure hanging over you?" Richard commented. "If I were you, I'd keep that to myself, Mack."

"Believe me, I'm not going over to Beth's to lay a guilt trip on her."

"Gee, bro, what are you going over there to do?" Ben inquired.

Destiny frowned at him. "That is none of your business, young man. I thought I raised you better than that."

"Sometimes these wild urges to poke around in Mack's personal life just overtake me," Ben said unrepentantly. "I live vicariously through him."

Destiny gave him a considering look. Mack could almost read her mind. If Ben was looking for vicarious thrills, then maybe, at long last, he was ready for another love affair of his own.

"You've stepped in it now," Mack taunted him. "I predict Destiny will have fixed you up with a nurse before she's out of surgery tomorrow."

Ben shuddered dramatically. "I don't think so," he said. "After all, Mack, she's not quite finished with you yet, is she?"

"You're sure you want to do this?" Beth asked Destiny for the tenth time, still unable to believe that a miracle was so close at hand. She felt compelled to keep asking, even though Destiny was losing patience with her.

"Don't you dare start in on me, too. I got enough of this from my nephews last night. It's not as if there's another option," Destiny said, giving Beth's hand a squeeze. She looked at her nephew. "I've known for months now that our lives were going to be forever intertwined. I think Mack finally understands the significance of that, too, don't you, darling?"

Mack gave her one of his irrepressible grins. "Stop trying to propose for me, Destiny. I'll handle that part myself, and I won't be doing it with you lying here on a hospital bed listening to every word."

Beth's head snapped around to stare at him. "What is she talking about?"

"We'll discuss it a little later," he said. "Let's get Tony well again, okay?"

"Some things are too important to wait," Destiny scolded.

Mack gave her an impatient look, seemed to reach some conclusion, then reached in his pocket. "I suppose I might as well get on with this," he told Beth, looking vaguely apologetic. "She's not going into that operating room until she sees this on your finger."

Beth stared at him, not comprehending the sudden turn the conversation had taken. Or maybe she was just a little terrified that she understood it too well and wasn't ready to hear it.

"Mack, what's going on?" she asked warily.

He looked into her eyes, holding her gaze until the room, Destiny, everything else seemed to fade into the background. It was as if they were completely alone.

"Finding out that we could lose Tony made me realize that life is far too short to waste a single minute on what-ifs," Mack told her quietly. "We don't know what's going to happen next year, next month or even tomorrow."

Beth's heart began to pound erratically. Surely he wasn't really going to do this, not here, not now. A part of her wanted him to get on with it so badly it terrified her. Another part was screaming that she wasn't ready.

"I do know that I want you at my side whatever happens. I love you, Beth. And I always will," Mack said, then waited.

"Well?" Destiny prodded, giving Beth an unsubtle poke. "He's waiting, Beth. Answer the man."

Beth's mouth gaped, her gaze never leaving Mack's face. "You're asking me to marry you?"

Destiny chuckled. "Maybe I'm biased, but I, for one, thought he was pretty clear about that. Don't make him ask twice. He could get cold feet."

"Not a chance," Mack said. "Not when it's this important. I'll ask as often as I have to."

Beth studied Mack intently and saw the certainty in his eyes. Instantly her heart was filled with the same conviction. If he could take this leap of faith, then she certainly could. "Yes," she whispered, choking back tears of joy. She shouldn't feel this happy when so much about this day was filled with uncertainty. "Yes."

"Put the ring on her finger, Mack," Destiny coached.

He gave her an irritated look. "I think I can take it from here. I got her to say yes, didn't I?"

"But time's awasting," Destiny retorted. "They're about to wheel me out of here, and I want this deal closed before I leave."

Mack took Beth's hand in his, then slid the simple diamond on her finger. "Now it's official, Doc."

Beth stared at the ring, then met his gaze. "You never back out of a deal, do you?"

"Never," he said solemnly. "Carltons are men of integrity and honor."

Beth beamed at him. "I think I knew that all along."

"Maybe not all along," Mack reminded her. "But you got the message when it counted." He winked at her. "I think I'll go give Tony the good news before he goes into the operating room. I promised him if you said yes, he could be best man at our wedding."

"You told him about this?" Beth asked incredulously.

"Hey, Destiny might have kicked off this relationship, but Tony was a critical player. He deserved to know it was all paying off."

"You could have told him after surgery," Beth reminded him quietly.

Mack nodded, his expression suddenly sad. "I know, but just in case…"

Beth went to him. "No doubts, Mack. Tony's a fighter. He'll dance at our wedding. I'm counting on it."

Slowly Mack's expression brightened. "Okay, Doc. That's good enough for me."

It was an eternity before Beth and Peyton finally emerged and pronounced the bone marrow transplant complete. Until then Mack, his brothers and Melanie huddled in the waiting room with Maria Vitale, passing the time with lousy coffee and prayers.

"They're both okay?" Mack asked, his gaze locked with Beth's. If there had been any unexpected twists, he would see it at once in her eyes, but they were clear and filled with an optimistic glint.

"Perfect," she assured him.

"How long will it be before we know if it was a success and that Tony's out of the woods?" he asked her.

"A while," she confessed. "But there's every reason for optimism."

Mack thought about his promise to Tony that he could be best man at their wedding. He pulled Beth aside and regarded her closely. "Do we need to set a wedding date soon?"

She studied him with surprise. "Are you anxious to get married for some reason?"

"You know what I'm asking, Beth."

"And I've told you, we have every reason to be optimistic. I'm not covering anything up, Mack. I swear it."

He nodded slowly and finally allowed himself to feel the first faint stirring of relief. He grinned then. "Maybe we shouldn't put the wedding off, anyway."

"Oh?"

"I'd hate to have you change your mind once the crisis is over."

"No chance of that," she assured him. "If anything, I'm the one who ought to be worried."

Mack pulled her into his arms and held her tight. For the first time in his life, he genuinely felt complete. "Sweetheart, you have nothing to be worried about. I told you earlier that I've never reneged on a major deal in my life."

"The Carlton integrity," she said.

"That," he agreed, then tilted her chin up until he could look directly into her eyes. "And the fact that this is the most important deal I ever closed."

A smile tugged at her lips. "Better than that defensive player you hired a couple of weeks ago?" she asked.

He stared at her in shock. "You know about that?"

"Hey, I read the sports pages."

Mack laughed. "Since when?"

"Since I fell in love with this celebrity jock, whose name is in there nearly every day. I can't have the entire world knowing more about you than I do."

"Never happen, darlin'. Never happen."

# *Epilogue*

It was the first Friday in October when Dr. Beth Browning married Mighty Mack Carlton before a crowd of dedicated doctors, somber scientists, raucous football players, loving family and still-stunned friends. Outside the church a throng of well-wishers had turned out, tipped off to the occasion by Pete Forsythe's column. Naturally he'd learned all of the supposedly secret details, though for once Destiny claimed total innocence.

Tony Vitale was the best man. His hair had grown back, his skin had a healthy glow and his smile was huge as he waited in front of the altar with Mack by his side.

When Tony whispered something, Mack leaned down to listen, then his gaze shot to the back of the candlelit church where Beth was waiting. A smile spread across his face, as well.

Beth heard the start of the organ music, but before she took her first step, she took a good, long look at her two guys, her heart in her throat. If Tony had a hopeful prognosis for a long and healthy life, it was thanks to Mack, as well as Destiny. This family she was marrying into was a remarkable one.

Destiny sat beside Maria Vitale in the front of the

church. The two had become fast friends since the transplant. Destiny was now dedicated to mothering both Maria and Tony to ensure their lives were a bit easier.

Richard and Ben stood next to Mack and Tony, looking handsome in their tuxes, though Ben had a slightly wary expression, as if he were all too aware that his days as a bachelor were likely to be short-lived now that Mack was about to be married.

Only a brief ceremony stood between Beth and the future she'd never anticipated on that long-ago day in the hospital cafeteria when Mack Carlton had walked into her life. A ceremony and a honeymoon, she thought, her blood suddenly humming.

The honeymoon had required a major concession on her part. Because neither of them had wanted to delay getting married until after the official football season ended in January, the honeymoon was built around the team's upcoming road trip, a week in San Francisco, followed by a week in St. Louis. Beth had bought a book on the finer points of football and ten scientific journals to read during the games.

The rest of the time she had other plans for Mack. It hardly mattered what city they were in. She didn't intend to leave the hotel suite until an hour before game time.

She met Mack's gaze and held back a smug grin. Something told her if she played her cards right, they might even miss the kickoff.

\* \* \* \* \*

*Turn the page for a sneak peek at*
*TREASURED,*
*The third book in the* PERFECT DESTINIES *series*
*by #1* New York Times *bestselling author*
*Sherryl Woods,*
*coming soon from MIRA Books.*

# 1

It had been one of those Friday-night gallery receptions that made Kathleen Dugan wonder if she'd been wrong not to take a job teaching art in the local school system. Maybe putting finger paints in the hands of five-year-old kids would be more rewarding than trying to introduce the bold, vibrant works of an amazingly talented young artist to people who preferred bland and insipid.

Of course, it hadn't helped that Boris Ostronovich spoke little English and took the temperamental-artist stereotype to new heights. He'd been sulking in a corner for the last two hours, a glass of vodka in one hand and a cigarette in the other. The cigarette had remained unlit only because Kathleen had threatened to close the show if he lit it up in direct defiance of fire codes, no-smoking policies and a whole list of personal objections.

All in all, the evening had pretty much been a disaster. Kathleen was willing to take responsibility for that. She hadn't gauged correctly just how important it was for the artist to mingle and make small talk. She'd thought Boris's work would sell itself. She'd discovered, instead, that people on the fence about a purchase were inclined to pass when they hadn't exchanged so much as a civil word with the artist. In another minute or two, when the few remaining guests had cleared out of her gallery, Kathleen was inclined to join Boris in a good, old-fashioned, well-deserved funk. She might even have a couple of burning shots of straight vodka, assuming there was any left by then.

"Bad night, dear?"

Kathleen turned to find Destiny Carlton regarding her with sympathy. Destiny was not only an artist herself, she was a regular at Kathleen's gallery in historic Old Town Alexandria, Virginia. Kathleen had been trying to wheedle a few of Destiny's more recent paintings from her to sell, but so far Destiny had resisted all of her overtures.

Destiny considered herself a patron of the arts these days, not a painter. She said she merely dabbled on those increasingly rare occasions when she picked up a brush at all. She was adamant that she hadn't done any work worthy of a showing since she'd closed her studio in the south of France over two decades ago.

Despite her disappointment, Kathleen considered Destiny to be a good friend. She could always be counted on to attend a show, if not to buy. And her understanding of the art world and her contacts had proven invaluable time and again as Kathleen worked to get her gallery established.

"The worst," Kathleen said, something she would never have admitted to anyone else.

"Don't be discouraged. It happens that way sometimes. Not everyone appreciates genius when they first see it."

Kathleen immediately brightened. "Then it isn't just me? Boris's work really is incredible?"

"Of course," Destiny said with convincing enthusiasm. "It's just not to everyone's taste. He'll find his audience and do rather well, I suspect. In fact, I was speaking to the paper's art critic before he left. I think he plans to write something quite positive. You'll be inundated with sales by this time next week. At the first whiff of a major new discovery, collectors will jump on the bandwagon, including some of those who left here tonight without buying anything."

Kathleen sighed. "Thank you so much for saying that. I thought for a minute I'd completely lost my touch. Tonight was every gallery owner's worst nightmare."

"Only a momentary blip," Destiny assured her. She glanced toward Boris. "How is he taking it?"

"Since he's barely said two words all evening, even before the night was officially declared a disaster, it's hard to tell," Kathleen said. "Either he's pining for his homeland or he had a lousy disposition even before the show. My guess is the latter. Until tonight I had no idea how important the artist's charm could be."

Destiny gave her a consoling look. "In the end it won't matter. In fact, the instant the critics declare Boris a true modern-art genius, all those people he put off tonight will brag to their friends about the night they met the sullen, eccentric artist."

Kathleen gave Destiny a warm hug. "Thank you so much for staying behind to tell me that."

"Actually, I lingered till the others had gone because I wanted a moment alone with you."

"Oh?"

"What are your plans for Thanksgiving, Kathleen? Are you going to Providence to visit your family?"

Kathleen frowned. She'd had a very tense conversation with her wealthy, socialite mother on that very topic earlier in the day, when she'd announced her intention to stay right here in Alexandria. She'd been reminded that all three current generations of Dugans gathered religiously for all major holidays. She'd been told that her absence was an affront to the family, a precursor to the breakdown of tradition. And on and on and on. It had been incredibly tedious and totally expected, which was why she'd put off making the call until this morning. Prudence Dugan was not put off easily, but Kathleen had held her ground for once.

"Actually I'm staying in town," she told Destiny. "I have a lot of work to catch up on. And I don't really want to close the gallery for the holiday weekend. I think business could be brisk on Friday and Saturday."

Destiny beamed at her. "Then I would love it if you would spend Thanksgiving day with my family. We'll all be at Ben's farm. It's lovely in Middleburg this time of year."

Kathleen regarded her friend suspiciously. While they had become rather well acquainted in recent years, this was the first time Destiny had sought to include her in a family gathering.

"Won't I be intruding?" she asked.

"Absolutely not. It will be a very low-key dinner for family and a few close friends. And it will give you a chance to see my nephew's paintings and give me a professional opinion."

Kathleen's suspicions mounted. She knew for a fact that Destiny's eye for art was every bit as good as her own. She also knew that Ben Carlton considered his painting to be little more than a hobby, something he loved to do. In fact, as far as she knew, he'd never sold his work. She suspected there was a good reason for that, that even he knew it wasn't of the caliber needed to make a splash in the art world.

Every article she'd ever read about the three Carlton men had said very little about the reclusive youngest brother. Ben stayed out of the spotlight, which shone on businessman and politician Richard Carlton and football great Mack Carlton. There were rumors of a tragic love affair that had sent Ben into hiding, but none of those rumors had ever been publicly confirmed. However, *brooding* was the adjective that was most often applied whenever his name was mentioned.

"Is he thinking of selling his works?" Kathleen asked carefully, trying to figure out just what her friend was up to. Being first in line for a chance to show them would, indeed, be a major coup. There was bound to be a lot of curiosity about the Carlton who chose to stay out of the public eye, whether his paintings were any good or not.

"Heavens, no," Destiny said, though there was a hint of dismay in her voice. "He's very stubborn on that point, but I'd like to persuade him that a talent like his shouldn't be hidden away in that drafty old barn of a studio out there."

"And you think I might be able to change his mind when *you* haven't succeeded?" Kathleen asked, her skepticism plain. Destiny had lots of practice wheedling million-dollar donations to her pet charities. Surely she could persuade her own nephew that he was talented.

"Perhaps. At the very least, you'll give him another perspective. He thinks I'm totally biased."

Never able to resist the chance that she might discover an exciting new talent, Kathleen finally nodded. She assured herself it was because she wanted a glimpse of the work, not the mysterious man. "I'd love to come for Thanksgiving. Where and when?"

Destiny beamed at her. "I'll send over directions and the details first thing in the morning." She headed for the door, looking oddly smug. "Oh, and wear that bright red silk tunic of yours, the one you had on at the Carlucci show. You looked stunning that night."

Destiny was gone before Kathleen could think of a response, but the comment had set off alarm bells. Everyone in certain social circles in the Washington Metropolitan region knew about Destiny's matchmaking schemes. While her behind-the-scenes plots had never made their way into the engagement or wedding announcements for Richard or Mack, they were hot gossip among the well-connected. And everyone was waiting to see what she would do to see Ben take the walk down the aisle.

Kathleen stared after her. "Oh, no, you don't," she whispered to Destiny's retreating back. "I am not looking for a husband, especially not some wounded, artistic type."

It was a type she knew all too well. It was the type she'd married, fought with and divorced. And while that had made her eminently qualified to run an art gallery and cope with artistic temperament, it had also strengthened her resolve never, ever, to be swept off her feet by another artist.

Tim Radnor had been kind and sensitive when they'd first met. He'd adored Kathleen, claiming she was his muse. But when his work faltered, she'd discovered that he had a cruel streak. There had been flashes of temper and stormy torrents of hurtful words. He'd never laid a hand on her, but his verbal abuse had been just as intolerable. Her marriage had been over within months. Healing had taken much longer.

As a result of that tumultuous marriage, she could deal with the craziness when it came to business, but not when it affected her heart.

If romance was on Destiny's mind, she was doomed to disappointment, Kathleen thought, already steeling her resolve. Ben Carlton could be the sexiest, most charming and most talented artist on the planet and it wouldn't matter. She would remain immune, because she knew all too well the dark side of an artistic temperament.

Firm words. Powerful resolve. She had 'em both. But just in case, Kathleen gazed skyward. "Help me out here, okay?"

"Is trouble?" a deep male voice asked quizzically.

Kathleen jumped. She'd forgotten all about Boris. Turning, she faced him and forced a smile. "No trouble, Boris. None at all." She would see to it.

Only a faint, pale hint of sunlight streamed across the canvas, but Ben Carlton was hardly aware that night was falling. It was like this when a painting was nearing completion. All he could see was what was in front of his eyes, the layers of color, the image slowly unfolding, capturing a moment in time, an impression he was terrified would be lost if he let it go before the last stroke was done. When natural light faded, he automatically adjusted the artificial light without really thinking about it.

"I should have known," a faintly exasperated female voice said, cutting through the silence.

He blinked at the interruption. No one came to his studio when he was working, not without risking his wrath. It was the one rule in a family that tended to defy rules.

"Go away," he muttered, his own impatience as evident as the annoyance in his aunt's voice.

"I most certainly will not go away," Destiny said. "Have you forgotten what day this is? What time it is?"

He struggled to hold on to the image in his head, but it fluttered like a snapshot caught by a breeze, then vanished. He sighed, then slowly turned to face his aunt.

"It's Thursday," he said to prove that he was not as oblivious as she'd assumed.

Destiny Carlton gave him a look filled with tolerant amusement. "Any particular Thursday?"

Ben dragged a hand through his hair and tried to remember what might be the least bit special about this particular Thursday. He was not the kind of man who paid attention to details, unless they were the sort of details going into one of his paintings. Then he could remember every nuance of light and texture.

"A holiday," she hinted. "One when the entire family gathers together to give thanks, a family that is currently waiting for their host while the turkey gets cold and the rolls burn."

"Aw, hell," he muttered. "I forgot all about Thanksgiving. Everyone's here already?"

"They have been for some time. Your brothers threatened to eat every bite of the holiday feast and leave you nothing, but I convinced them to let me try to drag you away from your painting." She stepped closer and eyed the canvas with a critical eye. "It's amazing, Ben. No one captures the beauty of this part of the world the way you do."

He grinned at the high praise. "Not even you? You taught me everything I know."

"When you were eight, I put a brush in your hand and taught you technique. You have the natural talent. It's extraordinary. I dabbled. You're a genius."

"Oh, please," he said, waving off the praise.

Painting had always given him peace of mind, a sense of control over the chaotic world around him. When his parents had died in a plane crash, he'd needed to find something that made sense, something that wouldn't abandon him. Destiny had bought him his first set of paints, taken him with her to a sidewalk near the family home on a charming, shaded street in Old Town Alexandria and told him to paint what he saw.

That first crude attempt still hung in the old town house where she continued to live alone now that he and his brothers had moved on with their lives. She insisted it was her most prized possession because it showed the promise of what he could become. She'd squirreled away some of Richard's early business plans and Mack's football trophies for the same reason. Destiny could be cool and calculating when necessary, but for the most part she was ruled by sentiment.

Richard had been clever with money and business. Mack was athletic. Ben had felt neither an interest in the family company nor in sports. Even when his parents were alive, he'd felt desperately alone, a sensitive misfit in a family of achievers. The day Destiny had handed him those paints, his aunt had given him a sense of pride and purpose. She'd told him that, like her, he brought another dimension to the well-respected family name and that he was never to dismiss the importance of what he could do that the others couldn't. After that, it had been easier to take his brothers' teasing and to dish out a fair amount of his own. He imagined he was going to be in for a ton of it this evening for missing his own party.

Having the holiday dinner at his place in the country had been Destiny's idea. Ben didn't entertain. He knew his way around a kitchen well enough to keep from starving, but certainly not well enough to foist what he cooked on to unsuspecting company. Destiny had dismissed every objection and arrived three days ago to take charge, bringing along the family's longtime housekeeper to clean and to prepare the meal.

If anyone else had tried taking over his life that way, Ben would have rebelled, but he owed his aunt too much. Besides, she understood his need for solitude better than anyone. Ever since Graciela's death, Ben had immersed himself in his art. The canvas and paints didn't make judgments. They didn't place blame. He could control them, as he couldn't control his own thoughts or his own sense of guilt over Graciela's accident on that awful night three years ago.

But if Destiny understood all that, she also seemed to know instinctively when he'd buried himself in his work for too long. That's when she'd dream up some excuse to take him away from his studio and draw him back into the real world. Tonight's holiday celebration was meant to be one of those occasions. Her one slipup had been not reminding him this morning that today was the day company was coming.

"Give me ten minutes," he told her now. "I'll clean up."

"Too late for that. Melanie is pregnant and starving.

She'll eat the flower arrangement if we don't offer an alternative soon. Besides, the company is beginning to wonder if we've just taken over some stranger's house. They need to meet you. You'll make up in charm what you lack in sartorial splendor."

"I have paint on my clothes," he protested, then gave her a hard look as what she'd said finally sank in. "Company? You mean besides Richard and Mack and their wives? Did you say anything about company when you badgered me into having Thanksgiving here?"

"I'm sure I did," she said blithely.

She hadn't, and they both knew it, which meant she was scheming about something more than relieving his solitude. When they reached the house, Ben immediately understood what she was up to.

"And, darling, this is Kathleen Dugan," Destiny said, after introducing several other strangers who were part of the rag-tag group of people Destiny had collected because she knew they had no place else to spend the holiday. There was little question, judging from her tone, that this Kathleen was the pièce de résistance.

He gave his aunt a sharp look. Kathleen was young, beautiful and here alone, which suggested she was available. He'd known for some time now—since Mack's recent wedding, in fact—that Destiny had targeted him for her next matchmaking scheme. Here was his proof—a woman with a fringe of black hair in a pixie cut that emphasized her cheekbones and her amazing violet eyes. There wasn't an artist on earth who wouldn't want to capture that interesting, angular face on canvas. Not that Ben ever did portraits, but even he was tempted to break his hard-and-fast rule. She was stunning in a red silk tunic that skimmed over a slender figure. She wore it over black pants and accented it with a necklace of chunky beads in gold and red. The look was elegant and just a touch avant-garde.

"Lovely to meet you," Kathleen said with a soft smile that showed no hint of the awkwardness Ben was feeling. Clearly she hadn't caught on to the scheme yet.

Ben nodded. He politely shook her hand, felt a startling jolt of awareness, then took another look into her eyes to see if she'd felt the same little *zing*. She showed no evidence of it, thank heavens.

"If you'll excuse my totally inappropriate attire," Ben said, quickly turning away from her and addressing the others, "I gather dinner is ready to be served."

"We've time for another drink," Destiny insisted, apparently no longer worried about the delayed meal. "Richard, bring your brother something. He can spend at least a few minutes socializing before we sit down to eat."

Ben frowned at her. "I thought we were in a rush."

"Only to drag you in here," his very pregnant sister-in-law said as she came and linked an arm through his, drawing him out of the spotlight, even as she whispered conspiratorially, "Don't you know that you're the main attraction?"

He gave Melanie a sharp look. They'd formed a bond back when Richard had been fighting his attraction to her. Ben trusted her instincts. He wanted to hear her take on this gathering. "Oh?"

"You never come out of this lair of yours," Melanie explained. "When Destiny invited us here, we figured something was up."

"Oh?" he said again, waiting to see if she'd drawn the

same conclusion about Kathleen's presence here that he had. "Such as?"

Melanie studied him intently. "You really don't know what Destiny is up to? You're as much in the dark as the rest of us?"

Ben glanced toward Kathleen, then. "Not as much as you might think," he said with a faint scowl.

Melanie gave the newcomer a knowing look. "Ah, so that's it. I wondered when Kathleen arrived if she was the chosen one. I figured it was going to be your turn soon. Destiny won't be entirely happy until all of her men are settled."

"I hope you're wrong about that," Ben said darkly. "I'd hate to disappoint her, but I am settled."

Richard overheard him and chuckled. "Oh, bro, if that's what you think, you're delusional." He, too, glanced toward Kathleen, whose head was tilted as she listened intently to something Destiny was saying. "I give you till May."

"June," Mack chimed in. "Destiny's been moping because none of us had a traditional June wedding. You're all she's got left, little brother. She won't allow you to let her down. I caught her out in the garden earlier. I think she was mentally seating the guests and envisioning the perfect area for the reception."

Ben shuddered. Richard and Mack had once been as fiercely adamant about not getting married as he was. Look at the two of them now. Richard even had a baby on the way, and Mack and Beth were talking about adopting one of the sick kids she worked with at the hospital. Maybe more. To his astonishment, those two seemed destined for a houseful. By this time next year, there would be the cries of children filling this house and any other place the Carlton family gathered. No one needed him adding to the clutter. He doubted Destiny saw it that way, though.

There were very few things that Ben wouldn't do for his aunt. Getting married was one of them. He liked his solitude. After the chaotic upheaval of his early years, he counted on the predictability of his quiet life in the country. Graciela had given him a reprieve from that, but then she, too, had died, and it had reinforced his commitment to go through life with his heart under the tightest possible wraps. Those who wrote that he was prone to dark moods and eccentricities had gotten it exactly right. There would be no more nicks in his armor, no more devastating pain to endure.

His resolve steady and sure, he risked another look at Kathleen Dugan, then belatedly saw the smug expression on his aunt's face when she caught him.

Ben sighed, then stood a little straighter, stiffening his spine, giving Destiny a daunting look. She didn't bat so much as an eyelash. That was the trouble with his aunt. She rarely took no for an answer. She was persuasive and sneaky. If he didn't take a firm stand right here, right now, he was doomed.

Unfortunately, though, he couldn't think of a single way to make his position clear over turkey and dressing.

He could always say, "So glad you could come, Kathleen, but don't get any ideas."

Or, "Delighted to meet you, Ms. Dugan, but ignore every word out of my aunt's mouth. She's devious and clever and not to be trusted."

Or maybe he should simply say nothing at all, just ignore the woman and avoid his aunt. If he could endure the next couple of hours, they'd all be gone and that would be that. He could bar the gates and go back into seclusion.

Perfect, he concluded. That was definitely the way to go. No overt rudeness that would come back to haunt him. No throwing down of the gauntlet. Just passive acceptance of Kathleen's presence here tonight.

Satisfied with that solution, he turned his attention to the drink Richard had thrust in his hand. A sniff reassured him it was nonalcoholic. He hadn't touched a drop of anything stronger than beer since the night of Graciela's accident.

"Darling," Destiny said, her gaze on him as she crossed the room, Kathleen at her side. "Did I mention earlier that Kathleen owns an art gallery?"

Next to him Melanie choked back a laugh. Richard and Mack smirked. Ben wanted nothing more than to pummel his brothers for getting so much enjoyment out of his discomfort at his aunt's obvious ploy. Kathleen was her handpicked choice for him, all right. There was no longer any question about that.

"Really?" he said tightly.

"She has the most amazing work on display there now," Destiny continued blithely. "You should stop by and take a look."

Ben cast a helpless look in Kathleen's direction. She now looked every bit as uncomfortable as he felt. "Maybe I will one of these days." When hell freezes over, he thought even as he muttered the polite words.

"I'd love to have your opinion," Kathleen said gamely.

"My opinion's not worth much," Ben said. "Destiny's the family expert."

Kathleen held his gaze. "But most artists have an eye for recognizing talent," she argued.

Ben barely contained a sigh. Surely Kathleen was smart enough not to fall into his aunt's trap. He wanted to warn her to run for her life, to skip the turkey, the dressing and the pumpkin pie and head back to Alexandria as quickly as possible and bar the door of her gallery from anyone named Carlton. He was tempted to point to Melanie and Beth and explain how they'd unwittingly fallen in with his aunt's schemes, but he doubted his sisters-in-law would appreciate the suggestion that their marriages were anything other than heaven-sent. They both seemed to have revised history to their liking after the wedding ceremonies.

Instead he merely said, "I'm not an artist."

"Of course you are," Destiny declared indignantly. "An exceptionally talented one at that. Why would you say such a thing, Ben?"

To get out of being drawn any further into this web, he very nearly shouted. He looked his aunt in the eye. "Are you an artist?"

"Not anymore," she said at once.

"Because you no longer paint?" he pressed.

Destiny frowned at him. "I still dabble."

"Then it must be because you don't show or sell your work," he said. "Is that why you're no longer an artist?"

"Yes," she said at once. "That's it exactly."

He gave Destiny a triumphant look. "Neither do I. No shows. No sales. I dabble." He found himself winking at Kathleen. "I guess we can forget about me offering a professional opinion on your current show."

A grin tugged at the corners of Kathleen's mouth. "Clever," she praised.

"Too clever for his own good," Destiny muttered.

"Uh-oh," Mack murmured, grinning broadly. "You've

done it now, Ben. Destiny's on the warpath. You're doomed."

Funny, Ben thought, glancing around the room at the sea of amused expressions, that was the same conclusion he'd reached about an hour ago. He should have quit back then and saved himself the aggravation.

# 2

Kathleen felt as if the undercurrents swirling around Ben Carlton's living room were about to drag her under. Every single suspicion she'd had about the real reason she'd been invited tonight was being confirmed with every subtle dig, every dark look between Ben and his aunt. Even his brothers and sisters-in-law seemed to be in on the game and were enjoying it thoroughly. In fact, she was the only one who didn't seem to get the rules. If she could have fled without appearing unbearably rude, she might have.

"Would you like to freshen up before dinner?" Beth Carlton asked, regarding her with sympathy.

If it meant escaping from this room, Kathleen would have agreed to join a trek across the still-green fields of winter wheat that stretched as far as the eye could see.

"Yes, please," she said gratefully.

"I'll show you where the powder room is," Beth said.

The minute they were out of earshot of the others, Beth gave her a warm smile. "Feel as if you're caught in an intricate web you didn't even realize was being spun?"

Kathleen nodded. "Worse, I have no idea how I got there. Am I some sort of sacrificial lamb?"

"Pretty much," Beth said. "Believe me, Melanie and I know exactly how you feel. We've been there. We were tangled up with Carlton men before we knew it."

"I don't suppose there's a way out?" Kathleen asked.

"Obviously neither of us found one," Beth said cheerfully. "Maybe you'll be the exception. Right now she's batting two for two, but Destiny's track record is bound to falter sooner or later."

Kathleen studied the pediatric oncologist who'd married Mack. Beth Carlton struck her as quiet, intelligent and lovely in an understated way, very much the opposite of Kathleen's eccentricity and flamboyance. It was hard to imagine that the same woman would have chosen them as potential marriage material for beloved nephews. Then, again, Ben was a far cry from his more outgoing, athletic brother. Destiny obviously knew her nephews well. As Beth had just noted, her knack for choosing the right women was outstanding.

"Then I'm not crazy," Kathleen ventured carefully. "Destiny is plotting to set me up with Ben? She didn't get me out here just to look at his art?"

Beth's grin spread. "Have you actually seen a single canvas since you arrived?"

"No."

"Were you asked to tag along when Destiny went to fetch Ben from his studio?"

"No."

Beth took a little bow, her expression amused. "I rest my case."

"But why me?" Kathleen couldn't keep the plaintive note out of her voice.

"Believe me, I asked the same thing when I realized what Destiny was up to with me and Mack. He was a professional football player, for heaven's sakes, and I'd never even watched a game. At least you and Ben have art in common. On the surface you're a much better match than Mack and I were."

"But Destiny got it right with the two of you, didn't she?" Kathleen concluded.

"Exactly right," Beth admitted happily. "She was absolutely on target with Richard and Melanie, too, though they fought it just as hard as Mack and I did. My advice is to go with the flow and see what happens. Assuming you ever want to get married, maybe having a woman with Destiny's intuition in your corner is not all bad."

"But I'm not looking for a husband," Kathleen protested. "Especially not an artist. I was married to one once. It did not turn out well."

Beth's expression turned thoughtful. "Does Destiny know about that?"

Kathleen shook her head. "I doubt it. I don't talk about it, and I took back my maiden name after the divorce."

"Let me think about this a minute," Beth said, then gestured toward a door. "The powder room's in there. I'll wait right here to show you the way to the dining room."

When Kathleen emerged a few minutes later, she found Beth and Melanie huddled together. They glanced up and beamed at her.

"So, here's the way we see it," Beth said. "Either Destiny knows about your past and figures that will make you a real challenge for Ben."

"Or she's made a serious miscalculation," Melanie said, grinning. "I like that one. Just once I'd like to see her get it wrong. No offense."

"None taken," Kathleen said, liking these two women immensely. She had a feeling their advice was going to be invaluable if she was to evade Destiny Carlton's snare. With any luck Ben would be equally appalled by this scheme, and the whole crazy thing would die for lack of participation by either one of them. He certainly hadn't looked especially happy earlier.

"We'd better go in to dinner before Destiny comes looking for us," Beth said, casting a worried look in the direction of the living room. "Destiny's allowed her conspiracies. Ours make her nervous."

"Why is that?" Kathleen asked.

"Because we're on to her," Melanie explained. "She was terrified I'd warn Beth away. Now she's equally worried that we might gang up and help you escape her clutches. I think she anticipates that the day will come when we'll get even with her, even though we're happy about the outcome of her machinations." She gave Kathleen the same sort of sympathetic look Beth had given her earlier. "We will, you know. If you need backup, just holler. We love Ben and we want to see him happy, but we also feel a certain amount of loyalty to any woman caught up in one of Destiny's matchmaking plots. It's a sisterhood thing."

Kathleen listened to the offer with amusement. Now that she'd been forewarned about the lengths to which Destiny might go, she felt much more confident that she was prepared to deal with her. "Don't worry. I think I can handle Destiny."

The declaration drew hoots of laughter. Despite her confidence in her own willpower and strength, that laughter gave Kathleen pause. That was the voice of experience responding. Two voices, in fact.

"Maybe I'd better get your phone numbers, just in case," she said as they walked toward the dining room where the other guests had now assembled.

In the doorway, Destiny gave them all a sharp look, then beamed at Kathleen. "Come, dear, I've seated you next to Ben."

Of course she had, Kathleen thought, fighting a renewed surge of panic. She avoided glancing at Melanie or Beth, afraid of the justifiable amusement she'd likely find in their eyes now. Instead she cast a look in Ben's direction, wondering what he thought of his aunt's blatant machinations. He had to find them as disquieting as she did.

Oddly enough, she thought he looked surprisingly relaxed. Maybe he was confident of his own ability to resist whatever trap Destiny was setting. Or maybe he hadn't figured out what she was up to. Doubtful, though, if he'd watched his brothers get snared one by one.

Kathleen took a closer look. He was every bit as handsome as she'd expected after seeing his brothers' pictures in the gossip columns of the local papers. There was no mistaking the fact that he was an artist, though. There were paint daubs in a variety of colors on his old jeans, a streak of vermilion on his cheek. Kathleen couldn't help feeling a faint flicker of admiration for a man who could be so totally unselfconscious showing up at his own dinner party at less than his best.

What a contrast that was to her own insecurities. She'd spent her entire life trying to put her best foot forward, trying to impress, trying to overcome an upbringing that had been financially privileged but beyond that had had very little to redeem it. She'd spent a lifetime hiding secrets and shame, acceding to her mother's pleas not to rock the family boat. Art had brought beauty into her life, and she admired and respected those who could create it.

As she stepped into the dining room, her gaze shifted from Ben to the magnificent painting above the mantel. At the sight of it, she came to a sudden stop. All thoughts of Ben Carlton, Destiny's scheming and her own past flew out of her head. Her breath caught in her throat.

"Oh, my," she whispered.

The artist had captured the fall scene with both a brilliant use of color and a delicate touch that made it seem almost dreamlike, the way it might look in the mind's eye when remembered weeks or months later, too perfect to be real. There was a lone deer at the edge of a brook, traces of snow on the ground with leaves of gold, red and burnished bronze falling along with the last faint snowflakes. The deer was staring straight out of the painting, as if looking directly at the artist, but its keen eyes were serene and unafraid. Kathleen imagined it had been exactly like that when the artist had come upon the scene, then made himself a part of it in a way that protected and preserved the moment.

Destiny caught her rapt gaze. "One of Ben's. He hated it when I insisted he hang it in here where his guests could enjoy it."

"But it's spectacular," Kathleen said, dismayed that it might have been hidden away if not for Destiny's insistence. Work this amazing did belong in a gallery. "I feel as if I looked out a window and saw exactly that scene."

Destiny smiled, her expression smug. "I just knew you would react that way. Tell my nephew that, please. He might actually believe it if it comes from you. He dismisses whatever I say. He's convinced I'm biased about his talent."

Excitement rippled through Kathleen. Destiny hadn't been exaggerating about her nephew's extraordinary gift. "There are more like this?" she asked, knowing the answer but hardly daring to hope that this was the rule, rather than the exception.

"His studio is packed to the rafters," Destiny revealed. "He's given a few to family and friends when we've begged, but for the most part, this is something he does strictly for himself."

"I could make him rich," Kathleen said with certainty, eager to fight to do just that. She was well-known for overcoming objections, for persuading tightfisted people to part with their money, and difficult artists to agree to showings in her small but prestigious gallery. All of Destiny's scheming meant nothing now. All that mattered was the art.

Destiny squeezed her hand. "Ben is rich. You'll have to find some other lure, if you hope to do a showing."

"Fame?" What painter didn't secretly yearn to be this generation's Renoir or Picasso? Disclaimers aside, surely Ben had an artist's ego.

Destiny shook her head. "He thinks Richard and Mack have all the limelight that the Carlton family needs."

Frustration burned inside Kathleen. What else could she come up with that might appeal to a reclusive artist who had no need for money or fame?

She drew her gaze from the incredible painting and turned to the woman who knew Ben best. "Any ideas?" she asked Destiny.

The older woman patted her hand and gave her a serene, knowing look. "I'm sure you'll think of something if you put your mind to it."

Even though she'd suspected the plot all along, even though Melanie and Beth had all but confirmed it, Kathleen was taken aback by the determined glint in Destiny's eyes. In Destiny's mind the art and the man were intertwined. Any desire for one was bound to tie Kathleen to the other. It was a diabolical scheme.

Kathleen looked from the painting to Ben Carlton. She would gladly sell her soul to the devil for a chance to represent such incredible art. But if she was understanding Destiny's sly hint correctly, it wasn't her soul she was expected to sell.

One more glance at Ben, one more little frisson of awareness and she couldn't help thinking it might not be such a bad bargain.

Ben watched warily as his aunt guided Kathleen into the dining room. He saw the way the younger woman came to a sudden halt when she saw his painting, and despite his claim that he painted only for himself, his breath snagged in his throat as he tried to gauge her reaction. She seemed impressed, but without being able to hear what she said, he couldn't be sure. It irked him that he cared.

"You're amazingly talented," Kathleen said the instant she'd taken her seat beside him.

Relief washed over him. Because that annoyed him, too, he merely shrugged. "Thanks. That's Destiny's favorite."

"She has a good eye."

"Have you ever seen *her* work?"

"A few pieces," Kathleen said. "She won't let me sell

them for her, though." She met his gaze. "Modesty must run in the family."

"I'm not modest," Ben assured her. "I'm just not interested in turning this into a career."

"Why not?"

His gaze challenged her. "Why should I? I don't need the money."

"Critical acclaim?"

"Not interested."

"Really?" she asked skeptically. "Or are you afraid your work won't measure up?"

He frowned at that. "Measure up to what? Some other artist's? Some artificial standard for technique or style or commercial success?"

"All of that," she said at once.

"None of it matters to me."

"Then why do you paint?"

"Because I enjoy it."

She stared at him in disbelief. "And that's enough?"

He grinned at her astonishment. "Isn't there anything you do, Ms. Dugan, just for the fun of it?"

"Of course," she said heatedly. "But you're wasting your talent, hiding it away from others who could take pleasure in seeing it or owning it."

He was astounded by the assessment. "You think I'm being selfish?"

"Absolutely."

Ben looked into her flashing violet eyes, and for an instant he lost his train of thought, lost his desire to argue with her. If they'd been alone, he might have been tempted to sweep her into his arms and kiss her until she forgot all about this silly debate over whether art was important if it wasn't on display for the masses.

"What are you passionate about?" he asked instead, clearly startling her.

"Art," she said at once.

"Nothing else?"

She flushed at the question. "Not really."

"Too bad. Don't you think that's taking a rather limited view of the world?"

"That from a man who's known far and wide as a recluse?" she retorted wryly.

Ben chuckled. "But a *passionate* recluse," he told her. "I love nature. I care about my family. I feel strongly about what I paint." He shot a look toward Richard. "I'm even starting to care just a little about politics." He turned toward Mack. "Not so much about football, though."

"Only because you could never catch a pass if your life had depended on it," Mack retorted amiably. He grinned at Kathleen. "He was afraid of breaking his fingers and not being able to hold a paint brush again."

"Then, even as a boy you loved painting?" Kathleen said. "It's always mattered to you?"

"It's what I enjoy doing," Ben confirmed. "It's not who I am."

"No ambition at all?"

He shook his head. "Sorry. None. Richard and Mack have more than enough for one family."

Kathleen set down her fork and regarded him with consternation. "How do you define yourself, if not as an artist?"

"A *reclusive* artist," Ben corrected, quoting the usual media description. "Why do I need to pin a label on myself?"

She seemed taken aback by that. "I don't suppose you do."

"How do you define who you are?" he asked.

"I own an art gallery. A very prestigious art gallery, in fact," she said with pride.

Ben studied her intently. He wondered if she had any idea how telling it was that she saw herself only in terms of what she did, not as a woman with any sort of hopes and dreams. A part of him wanted to unravel that particular puzzle and discover what had made her choose ambition over any sort of personal connection.

Because right here and now, surrounded by people absorbed in their own conversations, it was safe enough to ask, he gazed into her amazing eyes. "No man in your life?"

A shadow flitted across her face. "None."

"Why is that?"

Eyes flashing, she met his gaze. "Is there a woman in yours?"

Ben laughed. "Touché."

"Which isn't an answer, is it?"

"No, there is no woman in my life," he said, waiting for the twinge of guilt that usually accompanied that admission.

"Why not?" she asked, proving she was better at the game than he was.

"Because the only one who ever mattered died," he said quietly.

Sympathy immediately filled her eyes. "I'm sorry. I didn't know."

"I'm surprised Destiny didn't fill you in," he said, glancing in his aunt's direction. Though Destiny was engaged in conversation with Richard, it was obvious she was keeping one ear attuned to what was going on between him and Kathleen. She gave him a quizzical look.

"Nothing," Ben said for her benefit. He almost regretted letting the conversation veer away from the safe topic of art. But since Kathleen had sidestepped his question as neatly as he'd initially avoided hers, he went back to it. "Why is there no special man in your life?"

"I was married once. It didn't work out."

There was a story there. He could see it in her face, hear it in the sudden tension in her voice. "Was it so awful you decided never to try it again?"

"Worse," she said succinctly. She met his gaze. "We were doing better when we were sticking to art."

Ben laughed. "Yes, we were, weren't we? I was just thinking the same thing, though I imagine there are those who think all the small talk is just avoidance."

"Avoidance?"

"Two people dancing around what really matters."

Kathleen flushed. "I'm perfectly willing to avoid delving into my personal life. How about you?"

"Suits me," he said easily, though a part of him was filled with regret. "Want to debate about the talent of the Impressionists versus the Modernists?"

She frowned. "Not especially."

"Know anything about politics?"

"Not much."

"Environmental issues?"

"I think global warming is a real risk," she said at once.

"Good for you. Anything else?"

She held up a forkful of turkey. "The food's delicious."

"I was thinking more in terms of another environmental issue," he teased.

"Sorry. You're fresh out of luck. I could argue the merits of free-range turkey over the frozen kind," she suggested cheerfully. "Everyone says free-range is healthier, but they're just as dead, so how healthy is that?"

Ben chuckled. "Now there's a hot-button topic, if ever I heard one."

"You don't have to be sarcastic," she said. "I told you I have a one-track mind."

"And it's totally focused on art," Ben said. "I think I get that." He studied her thoughtfully. "This man you were married to, was he an artist?"

She stiffened visibly. "As a matter of fact, he was."

Ben should have taken comfort in that. If an artist had hurt Kathleen so badly that she wasn't the least bit interested in marriage, then he should be safe enough from all of Destiny's clever machinations. She'd miscalculated this time. Oddly, though, he didn't feel nearly as relieved as he should. In fact, he felt a powerful urge to go find this man who'd hurt Kathleen and wring his neck.

"People get over bad marriages and move on," he told her quietly.

"Have you gotten over losing the woman you loved?"

"No, but it's different."

"Different how?"

Ben hesitated. They were about to enter into an area he never discussed, not with anyone. Somehow, though, he felt compelled to tell Kathleen the truth. "I blame myself for her death," he said.

Kathleen looked momentarily startled by the admission. "Did you cause her death?"

He smiled sadly at the sudden hint of caution in her voice. "Not the way you mean, no, but I was responsible just the same."

"How?"

"We argued. She was drunk and I let her leave. She ran her car into a tree and died." He recited the bare facts without emotion, watching Kathleen's face. She didn't flinch. She didn't look shocked or horrified. Rather she looked indignant.

"You can't blame yourself for that," she said fiercely. "She was an adult. She should have known better than to get behind the wheel when she was upset and drunk."

"People who are drunk are not known for their logic. I could have stopped her. I *should* have," Ben countered as he had to every other person who'd tried to let him off the hook.

"Really? How? By taking away the car keys?"

"That would have done it," he said bleakly, thinking how simple it would have been to prevent the tragedy that had shaped the last three years of his adult life.

"Or she would have waited a bit, then found your keys and taken your car," Kathleen countered.

"It might have slowed her down, though, given her time to think."

"As you said yourself, it doesn't sound to me as if she was thinking all that rationally."

Ben sighed. No, Graciela hadn't been thinking rationally, but neither had he. He'd known her state of mind was irrational that night, that she was feeling defensive and cornered at having been caught with her lover. He'd told her to get out anyway. Not only hadn't he taken those car keys from her, he'd all but tossed her out the door and put her behind the wheel.

"It hardly matters now," he said at last. "I can't change that night."

Kathleen looked directly into his eyes. "No," she said softly. "You can't. The only thing you can do—the thing you *must* do—is put it behind you."

Ben wanted desperately to accept that, to let go of the past as his entire family had urged him to do, but blaming himself was too ingrained. Absolution from a woman he'd known a few hours counted for nothing.

He forced his gaze away from Kathleen and saw Destiny and his brothers watching him intently, as if they'd sensed or even heard what Ben and Kathleen had been discussing and were awaiting either an explosion or a sudden epiphany. He gave them neither.

Instead, he lifted his glass of water. "To good company and wonderful food. Thanks, Destiny."

"To Destiny," the others echoed.

Destiny beamed at him, evidently satisfied that things were working out exactly as she'd intended. "Happy Thanksgiving, everyone."

Ben drank to her toast, but even as he wished everyone a wonderful Thanksgiving, he couldn't help wondering when this dark, empty hole inside him would go away and he'd truly be able to count his blessings again. He gazed at Kathleen and thought he saw shadows in her eyes, as well, and guessed she was feeling much the same way.

He knew Destiny wanted something to come from this meeting today, but it wasn't in the cards. Whatever the whole story, Kathleen Dugan's soul was as shattered as his own.

*Don't miss this exclusive first look at*
*DESTINY UNLEASHED,*
*the exciting conclusion to*
*the* PERFECT DESTINIES *series*
*by #1* New York Times *bestselling author*
*Sherryl Woods,*
*coming soon from MIRA Books.*

# *1*

If she'd had any idea that reinventing herself would require so much self-doubt and soul-searching, Destiny Carlton might have left it for another day. Perhaps another lifetime.

Her agitated pacing slowed at last, and she turned to the woman who had been her personal secretary and confidante for nearly two decades.

"Am I crazy to even be thinking about this?" she asked Miriam Thomas. "Have I finally lost it completely? Give me your honest answer."

Miriam's lips quirked. She'd never been anything less than brutally honest. "You're the most sane person I know," she said loyally.

"But this," Destiny said doubtfully, "this is huge. It's not as if I want to get a little job in the corner card shop."

"Hardly," Miriam agreed wryly.

"I haven't worked in years," Destiny pointed out.

"Ha!"

"Okay, okay, I've run charity events and I've certainly kept my eye on all the decisions at Carlton Industries, but that's not the same as actually being in business. It's not the same as going in to my nephew and asking him to trust me to take over an entire division of the family company."

"Isn't that the point?" Miriam asked. "It *is* the family company and you're a very important part of this family, the matriarch, in a manner of speaking."

"True, but I turned my back on it years ago and left it to my brother. The only reason I gave up my art and my studio in the south of France was because of the plane crash that killed my brother and his wife. I couldn't leave Richard, Mack and Ben all alone. They were mere boys at the time. They needed me. Now they're grown men with wives of their own."

"Thanks to you," Miriam reminded her.

Destiny allowed herself a small smile. "Yes, all that meddling did work out rather well, if I do say so myself. There was no telling how long it would have taken them to get around to settling down if I hadn't given fate a bit of a nudge."

"So they owe you," Miriam suggested. "If you want to try something totally new, if you want to reinvent yourself completely at this stage of your life, why shouldn't you? And why shouldn't they give you their blessing?"

"It's not just their blessing I want," Destiny said. "I'm asking to take over the European division. Richard has me tucked into this nice, predictable niche in his life. I'm the doting, slightly madcap aunt. He doesn't see me as any kind of businesswoman. I'm partly to blame for that. I've never shown the slightest inclination to work for Carlton Industries before, at least not in any formal capacity."

"Sit down," Miriam ordered in one of her rare displays of impatience. She actually scowled until Destiny complied. "Bottom line, you know this company inside out, whether you've ever held an official job here or not. You're on the board of directors, for goodness' sake, and no one goes into those meetings more informed than you do. Am I right?"

"I try," Destiny agreed. It was a point of honor to her that she do her homework if she was going to hold a seat on the board.

"And you're uniquely suited to this particular job, isn't that right?"

Destiny thought of the problems in the European division. Most of them had been caused by the persistent stealth attacks of one man in particular, William Harcourt, the man she'd once loved with all her heart, the man she'd walked away from more than twenty years ago when she'd come back to the States to take care of her suddenly orphaned nephews.

"I do know how William's mind works," she agreed. "And the fact that he's become a threat to my family's company—perhaps because of me—makes me highly motivated to put a stop to it."

"Well, then, I don't see how you have any choice. You have to do this," Miriam concluded. "Not just for your own sake, but for the company."

"What if I botch it up?" Destiny asked, unable to shake her own self-doubts.

Miriam gave her a scathing look. "Don't be ridiculous. You won't." She grinned. "For one thing, you'll have me right there beside you."

Destiny stared at her. "You'd go to London with me?"

"I certainly wouldn't let you set off alone," Miriam said emphatically. "Besides, with Darryl dead and Dwayne in college, my life is as much of an empty nest as yours. It will be good for both of us to dive into something new and exciting."

Yes, Destiny thought, that was exactly it. She needed a challenge. Ever since the marriage of her youngest nephew, she'd been essentially at loose ends. If she wanted to go back to her house in France, she could. If she wanted to spend her time painting, she could do that, too. If she merely wanted to travel, that option was open as well.

But all these years of running a household, of overseeing her nephews' education, of taking a more active role on the Carlton Industries board of directors had given her a jaundiced view of idleness.

She wanted to be productive. She'd made the transition from eccentric artist to instant mother rather successfully. Now she wanted to reinvent herself yet again. There was someone inside her still to be discovered. She had a lot left to prove, not to her nephews, but to herself. Leading a wildly madcap lifestyle in her twenties or even at thirty had been one thing. It was quite another to consider going back to it in her fifties.

It wasn't too late to find an entirely new direction that suited her, she assured herself. At fifty-three, she was still vibrant, intelligent and capable. In fact, in no small measure thanks to her success in getting her nephews settled, she felt ready to tackle anything.

For months now this idea had been brewing in the back of her mind. She'd tossed out an occasional hint, just to see if Richard would jump at the bait, but he didn't seem to be taking her seriously. It was time he did. After all, he was the one who'd indirectly planted the idea in her head.

It was all tied up with William Harcourt, who had turned out to have an astonishing head for running his own family's business. In recent years he had made it his apparent mission in life to go after every European contract previously held by Carlton Industries. He'd won some, lost more, but there was no mistaking his use of inside information—her own pillow-talk revelations, damn him—to make her family's company pay dearly for every deal it made. Until very recently his actions had been more annoyance than threat, but lately his tactics had grown bolder and more damaging. It was time to put a stop to it.

Destiny had made a lot of impulsive decisions in her life, but she didn't intend for this plan for her future to be one of them. She'd given the matter of William Harcourt targeting Carlton Industries a lot of thought and finally concluded that she was the only one who could make him rue the day he'd decided to betray her and go after her family. Revenge would be so much more challenging—so much more *fun*—than going back to claim an idle life that no longer held any meaning.

She simply had to convince Richard—the entire family, in fact—that she was up to the task.

"You honestly believe I can do this?" she asked Miriam one last time.

"Without question," Miriam said confidently.

Destiny nodded. "Then it's time I get Richard on board with the idea. He is the CEO, after all. I don't suppose you have any idea how I'm going to accomplish that, do you?"

"Pull rank," Miriam suggested, the glint in her eye suggesting she wasn't entirely joking.

"I think finesse is probably a better approach," Destiny scolded mildly, then grinned. "I'll save pulling rank as a last resort."

"You want to do what?" Richard's head snapped up from the stack of papers on his desk. He studied his aunt as if she'd announced she intended to take up skydiving, though come to think of it that was something Destiny was entirely likely to do if boredom set in. This announcement was far more unexpected.

"Don't glower at me like that," she scolded. "It's not as if I haven't grown up around this company. I know its inner workings almost as well as you do. It was my grandfather who started it, after all, and my father who turned it into a worldwide conglomerate. I've held a seat on the board for years now, and believe me, I do not let the reports sit on my desk gathering dust. I may be the only person on the board besides you who actually reads them."

"But you've never shown the slightest interest in working for Carlton Industries," Richard said, totally perplexed. "When your father tried to groom you for a position here, you ran away to France. When you came back after my father died, you left it to his executive vice president to run things until I was old enough to take over."

"Because, just like you, your father lived and breathed this company. I simply let him have it because it was the sensible, fair thing to do. I had more interesting things to pursue. And when I came back, I had far more important responsibilities—you and your brothers. The company was running smoothly and you were already being groomed to take over. There was no need for my interference or involvement."

"Okay, I can accept all that," he said, still perplexed. "What's changed?"

"I've changed," she said simply. "Now I want to run the European division. If you agree to this, Richard, I can promise you won't regret it."

"But why?" Richard persisted.

"Because it's there," she snapped impatiently. "Don't be dense, Richard. I want to do it because now that you and your brothers are married, I need something to do. I want to find out what I'm really made of."

He was still bewildered. His aunt's days were jam-packed with things to do. "When was the last time your calendar wasn't crammed with foundation meetings, fund-raisers, luncheons and social engagements?"

Destiny waved them off as if they were of no consequence. "There was a time when that lifestyle suited me. Now it doesn't. I need a real purpose. I want to make a contribution to this family. I think I have something unique to offer Carlton Industries. All those years coaxing dollars out of tightwads for various charities ought to be good for something."

"Hold it right there," Richard said, regarding her with exasperation. "Don't you think you made an incredible contribution by coming back here to take over when Mom and Dad died? You gave the three of us a home and stability. You brought fun and adventure into our lives. Rosalind Russell in that old *Auntie Mame* movie you showed us had nothing on you. You saw that we became decent, well-educated men. Hell, you even meddled until we were married to women you approved of. There's a whole new generation of Carltons coming along, thanks to you."

"Exactly my point," Destiny responded. "You're all

settled. You have your own families. You don't need me anymore."

"We'll always need you," Richard protested, indignant that she could think otherwise. "Have we not shown you that?"

"You need me as the doting great-aunt who spoils your children rotten, nothing more. I can't be content with that. I want more."

He decided to try another tack to dissuade her from this insane idea. "What about your house in France? I always thought you'd want to go back there someday to live, get back to your painting and your gardens. You always talk about that time in your life as if it were magical. Now's your chance. Go for a few months. Open your studio and paint again."

"All that's in the past," she said blithely, as if she hadn't talked incessantly about doing that very thing at some distant point in the future. "You can't recapture something that was lost. In fact, I'm thinking of selling the house."

Shocked by the blasé announcement, he stared at her. "Now I know there's something wrong. What aren't you telling me? You always swore you would never sell that house, that you wanted to know it was there for your old age."

She shrugged. "Times change. I was young and impetuous back then. While you boys were growing up, so was I. I have new dreams now."

Richard regarded her skeptically. "And one of those dreams is to run our European division?"

"Yes," she declared flatly, her gaze unblinking.

Truthfully, he didn't doubt for a second that she could do it. Destiny was an amazing woman. She had a huge and generous heart, an astounding zest for life, and a mind that could grasp the details of a business merger even more quickly than his.

In her fifties, she was still a beautiful woman, trim and lithe with a cloud of soft brown hair framing a face that time had treated kindly. Her generous mouth was usually curved in a brilliant smile and laugh lines fanned out from eyes that sparkled.

There was no shortage of available men to fill her evenings, and yet she kept most of them at arm's length. His wife said it was because Destiny still longed for the love of her life, whoever the hell that was, the man she'd left behind when she'd come home to take charge of her nephews. Maybe that was true, though Richard didn't like thinking that she'd sacrificed someone so irreplaceable that she'd spent the last twenty years yearning for him. It would be even worse if that man turned out to be William Harcourt, as he once suspected. Harcourt was the very man who'd become the bane of Richard's existence by mucking about in every deal Carlton Industries tried to make in Europe.

He pushed all of that from his mind and tried to view this request from Destiny's perspective. In all these years she had never asked for anything for herself. She'd thrown herself into sudden and unexpected motherhood with complete abandon, mastering it with her own unorthodox style. After all she'd done for him and his brothers, if she wanted this one thing from him now, how could he deny her?

Still, the decision seemed so impulsive, so out of character, he had to be sure it wasn't a whim. Carlton Industries wasn't some playground for a woman who was simply bored with her life.

"Destiny, have you really thought this through?" he asked. "There are downsides. Serious downsides, in fact. Tackling such a huge job will mean long days in an office. There will be a lot of stress involved."

Her gaze narrowed. "Are you suggesting I'm not physically or mentally up to it?" she asked, her tone suddenly icy.

Richard knew better than to say any such thing. "Of course not."

"Well then, why are you hesitating?"

"Because this is so unlike you. In fact, every time I've brought up the European division and the problems it was having, you've told me to deal with it myself."

She regarded him blandly. "But you haven't, have you?"

Richard sighed. She had him there. William Harcourt was still insinuating himself into every single negotiation Carlton Industries was involved in. Richard had managed to thwart most of Harcourt's attempts to steal business, but he hadn't really dealt the man a final, knockout blow that would end the nonsense.

He couldn't help wondering yet again if there was a link between Harcourt and Destiny he didn't know about. He'd asked Destiny before if she had known the man years ago, but she'd avoided giving him a direct answer. Ben had managed to finagle an admission that she'd known Harcourt, but had gotten nothing more. That rather incomplete acknowledgment had raised Richard's suspicions that there was more going on with Harcourt than business, but without proof he hadn't been able to call her on it. He needed to try again.

"Does this have something to do with Harcourt?" he asked her.

"No, it has to do with me," she insisted, regarding him with an unblinking gaze that gave away nothing. "It's time to find out what I'm made of."

"You're an incredible woman!" Richard said impatiently. "Why are you questioning that now? Don't start spouting some nonsense about low self-esteem to me. I'll laugh you right out of here."

"Darling, it's not that I don't think I did a good job raising you and your brothers or that I haven't made a contribution to the community, but I don't know who I am, not really. I don't paint anymore. I'm not your surrogate mother. I'm bored by running events. Somewhere along the way I've lost myself."

Richard was completely bewildered by her claim. "That's crazy."

"Is it? I was very young when I first went to Europe. I had plenty of money and virtually no responsibilities. I painted because I enjoyed it, not because I was passionate about it. I was surrounded by people who were as irresponsible as I was."

"Including William Harcourt?" he asked again, wondering if she would finally give him an honest answer.

She gave him a sour look. "Yes, if you must know, including William."

When Richard began to press her on that, she held up her hand. "The point I'm trying to make is that when your parents died, I came back here and had the responsibility of a family thrust on me. I think I lived up to that responsibility reasonably well—"

"Of course you did."

"But," she added with a trace of impatience, "those years were a gift, something unexpected, that shaped my life for a time, but now I'm ready to move on. I need to find out who Destiny Carlton really is."

"And you think you could be a successful business-woman?"

"Why not?" she asked. "It is in my genes, after all." She gave him a hard look. "I honestly don't know why you're making such a fuss or why you're so surprised by this. I've been talking about it for months now, ever since Ben's wedding. I've been waiting for you to come up with this idea on your own, but you've ignored every hint I've dropped."

"I honestly didn't think you were serious."

"In other words, you were certain it was just another one of Destiny's flighty whims," she scoffed. "And that says it all, doesn't it? Is it any wonder I want my family to start to take me seriously?"

He could see that he'd hurt her, but he didn't know how else he could have reacted to this crazy idea. He couldn't just turn over an entire division to her because it was what she wanted. He had as much responsibility to the company as he did to her.

"Destiny, why don't you think it over for another day or two? Or take a vacation, go to France and see if that fits you the way it once did," he suggested finally, hoping to buy himself enough time to formulate a plan to steer all this energy in a different direction. Surely there was some other satisfying pursuit she could take up that would keep her right here at home. Maybe they could encourage her to accept one of the marriage proposals constantly being tossed her way by high-profile men in the region. The prospect of a little turnabout meddling struck him as a fine idea.

Meantime, though, he gave her a placating smile. "Think about it for a few days or even a few weeks and we'll talk again."

"Meaning you want to check with your brothers to make sure I haven't gone round the bend," she said dryly. "Okay, fine. I'll compromise, but I won't put this off for weeks. For one thing, William is nipping at our heels on another deal, and this time there's a good chance we can lose if we don't act quickly. I can wait twenty-four hours while you hold a family powwow, as long as it gets me what I want. Trust me, Richard, I won't change my mind."

It wasn't the delay he'd hoped for, but he could see she wasn't prepared to bend any further. "Fine. We'll get together at the end of the day tomorrow."

She gave him an innocent look. "I really do hope you'll see this my way."

"I promise to give it serious consideration," he told her.

"I know you will," she said cheerfully. "I'm sure you're aware that I'd hate to have to pull rank on you."

His gaze narrowed. "Meaning what, exactly?"

"Meaning that I'd prefer not to go straight to the board to explain that the European operation has been in a shambles for some time and that you haven't taken any definitive action to shore it up and turn it into the gold mine it could be."

As her words sank in, Richard stared at her. If he had ever doubted Destiny's business acumen or her ability to be a tough negotiator, he didn't any longer. She'd obviously done her homework rather thoroughly before coming to him. And she'd delivered that threat without so much as a blink of her steady gaze.

"You would do that?" he asked, stunned by her audacity.

She beamed at him. "I don't think it will be necessary, do you?"

With that, Destiny swept out of his office, looking as regal and smug as a queen.

Richard watched her exit and sighed. Heaven help the European division! There was little doubt that Destiny was taking over. He considered himself to be a tough-minded businessman and a seasoned negotiator, but she'd put him in his place in no time flat. He'd just have to find some way to keep her on a tight rein.

But even as he reached that conclusion, Richard had to laugh. Keeping his aunt under control was going to be a little like trying to contain a hurricane. It simply couldn't be done.

Destiny thought her meeting with Richard had gone rather well. There was little doubt that he would come around to her way of thinking, eventually, at any rate. It might take a bit more persuasion, but she thought that subtle threat at the end of their conversation had probably done the trick. He definitely hadn't been anticipating that. She had a feeling he'd been as impressed as he'd been shocked. Hard truths and uncompromising stands were something her nephew understood.

She poured herself a cup of tea and settled into a chair in front of the fire, her feet tucked under her, and thought about what she would do first when she got to London, where Carlton Industries was headquartered.

She'd been studying the reports for months now. Goodness knows, there was a lot to do and not all of it had to do with William. There were some very stuffy people in charge and the entire operation needed a good shake-up.

She was still happily contemplating all that when the front door burst open and Mack and Ben called out to her.

"In here," she responded, not the least bit surprised by their arrival. "Having tea by the fire. If you want some, get cups before you come in."

They came in a few minutes later, not only with cups, but with another pot of tea and a plate of the house-keeper's chocolate chip cookies, which were always on hand, especially for Ben. Not that there was any short-age of sweets in his life since he'd married Kathleen, who baked like a fine pastry chef, but he still loved Mrs. Darlington's cookies.

"I imagine you've been talking to your brother," she said when they were seated. "If you've come to change my mind, you can forget it."

"Not to change your mind," Ben said gently. "Just to see if we've done something to make you feel that you're not needed here."

"Don't be silly," she said at once. "Why can't any of you see that this isn't about you? It's about me and what I need to do."

"You really want to move halfway around the world?" Mack asked doubtfully.

"Yes. And it's not as if we don't own a corporate jet that can bring me home anytime I'm needed here." She reached for Ben's hand and gave it a squeeze. He was the real worrier, and she could see the concern in his eyes. "Darlings, this really is what I want to do. I'm looking forward to having a brand-new challenge in my life. Think how exciting that will be for me. If we don't take on new things once in a while, we stagnate."

"Is this really about a new challenge or an old love?" Ben asked directly.

"Perhaps both," she admitted. "But I'm not hoping to reignite an old flame, in case that's what's worrying you. If anything, quite the opposite. William has made a nuisance of himself in our company's business for far too long now. The fact that he has dared to become an increasingly serious threat to my family cannot be tolerated. I intend to see that he realizes that."

Mack regarded her intently, then slowly nodded. "You really are excited about this, aren't you? You're looking forward to busting some serious butt over there?"

"Excited, stimulated, determined," she said. "In fact, I haven't felt like this in years. I feel young again, as if there are endless possibilities spread out before me."

Her nephews exchanged a resigned look.

"I still don't like it, but I suppose we have no right to stand in your way," Ben said. "We'll talk to Richard and convince him that you know exactly what you're doing."

"Thank you, darling."

"Don't thank me," Ben said, his expression gloomy. "I still wish you weren't dead-set on doing this."

"Me, too," Mack said. "But I think I understand your reasons for wanting to. When that knee injury killed my football career, I was at loose ends for a while, too, until you and Richard convinced me that I could use my love of the game in a whole new way by buying into the team. If I could reinvent myself from a professional athlete into a businessman, then you can surely be anything you set out to be."

"Oh, Mack, what a sweet thing to say," she told him, her eyes misting up.

"Just one question, you won't leave before Beth has the baby, will you? She'll never forgive you," Mack said.

"Absolutely not," Destiny assured him. "And once Richard agrees to this, I'm sure it will take weeks and weeks for him to drill me on all the little odds and ends he thinks I must know to be successful. I would like to be over there before Christmas, though."

"Christmas?" both men said, clearly appalled.

"You could all fly over," she reminded them. "I was there for the holidays years ago. There's nothing quite like a Christmas in London."

Ben sighed. "I think we're getting a little ahead of ourselves here. Let's take one step at a time. Let's get Richard on board with this."

Destiny beamed at him. "Oh, I think once you two speak up, it will be a foregone conclusion."

"Oh?" Mack said. "He didn't sound so convinced when I spoke to him."

"Let's just say I left him with a little incentive to mull over," Destiny said coyly. "I'm not surprised he didn't mention it. I think he was caught off guard."

"An incentive? He didn't mention any incentive to me," Mack said.

"Nor to me," Ben agreed, giving her a sharp look. "Was it an incentive or a threat, Destiny? What are you up to?"

"Nothing that an outstanding businessman like Richard won't understand," she assured them both.

Mack began to chuckle. "Oh, Destiny, something tells me Europe is not ready for you."

She laughed with him. "Well, darlings, ready or not, here I come."

# 2

William Harcourt was on a golf course in Scotland when he got word that the European office of Carlton Industries was soon to be operating under a new chairman. Sir Lloyd Smedley gave him the news just as William took his shot on the seventh hole tee.

"Is that so?" William asked, distracted. The seventh hole was a tricky one. It had gotten the better of him yesterday, but he'd be damned if it would again.

"Destiny Carlton is taking over," Lloyd added, his expression totally innocent. "Believe you knew her, didn't you?"

William's golf ball dribbled off the tee and died, which was precisely the result his sneaky companion had obviously been hoping for. Lloyd was losing today. He'd clearly intended his little bombshell to ruin William's concentration, not just on this hole, but for the rest of the round.

William felt a little *zing* in his blood, something that hadn't happened nearly often enough since Destiny had walked out on their relationship twenty years before.

Back then, he'd stubbornly resisted following her to

the States, deluding himself for the longest time that a love like theirs wasn't something she could possibly forget or abandon forever.

But she had. He'd totally misjudged her sense of family loyalty. The Destiny he'd known in France hadn't had a maternal bone in her delectable body. She'd been carefree, impetuous and a bit of a Bohemian. But to his shock, she'd thrown over all traces of her carefree ways to settle down and mother her three orphaned nephews.

After a time, when he'd heard barely a word from her, his pride had kicked in. She'd chosen children who were virtual strangers over him, the man she'd claimed to love. It had grated.

It had taken him a long time to catch on to the fact that nothing on earth was worse than a man more devoted to pride than common sense. If she'd abandoned those boys, as he'd anticipated, she wouldn't have been the kind of woman he wanted in his life. *That* was what he should have realized from the beginning. He was the fool who'd forced her to make an impossible choice, rather than going after her and being supportive when her entire world had been turned upside down. All these years, he could have had her love and the love of three stepsons, plus maybe some children of their own. Any children of Destiny's would have been astonishingly bright and handsome. Destiny hadn't cost the two of them a future. He had.

William had found his own shortsightedness to be so incredibly annoying, so completely perplexing, that he had spent the last ten years mucking up every business deal Carlton Industries set out to make in Europe. It wasn't something he'd done to get rich. Hell, he had more money than he could spend in ten lifetimes. It wasn't even the satisfaction of winning that had drawn him into the game. It was an idiotic, half-baked attempt to get Destiny's attention.

And now he had.

He grinned as he set his ball back on the tee and slammed it straight down the fairway toward the green, gazing at its trajectory with satisfaction. About damn time she got the message. He'd wasted a lot of years waiting for life to get interesting again.

Harcourt & Sons was one of those long-established London companies that dabbled in a wide variety of businesses, assembled over generations less with logic than with the various passions and needs of prior generations. William appreciated that aspect of the company's history. It made his own acquisition tactics in recent years seem perfectly fitting. His ancestors had acquired whatever companies appealed to them, just as he was intent on acquiring those most likely to annoy Destiny.

Harcourt owned a small chain of exclusive haberdashers, founded due to William's grandfather's girth and demand for excellent tailoring. The chain had begun on Saville Row, then spread through the countryside, thanks to his grandfather's contacts in Parliament who wanted the shops that specialized in personalized service conveniently located in their home districts. It was also a small way to support their local woolen manufacturers.

Another company was renowned throughout the country for its exotic selection of teas, acquired when William's grandmother had had difficulty obtaining the blends she wanted. Those shops had later been expanded to serve an elegant afternoon tea, when his mother had wanted a place to take her friends after a day's shopping.

The whole conglomerate had begun quite unexpectedly with an antiquarian bookshop, opened after his great-grandfather's bookshelves were filled to overflowing with leather-bound editions of the classics, as well as the lighter novels preferred by William's great-grandmother. This remarkable woman had not been content to sit idly in the country when her husband came to London. Far ahead of her time, she'd wanted something productive to do. She'd found a location and badgered her husband until he'd helped her to set up the shop. Their friends had been scandalized that Amanda Wellington Harcourt would ignore the family's noble heritage and go into trade.

To everyone's surprise, except her husband's, she'd made an enormous success of it. *She,* not William's great-grandfather, was the Harcourt of Harcourt & Sons. H&S Books now had stores all over Great Britain, still dealing primarily with rare books and first editions, though a rack of current bestsellers was beginning to appear in some of the stores along with important biographies and books on travel.

Recalling the oft-told tale now, William couldn't help being reminded of Destiny. She and Great-grandmother Amanda had a lot in common. Both were bold, strong women, who refused to be confined by society's constraints. They both had vision and the drive to succeed.

He'd been little more than a toddler when his great-grandmother had died, but he could still remember the fire in her eyes and the enthusiasm in her voice as she'd talked about books and read to him from the classics. She, more than any teacher he'd ever had, had taught him to love learning and to be open to new ideas. She'd been the one who'd made him into the kind of man who'd be drawn to an unconventional woman like Destiny.

Sitting behind the desk in his office, William pulled a signed volume of Charles Dickens's *A Christmas Carol* from the shelf behind him and rubbed his fingers over the fine, gold-embossed leather. This rare treasure had been a gift from Destiny when she'd discovered his love of old books. Inside, he found the card she'd written in her neat hand. "To my love. May you always know the true meaning of Christmas and feel the joy in my heart when I think of you. You, too, are rare and wonderful. Love, Destiny."

Carefully, he replaced the book in its place of honor on his shelf, then buzzed for his assistant. Malcolm Dandridge had been with Harcourt & Sons since William's father's day. There was little Malcolm didn't know about what went on inside the company and in corporate London. William counted on Malcolm's loyalty and his discretion. Over the years both had proved invaluable.

"Yes, sir?" Malcolm said, entering with pad in hand, ready for whatever business William needed him to tend to.

"Sit, Malcolm. Tell me what you've heard about Carlton Industries lately."

To his credit, Malcolm had never asked about William's seeming obsession with the American conglomerate. Nor had he criticized the sometimes inexplicable decisions William had made to go after companies that were ill suited for Harcourt & Sons. If he thought William's behavior was reckless, he was far too polite and loyal to mention it.

"It's been a bit quiet lately," Malcolm reported. "It's my opinion, sir, that the last negotiation rattled them. It proved rather costly, thanks to your clever strategy. I'm sure they're busy trying to conserve capital in order to offset that particular deal."

"Anything about the new chairman?" William asked, wondering if Lloyd had gotten it right and Destiny truly was coming to take over. "Has one been appointed?"

"Yes, sir. A Ms. Destiny Carlton, a rather surprising choice according to my sources."

William's heart did another little stutter step, even though it was old news to him. Having it confirmed made it seem that much more real.

"When will she be taking over?" he asked, hoping his expression was totally bland.

"I believe Ms. Carlton is expected in early December, sir."

"Not until then?" William asked, both surprised and more than a little disappointed. It was only the beginning of October now. "Any explanation for the delay?"

"None, sir, though it is my opinion that she's probably being groomed for the position. My sources tell me that she's had virtually no hands-on experience at the company. I believe that we will be able to make some solid inroads against them once she's on the scene."

"Don't sell her short," William warned.

Malcolm looked startled by his sharp tone. "You know her, sir?"

"Quite well, as a matter of fact. She might not have spent much time working with the company, but it would be naive to assume she can't handle the job. She's a Carlton, after all. I suspect we'll have our work cut out for us, if we intend to get the better of her." He was not about to admit how much the prospect excited him. There was a deal on the table right now for a group of faltering travel agencies. The notion of battling wits with Destiny to acquire it right out from under her was stimulating. This was one fight he intended to win at any cost, a metaphor of sorts for his intentions toward Destiny.

"As you say, sir. But as brilliant as she may be, she'll be no match for you. The nephew certainly hasn't been."

"Because his mind hasn't been on it," William guessed. "And the stakes haven't been high enough." He paused thoughtfully. "I imagine Destiny's going to come in and do something dramatic, if only to get our attention. She won't be satisfied to win this skirmish for Fortnum Travel. I wonder what her first target for acquisition will be?"

"Shall I see what I can find out?" Malcolm asked. "Perhaps there are rumors inside the company."

William nodded. "Yes, definitely, see what you can learn, Malcolm. A preemptive strike might be just the thing. We'll want to keep her on her toes."

In fact, he thought cheerfully, a preemptive strike might bring Destiny roaring straight into his office, eyes blazing and temper high. Now, there was a sight he'd been longing to see for far too long now.

Destiny was growing weary of all the admonitions and instructions and piles and piles of detailed reports, most of which she'd read long before she'd put her plan into play. She knew perfectly well that Richard was merely trying to overwhelm her with so much information, to make the task seem so daunting and formidable that she'd give up in frustration and declare herself no longer interested in taking over the European division. He still wasn't entirely reconciled to this whole idea of her as an integral part of the company.

She frowned as Richard went over ground he'd covered just last week…and the week before that.

"Do you truly believe that I am so forgetful that I don't know we've been over this twice before?" she asked finally, her voice filled with undisguised frustration.

He seemed startled by her question. "Have we?"

She rolled her eyes. "Either you're the forgetful one or you've gotten your strategy completely muddled."

"Strategy? What strategy?"

"To make me forget what you still believe is a crazy idea," she said mildly. "Mack and Beth's baby is due any day now. I'm leaving in two weeks, Richard. Get used to it."

"I just want you to be fully prepared to pull off this Fortnum Travel acquisition. We can't afford any missteps," he retorted defensively. "This deal will set the tone for everything you do from now on. After all, you're not just someone new coming in. You're a Carlton. How would it look if you're not on top of things?"

"I'm sure the earth would keep spinning," she responded.

"But you need to have everyone's respect from the moment you set foot into the building," he said. "You only have one chance to make a first impression. How many times did you drill that little maxim into my head?"

"A first impression is one thing," she responded. "Respect is something else entirely. No one gains respect just because they show up, I don't care what their name is. Respect is earned. I expect to pay my dues in that regard, which is why we will acquire Fortnum Travel. I won't let it slip away. I promise."

"I'm just trying to make it a bit easier," he grumbled.

"I know," she soothed. "And I do appreciate it, but this is getting old, Richard. It's not as if there aren't phones and faxes over there. I'll be able to reach you at a moment's notice if something comes up that I can't handle. I'm neither proud nor foolish. I'll ask for any help I need."

"Yes, of course," he said finally, his expression resigned. "Is there anything I can help with now?"

Destiny had been waiting for just this moment. She'd been toying with an idea for a few weeks now, something guaranteed to get William's attention and show him that she was about to make his life the same sort of hell he'd been trying to create for Carlton Industries. It would be solid proof that she was just as capable as he of capitalizing on the intimate secrets they'd shared all those years ago. She reached into her briefcase and pulled out a thick folder. She'd left absolutely no stone unturned in accumulating her research to make her case to Richard. The cover sheet was concise, but there were pages of backup material for every premise she'd stated.

"Take a look at this," she said, handing it to Richard. "Tell me what you think. I want your honest opinion. Don't sugarcoat anything."

Richard's eyes widened as he glanced through the detailed research. "You've spent a lot of time on this," he said eventually in a cautious tone that could only be construed as less-than-a-ringing endorsement.

"I wanted to be sure I could answer any questions you might have."

"The numbers make sense," he admitted.

"But?"

He gave her a perplexed look. "Why on earth would

you want to acquire some nothing little bookstore? I don't get it. It's not the kind of business that's a good fit for us. It's too small. There's no real growth potential."

She smiled at his logic. It was exactly what she'd expected. Richard was very much a bottom-line kind of man.

"But it is the kind of business that fits quite nicely with Harcourt & Sons," she explained. "It's the only major antiquarian bookseller in London that's on a par with H&S Books. The owner is old. He wants to retire, but he doesn't want to sell to just anyone. He's been annoyed at Harcourt & Sons for some time now for the aggressive way they've gone after rare books. He finds it a bit unseemly. He's from an era that considered the pursuit of rare editions to be a gentleman's sport."

"So we help him to get his revenge," Richard said slowly. "And in the process, we annoy the daylights out of William Harcourt."

Destiny beamed at him. "Precisely. It's the last thing he'll be expecting. Right now all of his attention is on the Fortnum Travel deal."

"But will he really care? This is nothing to a man like Harcourt."

"In dollars and cents, yes," she agreed. "But not in importance. H&S Books is the cornerstone of the company, their prestige division. It was William's great-grandmother's creation. It has huge sentimental value, if not financial significance. William won't be happy if he thinks we're about to invest major money in his competition and target it for expansion. And it will send a clear message that if he continues to go after us, we'll go after him, business by business, first books, then tea, then clothing, until we have competition not just in England, but all over Europe."

Richard regarded her with evident surprise. "You really do have a knack for this, don't you? And a rather bloodthirsty eagerness to go for the jugular."

"Well, of course I do," Destiny said impatiently. "Nobody messes with my family and gets away with it. Making William sit up and take notice will be my pleasure."

"It's not all about getting even with Harcourt," Richard warned. "We do have a company to run over there. Some of our existing businesses are not performing to our expectations. Those need to be addressed, too."

"I know that and I have plans for each and every one of them. This," she said, gesturing toward the folder, "is just for the fun of it."

Richard laughed. "Let me go over these figures again tonight."

"Don't take too long. I want to arrive in London with guns blazing."

"This is only a BB shot," Richard reminded her.

"Even a BB shot hurts when you're not expecting it and it hits you where you live," Destiny retorted.

"Remind me never to get on your bad side," Richard said, regarding her with evident approval for the first time since they'd set off down this road.

"Darling, you could never get on my bad side," she assured him. "You're family, and no matter how annoying you might become, family always forgives and forgets."

"Good to know."

Even as she left her nephew to ponder her suggested strategy, she couldn't help wondering if William was going to be shocked that she could come after him the way she intended to, given the feelings they'd once shared. Probably. He seemed to have missed the fact that nothing was more important to her than family. He hadn't gotten it twenty years ago, and it was plain he didn't get it now.

That was just one reason she wanted to arrive in London with an unmistakable message. Apparently William wasn't too smart about subtleties and nuances. She was going to have to deliver a direct hit, then see to it that she kept them coming until he abandoned the fight and went crawling back to whatever country estate he was living on these days.

Richard had an odd feeling in the pit of his stomach as he reread Destiny's proposal for taking over the small but prestigious London bookseller she'd targeted. On the one hand, it didn't make a lick of sense to acquire Jameson's Booksellers. It would be a nuisance purchase, requiring them to track down or train someone with the necessary expertise to make a success of it, to make it a worthy rival for H&S Books. On the other hand, he could see precisely why Destiny thought it would be a nice opening salvo against Harcourt.

He tried to put his finger on what was really bothering him. It wasn't the cash outlay. That was peanuts to a corporation the size of Carlton Industries. It wasn't the energy likely to be expended on making and then following through with such an acquisition. So what was it?

Melanie came into his den after putting their daughter down for the night, took one look at him and murmured, "Uh-oh."

He met her gaze. "What?"

"I know that expression." She came and sat on his lap and traced the crease in his brow. "You're worrying about something. And since I recognize Destiny's handwriting on that file, I assume it has something to do with her."

"You're too smart for your own good," he murmured, breathing in the flowery scent she'd dabbed on while she was upstairs. It would be very easy right now to forget all about business and spend the rest of the evening in bed with his wife, working on the expansion plan they had in mind for their family. Maybe the prospect of another baby would cut short Destiny's European adventure and get her back home again.

"I have to be smart to keep up with you two," Melanie said. "What's Destiny done now?"

"Nothing yet," he admitted. "But she has an idea she wants to pursue the minute she gets to London."

"A bad idea?"

"Not really."

"An expensive idea?"

"Not at all."

"Is it dangerous? I mean to her, personally."

"No," he admitted.

"Then what's the problem?"

Richard sighed. "I can't put my finger on it. Maybe you can." He described Destiny's scheme, then asked, "What do you think?"

"I think it's ingenious," she said at once. "She's going to be an invaluable asset, you know. Is that what you're having trouble admitting?"

"Of course not. I've always respected her intelligence. And I've always known she was clever. She got the two of us together, didn't she?"

"Over your vehement objections, in fact," Melanie concurred. "And my somewhat less strenuous ones."

"Wise woman," Richard admitted, grinning.

"Her or me?"

"Both of you, in fact, but not half as smart as I was to go along with the plan in the end."

Melanie kissed him, which momentarily served as a rather effective distraction.

"Want to know what I think your problem is?" Melanie asked eventually.

"Sure."

"You don't like the fact that she's the one who came up with the idea."

Richard scowled at her implication. "Don't be ridiculous. I am not jealous of my own aunt. That would be childish and immature."

"Yes, it would," she agreed readily. "And I'm not suggesting that, but you can't deny that it is nagging at you that she apparently has enough insight into what makes William Harcourt tick to come up with a plot like this."

The explanation resonated with him a little too clearly. "You could be right," he admitted slowly. "I don't like anything I don't understand, and Destiny has never been forthcoming about just what this man meant to her. I'm beginning to get the nasty feeling that he was quite important to her once, more important than any of us have suspected."

"And if he was?"

"Then he's a real danger to her and to the company," he said.

Melanie regarded him with shock. "You can't honestly think she would ever betray Carlton Industries."

He heard her scandalized tone and tried quickly to explain that he didn't doubt Destiny's honesty or integrity. "I don't think she would do anything intentionally," he began carefully. "But people who think they're in love do all sorts of crazy things they might not do if they were thinking clearly."

"Like us?"

"This is nothing like us," he protested. "There was never any conflict of interest with the two of us."

Melanie stood up, her disapproval plain. "I suggest you not repeat your concerns to Destiny," she told him quietly but emphatically.

He stared at her blankly, not quite getting why she was suddenly seething. "I have an obligation to the company. Why the hell shouldn't I say something if I think she's putting our interests at risk?" he demanded.

"Because your implication is insulting, and frankly, if I were Destiny, I'd slap you silly. I'm very tempted to do it myself on her behalf."

She stalked off then, obviously every bit as insulted as she insisted Destiny was likely to be.

Richard stared after his wife in consternation. Give him a complex business situation to resolve anytime, because if he lived to be a hundred, he would never understand the women in his life.

Join #1 *New York Times* bestselling author

# SHERRYL WOODS

### in Serenity, South Carolina, with a *Sweet Magnolias* story of newfound love and unwavering friendship.

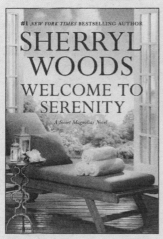

When Jeanette Brioche helped launch The Corner Spa in Serenity, South Carolina, she found a whole lot more than professional satisfaction. She discovered the deep and loyal friendships that had been missing from her life. But even the Sweet Magnolias can't persuade her that the holidays are anything more than a season of misery.

Pushed into working on the town's much-loved annual Christmas festival, Jeanette teams up with the sexy new town manager. Tom McDonald may be the only person in Serenity who's less enthused about family and the holidays than she is.

But with tree decorations going up on the town square and a bit of romance in the air, they discover that this just may be a season of miracles after all.

## Available now, wherever books are sold!

# SHERRYL WOODS

| | | | |
|---|---|---|---|
| 32979 | MOONLIGHT COVE | ___$7.99 U.S. | ___$9.99 CAN. |
| 32976 | ALONG CAME TROUBLE | ___$7.99 U.S. | ___$9.99 CAN. |
| 32975 | ABOUT THAT MAN | ___$7.99 U.S. | ___$9.99 CAN. |
| 32947 | DRIFTWOOD COTTAGE | ___$7.99 U.S. | ___$9.99 CAN. |
| 32814 | RETURN TO ROSE COTTAGE | ___$7.99 U.S. | ___$9.99 CAN. |
| 32641 | HARBOR LIGHTS | ___$7.99 U.S. | ___$9.99 CAN. |
| 32634 | FLOWERS ON MAIN | ___$7.99 U.S. | ___$9.99 CAN. |
| 32626 | THE INN AT EAGLE POINT | ___$7.99 U.S. | ___$7.99 CAN. |
| 31791 | THE CALAMITY JANES: CASSIE & KAREN | ___$7.99 U.S. | ___$8.99 CAN. |
| 31788 | THE CALAMITY JANES: LAUREN | ___$7.99 U.S. | ___$8.99 CAN. |
| 31778 | THE CALAMITY JANES: GINA & EMMA | ___$7.99 U.S. | ___$8.99 CAN. |
| 31766 | WILLOW BROOK ROAD | ___$8.99 U.S. | ___$9.99 CAN. |
| 31732 | DOGWOOD HILL | ___$8.99 U.S. | ___$9.99 CAN. |
| 31679 | THE DEVANEY BROTHERS: DANIEL | ___$7.99 U.S. | ___$9.99 CAN. |
| 31668 | A SEASIDE CHRISTMAS | ___$7.99 U.S. | ___$8.99 CAN. |
| 31630 | THE DEVANEY BROTHERS: MICHAEL AND PATRICK | ___$7.99 U.S. | ___$8.99 CAN. |
| 31607 | THE DEVANEY BROTHERS: RYAN AND SEAN | ___$7.99 U.S. | ___$8.99 CAN. |
| 31589 | HOME TO SEAVIEW KEY | ___$7.99 U.S. | ___$8.99 CAN. |
| 31581 | SEAVIEW INN | ___$7.99 U.S. | ___$8.99 CAN. |
| 31466 | AFTER TEX | ___$7.99 U.S. | ___$9.99 CAN. |
| 31442 | WIND CHIME POINT | ___$7.99 U.S. | ___$9.99 CAN. |
| 31414 | TEMPTATION | ___$7.99 U.S. | ___$9.99 CAN. |
| 31391 | AN O'BRIEN FAMILY CHRISTMAS | ___$7.99 U.S. | ___$9.99 CAN. |
| 31326 | WAKING UP IN CHARLESTON | ___$7.99 U.S. | ___$9.99 CAN. |
| 31288 | FLIRTING WITH DISASTER | ___$7.99 U.S. | ___$9.99 CAN. |
| 31262 | A CHESAPEAKE SHORES CHRISTMAS | ___$7.99 U.S. | ___$9.99 CAN. |

*(limited quantities available)*

TOTAL AMOUNT                         $ _____
POSTAGE & HANDLING           $ _____
($1.00 for 1 book, 50¢ for each additional)
APPLICABLE TAXES*             $ _____
TOTAL PAYABLE                   $ _____
*(check or money order—please do not send cash)*

To order, complete this form and send it, along with a check or money order for the total above, payable to MIRA Books, to: **In the U.S.:** 3010 Walden Avenue, P.O. Box 9077, Buffalo, NY 14269-9077; **In Canada:** P.O. Box 636, Fort Erie, Ontario, L2A 5X3.

Name: _____
Address: _____ City: _____
State/Prov.: _____ Zip/Postal Code: _____
Account Number (if applicable): _____
075 CSAS

        *New York residents remit applicable sales taxes.
        *Canadian residents remit applicable GST and provincial taxes.

**MIRA®**

**www.MIRABooks.com**

MSHW0416BL